MW00588392

MERGED WITH HIM

The Merge Series, Book 1

KYLIE KENT

McCartney Industries Pty Ltd.

ISBN 13: 978-0-6489981-0-5 (ebook)
Paperback: 978-0-6489981-1-2

Cover Illustration by
RJ CREATIVES GRAPHIC SERVICES

Editing services provided by Editor Shannan Saunders
–https://www.lovebooksediting.com

Re-edited July 2021 by - Kat Pagan - https://www.facebook.com/
PaganProofreading

Please Stalk Me

Come and check out my website and join my mailing list to stay up to date and gain access to bonus materials.
Website & Newsletter: https://www.kyliekent.com/

If you want early access to everything, yes everything come and join my Patreon Group Kylie Kent Patreon

Want to be involved in discussions and have access to tons of give-aways? Join my readers group on Facebook Kylie's Steam Room

Facebook: @kyliekent2020
Instagram Follow: @author_kylie_kent_

To my husband, who was my very own insta-love. The one who has supported me in everything I do for twenty years. Without his support and encouragement, this story would never have been told.

Merged

MERGED
"COMBINE OR CAUSE TO COMBINE TO FORM A SINGLE ENTITY"

One

ALYSSA

"*S*ARAH, I CAN'T WEAR THAT!" I exclaim to my best friend, who is holding up the tiniest black dress I have ever seen. "That dress looks like something you took off a doll; no way is all of *this* going to fit into that bit of fabric." I emphasize my curves by waving my hands down my body.

"Don't be dramatic, Lyssa. You want to look hot for this date with Ethan, right?"

I have absolutely no idea who the heck Ethan is, other than some guy that my best friend so helpfully set me up with. I'm not sure if I want to make the impression of a sexy kitten, or the girl you immediately friend zone and never try to hit on again.

"I want to look somewhere between Sex on the Beach and a Dirty Margarita," I try to explain in my friend's true language of cocktails.

"Okay. Okay, I get it. You want to look more like a piña colada. Fifty percent girl you take home to mother, and fifty percent hit it and quit it," Sarah animatedly calls out as she continues to dig through her wardrobe. We shared the townhouse together, and I couldn't want for a better flatmate than my best friend. However, she was delusional if she thought I was squeezing my body into one of her barely-there dresses.

Where Sarah was tall and slim with a runner's body, I was on more of the curvier side with the body of a person who would rather sit at home reading the latest romance on my Kindle, than endure any form of the hell they call exercise. Sarah, though, was a health guru to the core, right down to the god-awful green stuff she drank every morning.

I guess her efforts were paying off; she was beautiful both inside and out. Sarah had those tanned, dark features that every girl would kill for or pay exuberant amounts of money to fake. With long, silky black hair and thick, pouty lips, she was stunning. Where she is tanned and toned, in comparison, I'm pale and curvy.

"*Ah-ha*, I found it!" she exclaims, walking out of the wardrobe triumphantly, holding up a strapless red dress.

Admittedly, the dress was gorgeous and would look so good on someone like Sarah. On someone like me? Let's just say I have a motto for clothes: just because you can squeeze into it, doesn't mean you should.

"I am not squeezing all of *this* into *that*," I plead, giving my best *don't make me pout* look.

"Lyssa, you have a killer bod. You know it. I know it. God knows it. And Ethan is about to know it. Just put the damn dress on already." She shoves the dress at me, waiting with a raised eyebrow.

"Fine." Stomping on the spot, I strip down to squeeze all my curves into the scrap of material that she claims to be a dress.

"Wow!" Sarah lets out a whistle as she grabs my shoulders, spinning me around to face the full-length mirror that stands in the corner of her room. I stand, staring back at my reflection and not believing what I'm seeing. First, the dress fit. It was not ripping at the seams to hold my curves in; instead, it looked like it was made for me, hugging me in all the right places.

My D-sized breasts were popping with the square-cut, strapless top—the fabric hugging at my hips before swaying out in a mermaid-shape that ended just before my knees. I was speechless as I looked at my reflection.

"Well, what do you think?" Sarah asks quietly from behind me.

"I think I love it! I think I love you. How do you always know how to dress me better than I can dress myself?" Turning, I hug her, squeezing tight.

"That's because I know the rocking body you possess underneath your baggy hoodies and jeans. Tonight, the rest of Sydney will know it too. Ethan won't know what to do with himself when he gets a look at you."

I finished the outfit off with a pair of black strappy Guess heels I scored in the clearance bin a few weeks ago and a shimmery black clutch. Sarah, being the makeup artist she is, beautifies my face and hair. Transforming my pale face into something that belonged on a magazine cover, she gave me just the right amount of smoky eye, paired with bright red shiny lips.

"The Uber will be here in ten!" Sarah yells from the living room.

Doing one last-minute check in the mirror, I make my way out to the living room. Nerves are eating at me; I'm not much of a people person. "Are you sure you don't want to tag along with me?" I plead with my best friend.

"Um, definitely not. I did not go to the effort of stalking that smoking hot groomsmen from the wedding I worked last weekend for myself. I did that all for you, sweet pea."

"Thanks?" It comes out as more of a question than a statement.

Grabbing onto my shoulders, she says, "I know you're nervous; you have every right to be after what that prick did to you, but this is different, okay?" I nod, trying to bury the memories that are creeping their way into my mind. Sarah hugs me and whispers, "You will thank me to the moon and back when you see him. Where did you say he was taking you again?"

4

I didn't give her any details because, knowing Sarah, she would turn up and spy on just how well I was not doing at this blind date thing, just to give me pointers for the next time.

"I didn't say." Smiling, I make my way to the door. "Don't wait up." As I say this, I know I'll be in early as I have a shift tomorrow. Sarah reads my face all too well, knowing I was thinking of having to go into work tomorrow.

"You can always call in sick if you stay out. You don't even like your job. Why not use all your personal leave for getting down and *personal* with a member of the opposite sex?" She wags her eyebrows up and down at me. Shaking my head, because there is no way to respond to all of that, I walk out the door.

SITTING in the back of the Uber, I rest my head against the headrest and contemplate cancelling this date and finding an open coffee shop, getting a vanilla latte and finishing the latest romance I was halfway through. Surely, my current book boyfriend could bring me more pleasure than a blind date with some guy named Ethan, no matter how hot Sarah claimed he was.

I hate meeting new people. I'm not a people person. I keep my close circle of friends small. That circle included Sarah and my other two BFFs, Holly and her identical twin Reilly; they were enough for me.

I process the list of pros and cons for cancelling the date. Pro: I can have a peaceful night with Ken, the current hot alpha book hero I'm crushing on. Con: I will undeniably have to endure Sarah's lecture when she eventually learns of my deceit. I decide to just meet this Ethan and avoid the day's long lecture on my lack of love life from my best friend.

The Uber pulls to a stop on the side of the street. Looking out the window, I double check the name of the restaurant that Ethan told me to meet him at—yes, *told me*. Not asked, not requested, just a simple message stating: *I'll meet you at Red Door Restaurant at 8 p.m.* That should have been my first red flag with this guy.

I can see the red door with a sign above proclaiming it to be the Red Door Restaurant, also taking note that next to the restaurant lays a carpeted

drink and contemplate how I will get out of here after this drink, *alone*.

There is so much beauty to take in. My eyes scan up and down the room, and that's when I see him. I lock eyes with possibly the most handsome man I've ever seen. His eyes pin me in place. I wish he were closer so I could see the colour. Leaning against the end of the bar, he lifts his glass to his lips—lips that look full and soft. I watch as he sips his drink, his throat as he swallows… Goddamn, even his throat is sexy. His beauty far outshines the opulence of this club. Inky hair that looks like it has a slight curl to it on top, tanned skin, a chiselled jaw with a little more than a five o'clock shadow. He's wearing a white dress shirt with the sleeves rolled up. *Mmm,* arm porn anyone? The top few buttons of his shirt are left undone, showing off just enough of a smooth chest. Paired with dark blue dress pants, he looks like he has just come from the cover shoot for GQ. As I'm contemplating this, a shadow falls across his face and his features become hard, almost like he's angry all of a sudden, like he wants to rip someone's head off.

I don't have time to dwell on his sudden change as a hand creeps up my leg. I turn to find Ethan with one hand on my leg and the other holding up my drink. Removing his hand from my leg, I smile as I go to take my drink from him, and my head spins. I lose my balance and fall into him. What the heck? I haven't even had the damn drink yet. I stumble as I try to find my way back onto my seat. His arms go around me like a vice and I push him back with both hands against his chest. Suddenly, he goes flying. Man, I'm stronger than I thought I was. I barely catch myself on the bar before I look up and into a pair of green eyes, emerald green eyes. Eyes that belong to the GQ model and he looks mad.

I try to focus on his eyes, but the world is spinning. Reaching up, I touch his face, thinking, "GQ, you are so pretty." Then I hear it, a rumble? A laugh?

A deep, husky voice mumbles, "Thanks," before his arms reach out and grab my waist. Thanks? Why is he thanking me? Why is the world spinning so fast? I think I just need to close my eyes for a bit. I close my eyes and then feel my body falling.

Two

ZACHARY

Two hours earlier

OUR HOURS, I've been sitting in this chair for four straight fucking hours. Stretching out the kink in my neck, I rub my thumbs over my temples to relieve some built-up pressure thumping through my head. I've been reading spreadsheet after spreadsheet, dealing with invoices and stock orders. I should hire someone to manage all of this day-to-day shit for me. The problem is I don't trust any fuckers with my accounts.

I'm reading through the latest revenue report—we've doubled our profit margin this month, compared to what it was this time last month. It seems the events and PR manager I hired two months ago has been doing her job this last month. I was close to firing her during her first month here. Her constant attempts at flirting and eye-fucking me were getting on my fucking nerves.

She must have finally got it through that plastic head of hers. It would never happen for her. I make it a rule to not fuck the employees on my payroll; it never ends well for me... *or them.*

The way the club is making legal money this month will make it a hell of a lot easier for the accountant to clean the money from the other business I run here. While owning one of the best night-clubs in Sydney is a very lucrative business, running the underground fight club, Club M, adds a lot more cash to the ever-growing pot.

Looking back through the extensive list of emails I have yet to reply to, I skim through to see which ones can wait, and which ones I will have to find the fucking time to get to before the night's through. I'm just about to click one open from my lawyer, as my office door flies open and my baby brother, all 6 ft 3inches of him, barges through. Obviously, he hasn't learnt the skill of fucking knocking.

"Bray, I see you still haven't mastered the art of knocking." I slide the Glock I was about to point his way back into the slot on the underside of my desk.

"Why waste precious time knocking when I can just turn the fucking handle and *boom*, here I am," he replies loudly as he slumps his big form onto the couch, pouring himself a glass of Glenfiddich 50-year-old whisky. Leaning back, he pops his feet up on the table.

"Help yourself, why don't you, and while you're at it, get your dirty fucking boots off my table." He grumbles as he removes his feet, placing them back on the floor. I give up on staring at the computer screen and join Bray at the couch, pouring myself a glass. "We have ten fully stocked bars in this building. Why are you in my office drinking my whisky?"

The bastard just smirks at me. "You've got the good stuff. Why wouldn't I be here?" I'm not buying that he just stormed into my office for whisky, however, I know my brother and I know when to pick my battles. This is one I don't need to pick right now.

Deciding to change tactics, I ask, "You ready for the fight tonight? Think maybe you should save your celebratory drink for after you win, winning me the thousands I'm betting on you?"

Bray shakes his head, smirking. "Please, I was born ready for this fight. Smith will wish he never challenged *the* Brayden fucking Johnson to an actual fight in the cage."

He's always been so damn cocky; the fact that he's undefeated does not help. I've placed a hundred grand on the line, so he better be fucking winning tonight. "You better be ready. I have a lot riding on this fight, Bray." I try to hit home with him just how much is at stake if he loses.

"I know, bro. Relax, I got this." He sips his drink before adding, "Also, I need you to be present on the floor tonight."

Ah, I knew there was a reason he was in my office,

and there it is. "And why, exactly, would you need me to be on the floor tonight?" I question.

I do my best not to be seen out on the floor. I would rather be in the basement watching over my fights, than watching over drunks and pushing off girls who have no sense of self-preservation.

They always come across like they're good for the one-night deal I offer, but then here they'll be, hanging around the following weekend with claws out and looking to stake a claim they have no right to stake. I don't do relationships, ever. No woman has ever kept my interest longer than a weekend to even make it seem worth considering putting myself through the hell of a monogamous relationship.

"I have it on good authority that Ella will be here tonight." And there it is, the one reason that would have my ass out on the fucking floor; our baby sister, and when I say baby, I mean fucking eighteen years old.

"Why the fuck would she come here? This is no place for Ella."

"You think I want her here? I have one fight tonight. I don't need to be fighting every other fucking arsehole in this joint who looks at her, on top of the one I have to win."

When I say nothing else, Bray sighs. "She's eighteen, Zac. We can't exactly lock her away, and better that she comes to our club where we can keep an eye on her, than she goes somewhere else where anything could fucking happen." I have to agree with that, not the locking away idea, because that's still a viable option to me.

"What am I supposed to do when she gets here? Just sit back and watch our baby sister get shit-faced and hit on by fucking drunks? Not happening."

He thinks on this for a moment before responding, "When she gets here, have one of your boys take her and her friends to the VIP floor. I've reserved a section for them."

"Fine, but I'm having two of my guys stay in her section all night, and when, not if but *when*, I'm getting locked up for murdering the arseholes who try to hit on her, you better fucking bail me out."

Brayden smirks before getting up and walking to the door. Looking back, he says, "I'll do better than bail you out, bro. I'll bury the fucking bodies so that no one ever finds them. You can't have a murder without a body, right?"

With that, he walks out the door. It wouldn't be the first time he's buried a body or two either.

AFTER REPLYING to about a billion emails, I look at the clock. I can hear the house music of the club pump. It's ten to nine, still early in club time, however, I have no idea what time Ella is planning on arriving. Shrugging out of my jacket, I remove my tie and fold the sleeves of my shirt up as I'm walking out of my office.

Dean, my best friend since high school and head of security, falls into step next to me. "What's on the agenda for tonight, boss?" he asks.

Grunting, I relay what little info I know, "Ella and some of her friends are planning to come in tonight. I need you to find two of your best guys to escort her straight to the VIP floor—make sure they stay in her section the whole night. I'm sure I don't need to tell you, but no one touches her."

He looks at me for a moment with a look I can't quite decipher, somewhat furious and confused. "What the fuck is she doing coming to a place like this? Isn't she only seventeen?"

"She just turned eighteen two weeks ago; you were there at her fucking party, you moron. Until now, I've kept her out of here. Fuck, I'm gonna have to kill some motherfuckers tonight, aren't I?"

Dean shakes his head, pulling out his phone. Ready to send off the orders to his men, he adds, "Don't worry, you won't be the only one doing the killing." With that, he turns the opposite way, walking up to the VIP floor, while I make my way down to the first floor.

I find a spot at the end of the main bar that extends the length of the building. From this vantage point, I can see the entrance to the club and every fucker who enters. As I look around, I see people are already filling the top floor balconies that overlook the dance floor. There are groups of people sitting around the sectioned areas that line the red walls of this floor. The tables that people sit around show the vision of The Merge: bodies entwined in a sexual embrace, when two or more souls become merged to unite as one.

Over the years, I've built The Merge up from the bottom. It's now the place to come for a good night out. What most don't know is the real action happens in the basement, below this very floor, where my underground fight events are held, and where I should be now, instead of sitting at this damn bar waiting for my sister to arrive.

James comes over with my drink before I even have to signal for him. "This is why you're my number one barman, James," I say in way of greeting, taking the drink.

"I'm your number one because my hot bod brings all the girls to the bar's more like it," he exclaims.

I have to admit he makes a killing in tips from the ladies here, even though tipping in Australia is not common. When he first started, James demanded we place a gold tip jar on the bar with his photo on it. According to him, the jar matched the décor (or some shit) so it shouldn't bother me.

The only time I've noticed it is when I see ladies strip their panties off right in front of it and place them in the jar. I keep my face turned towards the door, waiting for Ella.

"If only they knew you would never make use of those numbers or panties they slip in that jar of yours." James laughs. "Nope, but I'd sure as shit make use of your number if you slipped it in." I shake my head at him. He has been trying to get me to swing to his team since he started working here four years ago.

"Waiting on someone?" James asks as he wipes the bar down—nosey bastard that he is.

"Ella," I say, not looking at him. That has him coughing and splattering all over the place. I wait for him to compose himself.

When he finally gets himself under control, his eyebrows raise in question. "What is she doing coming to a place like this?"

"Apparently, she is eighteen now, and this is what eighteen-year-olds fucking do on a Friday night."

"Well, eighteen or not, she's not likely to have any fun here with you and Bray around supervising."

That thought makes me smile. Looking at him, I say, "You know what? You're right. With any luck, she'll hate it and not want to go clubbing again." I raise my glass in cheers as he walks back down the other end of the bar to serve some early customers.

I turn back to keep watch on the door again and almost choke on the drink I was attempting to swallow. Standing in the doorway is a fucking angel. Long, blonde, wavy hair, curves in all the right places and those breasts… Holy mother of god, what I wouldn't do to get a taste of them. Even in the dark, she looks like a ray of fucking sunshine.

She stands there in a red dress, looking every bit a fifty's pinup model. Why is she just standing there? She seems to look around, taking it all in. Just as I'm about to get up and offer her a privately guided tour, particularly to my office, some pencil-dicked douche comes up behind her and squeezes her ass.

I'm ready to rip the douches hand right off his arm. She spins so quickly with her arm raised and I wait for the slap that doesn't come. She hesitates before lowering her arm.

The douche grabs her hand and starts tugging her towards the bar. I'm ready to put him in his place for her, before she tugs her hand free and takes up a seat right next to him. Maybe he's her boyfriend? The thought makes me irrationally mad. I don't know this woman. I don't have any kind of claim on her… yet. I watch as she orders a drink from James before spinning around in her chair and watching the room.

Her gaze finally makes it to my side of the bar and as soon as our eyes lock on each other, I'm hypnotised, caught in a trance and soaking in all that she is. She isn't looking away either. I don't know what it is, but this woman has cast a spell. I know I need to look away, but I can't seem to make my eyes move.

Just behind her, I see James place their drinks on the bar top before turning away to serve another customer, and that's when I see the same pencil-dicked douche empty some kind of white powder into her drink.

This has me seeing red. Just as I'm getting up to go over, the douche slides his hand up her leg and she turns around, about to accept the drink, but she stumbles. When he grabs her, I know I'm about to cash in on Bray's offer to bury bodies.

The angel attempts to push him off, but it's useless —he's twice her size. Walking up behind him, I throw him across the room before turning back to my sunshine. Huh, *my* sunshine? I give a hand signal to the security grabbing him, so they know to take him down to the basement and wait for my orders on what to do with him.

I turn just in time to catch the angel as she falls again, steadying her with my hands on her waist. I know she can't be drunk. I watched her walk into the club less than five minutes ago. She was stable, not a wobble to her. Now she can barely stand.

She reaches up and touches my face. "GQ, you are so pretty." I laugh, but before I know it, she's falling into me.

"Shit." Scooping her up into my arms, I instruct James to have her drink, the one I know was roofied, sent downstairs and to tell the boys to wait for me.

I pick up her purse off the bar, carry her up to my office and lay her on the couch. Just as I'm doing this, Dean comes through the door. He looks at me, then at the couch, then at me again.

Yeah, mate, I know. It's strange to see a woman on my couch in her clothes. Although, now that I think about it, that dress doesn't do a damn thing to cover her body from roaming eyes. Before I think about what I'm doing, I walk over to my chair and grab my jacket, placing it over the top half of her body.

As I look back up, Dean is staring at me, mouth gaping like a damn fish. "What?" I demand, getting more and more frustrated at the situation. I need to get my hands on the fucker who did this to her.

He shakes his head and smirks. "*Umm*, nothing, boss. What do you want me to do with the prick the boys brought downstairs?"

"Ella here yet?" I ask.

"Just got here. She's in VIP with her friends—got Steve and Jonno with them."

I nod. "Tell them to bring her up here. Make sure Steve and Jonno come too."

He pulls out his phone, firing off text messages as I empty the woman's purse contents onto my desk. Picking up her ID, I discover she is twenty-three years old. Alyssa Summers. Nice name—it feels like it just rolls off the tongue.

ELLA COMES STUMBLING into my office giggling with one of her friends, who suddenly stops and stares at me. Ella is oblivious until I call her out. "Ella, how much have you had to drink?"

She looks up and smiles at me, knowing she can usually get away with murder with that damn smile. This time, I'm not smiling back. She takes a minute, but she sobers and looks around. Noticing the woman passed out on the couch, she looks back to me.

"I've only had one drink, Zac. Why?"

"I need you to stay here and watch over her for a bit," I say, pointing at the passed out and oblivious woman.

"Who is she? And why am I babysitting one of your floozies?"

"She," I say, pointing at the woman, "is Alyssa, and was roofied by some asshole who I need to teach a lesson to. She is not one of my *floozies* as you call them."

Ella takes a moment to digest what I've said before taking a seat on the opposite couch, her silent friend following suit. "Wow, I can't believe someone was stupid enough to drug a girl in your club, Zac."

I don't reply to the comment; the motherfucker won't be doing it again once I'm finished with him.

"I need you to stay outside the door. No one gets in; no one touches her," I demand, pointing at Steve and Jonno, both of whom nod their heads before turning to stand out front of the door.

Turning to Ella, I instruct, "Do not let anyone touch her."

She stares at me, mouth open, before composing herself and replying, "Sure thing, big brother. No one touches her."

I kiss Ella on the head as I walk out of the office. "Don't leave until I get back." I don't bother waiting for her reply. I know she won't leave Alyssa alone.

STANDING in a corner of the dark room, I know he doesn't realise I'm here yet. He doesn't know that I relish the sound of his cries and pleas for help... help that's never going to come.

Down here, there is nobody to hear him scream. I

wait a few more minutes for the fight that's about to happen in the cage between Bray and Smith to start. The noise of the crowd will drown out this fucker's screams. When I hear the roar of the crowd, I take a breath in, inhaling the smells of the basement— dampness mixed with blood. Counting down in my head, I know that I am going to get my hands on the douche any time now.

I wait until I hear the ref's whistle before I make myself known to the arsehole tied to my chair. "Smell that?" I ask, watching as he jumps, turning his head left and right and attempting to see where I am. It's useless though; he's blindfolded and can't see for shit.

"Who are you? Why am I here? Let me go," he pleads, already begging before the fun begins. *Figures*.

"I'm the guy about to give you a lesson on what happens to fuckers who drug innocent women in my fucking club." I get right up to his face before whispering in his ear, "And I will enjoy every damn minute of this lesson."

He pisses himself, literally just fucking pisses himself, the wet patch growing on the front of his jeans. Not surprising, as any guy who needs to resort to drugging a woman is a weak piece of shit.

Landing a punch to his stomach, then another to his face, I relish the blood splatters that come from his mouth. Now I'm smiling. It's a shame he can't see how damn much I'm enjoying this.

The sight of his blood, and the fact that I caused it, releases something in me.

His cries get louder. "Please… please let me go, man. I did nothing."

Pathetic is what he is. "Scream all you want, mate. No one can hear you down here. And even if they could hear, they wouldn't save you."

He struggles against the ropes on his arms. Holding his head still, I land another punch to his ribs then one to his face. I let go and he falls backwards, chair and all.

"Fuck you! Untie me and fight me like a real man." Now, he tries to be brave—the fucker probably thinks I won't fight him if he's not tied down. Think again, motherfucker. Bending down, I remove the blindfold and nod to Dean, giving him the signal to cut the ties loose.

"Wha… what… what are you doing?" he sputters as Dean approaches, flicking the knife between his fingers.

"Making your wish come true, fucker. I'm cutting those ties, so you can fight the boss *like a real man.*"

Dean laughs and kicks him in his stomach before leaning down and cutting the ties loose. The douche scoots backwards on his arse until he hits the wall.

"Stand up!" I command.

"N… n… no, please. You don't have to do this. Just let me go. I won't say nothing to nobody." He's shaking his head back and forth violently.

"I thought you wanted to fight me like a real man? Now get the fuck off the floor!" I approach him, and he still doesn't stand up to fight. I kick him in his ribs and he goes into the foetal position, crying like the motherfucking pansy arse he is.

I go at him, landing punches to his face and torso, before I turn back to Dean, who's watching with a huge-arse grin on his face—sadistic bastard that he is.

"Got that drink I had James send down here?" I ask.

"Yep," he says as he walks over to the table, picking up the drink.

"Good, make sure he drinks the whole thing before you throw his ass out to the back alley." I walk out, hearing the asshole screaming and begging. I don't need to be there for the rest. I have an angel who needs taking care of back in my office.

Three

ALYSSA

*M*Y HEAD FEELS like a hundred little men with big hammers are pounding away on my brain. *Pound. Thump. Pound. Thump. Argh,* I slowly try to open my eyes to the world. "Bright," I mumble out to nobody but myself.

My angel fairy must be listening today because I hear the shifting of fabric and the room becomes darker. Much better. I try to open my eyes again, slowly coming back to reality.

Why is my bed so damn hard? *Wait.* I open my eyes. That's when I see him. That's when I realise I am most definitely not in my bedroom. Because, one thing I know for sure, the god sitting in the chair across from me would not be following a girl like me to my bedroom, or any room.

"Morning, sunshine." Oh god, he talks. His voice.

A husky rumble that goes straight through to my core. He's looking straight at me with a smirk on his face and one raised eyebrow, like he's waiting for something.

"*Ah… umm.*" I stumble over my words.

"Usually, the response would be good morning. I'd even accept: Morning, handsome. Morning, sexy. Your choice really. I'm not picky." Picky, maybe. Cocky, definitely.

"Morning?" My greeting comes out as more of a question than an actual greeting. "Where am I? Do I know you? Oh god, we didn't, did we?"

I freak out as I look underneath the jacket that lies on top of my dress—my dress, which is still in place, thank god. I mentally run an internal category of my body: my head hurts for sure, my stomach is seedy, but other parts (the important parts) nothing. Surely if we did anything, I would feel something, right?

Looking at him, I don't see how I wouldn't have jumped at the chance to get him naked. He's wearing a pair of faded jeans, a black V-neck shirt that stretches across his chest and broad shoulders, and black boots. Did he just come from a photoshoot? His biceps are on show from the short sleeves of the shirt.

He's not disgustingly huge like a bodybuilder. Just the right amount of muscle, enough to know he takes care of himself and spends time in a gym. His shirt is tucked in slightly to the waist of his jeans, which hang low on his hips.

His hair is damp like he's just stepped out of the shower—*mmm,* now *that* I would like to see, him in a shower, water running down his body. I'm pulled from my thoughts as I hear his laugh; it's deep and rough, almost like his voice is not used to the concept of laughing.

He's laughing at my obvious distress. "Trust me, sunshine, if we did," he says, raising his eyebrows, "you would most certainly remember, and not to mention, feel it for the next few days."

Yep, most definitely a cocky-ass, probably has girls falling at his feet left and right. Why does that thought make me want to throw up even more?

He hands me a bottle of water and some aspirin that were sitting on the table. "Take these and drink this; you can thank me later."

I swallow the pills and drink half the bottle of water before looking back at him. "Thank you, but you didn't answer my question. Where am I, and how did I get here?" I wave my arm around the office I woke up in, then take a moment to look around the space. It's obvious no money was spared fitting out this office. A huge mahogany desk sits centred in front of wall-to-ceiling windows that overlook the view of the Sydney Harbour. Dark timber shelving lines the walls; some stacked with bottles and glasses, and others with photographs, books and ornaments.

"You're in my office. I carried you up here after you collapsed on me down at the bar."

Bits of the night start coming back. I remember sitting at the bar, I remember staring at the man who now sits in front of me (GQ), and then I remember Ethan.

"Ethan?" I question, unsure what happened to my date, and unsure if I exactly care what happened to him either.

At the mention of the name, Mr. GQ looks away from me, face hard as stone while clenching his jaw. "He your boyfriend or something?" he asks through clenched teeth.

"Or something," I answer, shrugging. He doesn't seem happy with my answer, just stares blankly at me like he's waiting for more. Well, he can keep waiting. I'm not one to discuss my ins and outs with strangers. "Have you got a bathroom I can use?" I ask as I stand up on wobbly legs, looking up at him as I regain my balance.

"Through there." He nods to a door. I pick up my clutch from the table and make my way into the bathroom, shutting and locking the door behind me.

"Shit, shit, shit," I say out loud as I try not to panic over my current situation. I pull my phone out to see a million missed calls and texts from Sarah, Reilly and Holly. Sarah must've told them I didn't come home. I read through Sarah's texts first.

SARAH: **Where are you? I thought you'd be home by now.**

Sarah: Seriously, Lyssa, text me back so I know you're still alive.

Sarah: Okay, if you don't call me back, I will come and hunt you down.

Sarah: You left me no choice. I had to call Holly and Reilly. Now you have three pissed off friends. Seriously, call me back so I know you're not dead in a ditch somewhere!!!

Sarah: Wait, you're not dead in a ditch, are you? Shit, because if you are, I will revive you just to KILL you myself for making me develop stress wrinkles.

Holly: Lyssa, there's no shame in getting your freak on. There is shame in making your friends worry. Text me back so we know you're still breathing.

Reilly: Is he hot?

AT THIS, I laugh a little and then stop myself as I realise I'm probably sounding like a crazy person to Mr. GQ on the other side of the door. I quickly send out a group text to the three of them.

ME: **Not dead, not in a ditch. Be home soon!**

NOT EVEN THREE SECONDS LATER, my phone vibrates in my hand. I don't bother opening their messages. Looking in the mirror, I audibly shriek at the reflection staring back at me. Racoon eyes much?

"Jeez, no wonder he was staring," I mumble to myself. I make quick work of doing my business, washing my hands and face before picking my phone back up and opening the Uber app.

I walk back out of the bathroom to find Mr. GQ standing at his desk—at least I think it's his desk. He looks like he belongs here. Realising I'm staring at him again, I look back down at my phone.

"I'm just going to call for an Uber and be on my way. Thanks for whatever it is you did for me last night."

"No," he says, staring straight at me. I swear he can see right into my soul; his stare is penetrating... *mmm*, penetrating. Damn it, now I'm thinking of him penetrating in other ways.

Shaking my head, I question him, "No? What do you mean, no?"

"Exactly that. No, you won't be getting an Uber home. I'll drive you." I must look like a confused nut job around this guy; he never seems to make sense to me.

"Well, that's nice of you, but I don't even know you. I'll just take an Uber."

"Do you know every Uber driver in Sydney?" he asks.

"What? Of course I don't know every Uber driver in Sydney," I respond, shaking my head at him.

"So, it's safe to get in a car with a complete stranger, but not safe to get a lift home with the guy who saved you from being date raped last night?" He's so matter of fact.

"What do you mean date raped? I wasn't..."

"No, you weren't, but you would have been had I not stepped in. That guy you were at the bar with, Ethan…" He clenches his jaw as he grinds out the name.

"I watched him put Rohypnol in your drink at the bar. Although he must have already given you something before you came in here, because you passed out without even touching the drink you ordered."

Holy shit, someone drugged me. No wonder my head feels like shit. I'm stunned. I don't know what to say to GQ, so instead, I stand, awkwardly staring at him.

I finally decide that I have manners. Reaching my hand out, I say, "Hi, I'm Alyssa, and thanks for helping me out last night. It's all a bit foggy for me. I remember being at the restaurant and then coming in here for a drink. I remember seeing you at the bar. I mean, how could I forget seeing you. That's not a face anyone would forget in a hurry, and… oh god, now I'm rambling. I'm just going to shut up now and go home."

Before I can even turn around, he grabs my hand and I'm stunned again at the zap of electricity going through my body. I wonder if he feels it too because he says nothing for a beat, just looks at me, confused.

He gives his head a subtle shake before speaking. "I'm Zac. Zachary Williams, but you can call me Zac, and I'm still driving you home."

With that, he picks up a pair of keys from his desk. He walks over to the couch to pick up his jacket before turning back to me and placing it over my shoulders, wrapping me up in his scent. It seems like such an odd and intimate gesture, something someone I don't know shouldn't be doing. It feels right though.

The fabric is soft. I gather the top of the jacket in my hands and bring it to my nose and sniff. It smells like him, woodsy with a mix of citrus. If he thinks it's strange that I literally sniffed his jacket, he doesn't say anything. He just smirks at me, showing me a dimple I can see myself licking. Before I can lose myself in my head again, he places his hand on my lower back as he leads me out of the office.

"Come."

I shiver at the demand—wild thoughts of him demanding me to come while spread out naked on his desk run through my mind. I contemplate how his hand feels warm, the complete opposite to how Ethan's hand felt when he touched me last night.

The thought of Ethan makes me furious. How dare he drug me. I don't have time to stew on my anger now. As Zac, aka GQ, leads me through the building, I'm focused on trying not to trip over myself with all the people around openly gawking at me? *At him?*

ZAC LEADS me out through a back door that opens to a carpark. Grabbing my hand, he takes me over to the passenger side of the closest car to the door—well, at least I think it's a car. It's shiny, black and has wheels, so it must be a car, right? Zac presses a button on the door, which has the door automatically opening out and then up. Okay, so definitely not an ordinary car.

"Get in," he grumbles.

I tentatively duck into the car, turning to him. "You know, you really don't need to drive me. I can find my way home."

He silently presses a button on the door, and suddenly I'm closed inside what is no doubt the fanciest car I've ever seen. I'm too frightened to move, on the off chance I dirty or break something. Sitting there frozen, I watch as Zac makes his way around the front of the car before climbing into the driver's side.

He shuts his door, turns the car on and then turns and looks at me like he's waiting for something. He doesn't say anything for a minute, and I squirm under his stare, not knowing what he's waiting for.

Unable to handle the intensity of his silent quest, I hesitantly try to break the silence. "*Umm, so…*" That's about as intelligent of a sentence I can put together right now.

"Buckle up, sunshine. It's a fast ride," he says as he reaches over, putting my seat belt on for me. I can feel the heat rise up my neck and reach my face as he plugs the seat belt in.

Zac takes off out of the carpark and into the easy Saturday morning city traffic. *Saturday morning.*

"Oh, shit," I mumble under my breath as I dig through my clutch for my phone to find out what the time is and how late I will be for my shift today. "Dammit!" My phone would choose this moment to be dead flat.

"What's wrong?" Zac questions with a deeply concerned look on his face.

"What time is it?" I attempt in the calmest voice I can muster, externally hoping to appear cool, calm, and collected. Internally, I'm a freaking mess, considering the worst possible scenarios. I'm late. I'm getting fired. I'm going to be jobless and homeless within the month. Maybe I'm being the glass is half empty kind of girl, but when you had the childhood I had, the glass is never half full.

Zac looks at the gold watch on his wrist, before looking back across at me. "It's 9:15."

9:15 a.m. Not so bad… I'm mentally calculating

the amount of time I need to get home, shower, and hike to the station. If I hurry, I can probably make the 10:15 train, which will get me to work at around 11:30.

"Fudge it, can this Batmobile of yours go any faster?" I plead.

"Batmobile?" he repeats, laughing a little. "This beauty…" He taps the steering wheel with pride. "… is a McLaren 570S. Yes, it goes faster."

"Well, do you think you can make *this beauty* go faster and get me home as quickly as you can?" I'm trying hard not to come across as panicked, but, by the look on his face, I don't think it's working.

"Look, if I'm going to go about breaking every road rule in the book, I need to know why you're in such a rush to get home?" He makes a scene of sniffing himself. "I showered while you were passed out on my couch, so I know it's not because I stink that you're in such a rush to get home, so what is it?"

Wow, just wow. *Well, here it goes. Try not to sound desperate in front of the hot guy, Lyssa.* I give myself a mental pep talk before admitting just how desperate I am. "You don't stink. I'm late. I have to be at work at 11:00. I need to get home. I need to shower, then I need to make the trek to the station—it's at least a forty-minute train ride to work. I can't be late… Oh god, I cannot be late!" Well, I think I totally came across as every bit as cool and collected as I was aiming for, right? *Yeah, probably not.*

"Sunshine, breathe. It's okay. I gotcha. I'll get you

home in no time. Hold on." Zac cruises through the streets, weaving in and out of traffic a little faster. He reaches over and gives my hand a little squeeze before turning his gaze back to the road.

I'm momentarily stunned by the electricity I feel run up my arm from his touch. I look at him, his muscles stretching out the black V-neck, his forearms tensing as he grips the steering wheel… damn. Unintentionally, I squeeze my legs together and suppress the moan that wants to escape. *What the hell is wrong with me?* This handsome stranger is nice enough to give me a lift home and all I can think about is jumping his bones.

I hear him curse under his breath. "Where do you work?" he asks, obviously trying to distract me with small talk. Could this moment get any more embarrassing? It's obvious he knows I was checking him out. "I work at RNS. I'm a nurse in emergency," I say with pride. Zac looks over and smiles briefly, before masking his face again.

"You should take the day off. You were drugged last night, remember?" he almost grunts out.

"I'm fine. I'm not taking the day off." We're turning onto my street when I realise I never gave him my address. "*Umm*, how did you know where I lived?" Zac looks over at me, supplying me with that GQ smile of his, and says, "I saw your address on your licence last night." As we turn into my street, he looks at the block of townhouses. "Which one is yours?"

I point out my townhouse. "That one, but you can

just stop here and I'll jump out. Thanks for the ride, and everything else."

Zac looks at me and shakes his head before pulling into a carpark and turning the car off. He gets out of the car and is around at my door before I can even comprehend what's happening. Zac opens my door, holding his hand out to help me out of the car.

I take his hand and the moment I do, I feel it again, that zap of electricity. Once I'm out of the car and have collected myself, I remove my hand.

"Thank you," I whisper as I walk towards my door. It's not until I get to the top step that I notice that Zac followed me to the door. Turning around, I squint at him. "*Umm*, what are you doing?"

He takes a moment, looking me over before answering. "First, I'm walking you to your door. Second, I'm waiting for you to shower and get ready for work so I can drop you off at the hospital."

I'm not really sure what is happening. Did I wake up in an alternative universe today? I pinch my arm. Okay, so I'm not dreaming, but I sure do look a little unstable to Mr. GQ in front of me.

"Why would you want to drive me to work?" I question. It's been my experience that people don't do anything expecting nothing in return.

"You're running late. You said you were planning on catching a train. Trains are not safe, and you would still be late. I can get you there in half the time, but you might want to get moving on that shower if you want to make it to work on time."

He's right—I know he's right—but it doesn't mean I have to be happy about it. Grumbling, I turn and open the door, before adding, "I'm only letting you give me a lift in the Batmobile because I really, really don't want to be late. You can wait on the couch."

He smirks and laughs as he follows me inside.

I POINT TO THE SOFA. "You can wait here. I'm just going to run upstairs and shower real quick."

Zac follows my gaze to look up at the narrow staircase before looking back to me. "Sure thing." He heads towards the sofa.

That's when I hear it… I thought just maybe something might go my way today and Sarah would be out already. She always leaves early on Saturdays, claiming she wants to make the most of the weekends by starting them early.

Sarah comes bounding down the stairs in a pair of cut-off shorts and bikini top, looking every bit the drop-dead gorgeous creature she is. She stops dead in her tracks when she sees me and Zac standing in our living room.

Sarah turns towards me and raises her eyebrows as she states, "*That* is not Ethan." Turning her head, she gives Zac the once-over. "Yep, definitely not Ethan. It is absolutely an improvement though."

I don't know why—I can't explain the feeling exactly—but something happens deep inside me when I see the way she's looking at Zac. Like he was a porterhouse steak she couldn't wait to sink her teeth into. I didn't like it, not one bit.

She must have noticed something flicker across my face because she comes up to me. "Are you okay? You don't look so hot." Concern is written on her face. "Did he do something to you? Because even serial killers can be beautiful, Lyssa." She turns towards Zac like she wants to bury him alive. Sarah is nothing if not the most loyal friend.

Unsure how to handle the situation, I turn to Zac, expecting him to be looking his fill at my beautiful friend, like every other man does in her presence. I'm stunned to silence when I see he isn't looking at her at all; his eyes are fixed on me. He looks pissed off again, jaw clenched tight.

Ignoring his pissed off look, I turn back to Sarah. "This is Zac; he helped me out last night, drove me home this morning, and has kindly offered to wait for me to shower and then drive me to work. Sorry, don't have time to chitchat. I'm late."

I'm just about to the first step when Sarah stops me. "Lyssa, stop right there!" She's using her *don't fuck with me* voice. I look over at Zac, who is now giving Sarah a death glare. I really don't have time to figure this guy out right now, or ever. "Why, and how exactly, did *Zac* have to help you last night?" Her voice rises in pitch as she shrieks and uses air quotes when she says his name.

"Oh, it was nothing. I'll fill you in later. In the meantime, make sure you lose Ethan's details and block him on all of your social media."

I turn to start back up the stairs when someone clears their throat. It's a deep, husky noise, one that sends shivers down my spine; a throat noise that most certainly does not belong to Sarah.

"I wouldn't say that getting roofied by your date and passing out in a packed nightclub is nothing, Alyssa. Your night could have gone a lot differently if I wasn't there," Zac so helpfully points out.

Sarah gasps. "You were roofied?" She doesn't give me time to answer before she starts on her tirade. "By Ethan, the hot groomsman? What the fuck? I'm going to kill him—no, I'm going to torture him. I'll start at his toes and make my way up his legs. I'll skip his manhood, make him think I'm sparing him, and move to his fingers. It can't be too hard to rip finger-nails off, right? Then I think I'll chop the fuckers off. Just when he thinks I'm done, that's when I'll strike him where it really hurts. Tie a string around his balls tight, then tie the other end to the door and slam it—

you know, like kids do for teeth. I'll keep slamming that door until his balls rip off."

Sarah paces as she continues mumbling to herself. I'm stunned into silence. I mean, I knew she was loyal as shit. What shocks me the most was how much I liked the picture she just painted in my head. I don't recall a time I've ever been this pissed off with someone, and that's saying something, because I've been in some shitty situations over the years.

When I come to this realisation, I tell her, "I'll help, and when were done, I'll help bury the body. We'll burn it in the grave before we shovel all the dirt back in too." Sarah smiles and nods, like it's a forgone plan.

Zac looks back and forward between us both. Fixing his gaze on me with a slight smirk, he says, "No need to get all Jekyll and Hyde, sunshine. I've already taken care of the fucker; he won't be bothering you again." He looks at his watch before looking back up. "Not that I'm not enjoying this episode of *Murder, She Wrote*, but you might want to get a move on with that shower if you want to make it to work on time. My car's fast, but it's no time machine, sweetheart."

That has me screeching my way upstairs and into the shower. I have the quickest shower in the history of showers, find a pair of scrubs, and pile my hair up into a messy top bun. Just before I'm about to turn to head downstairs, I stop and add a layer of nude lip gloss to my lips.

Four

ZAC

I LOOK over to Alyssa sitting in the seat next to me. It feels right to have her there. She's only wearing scrubs, but I swear when she came down the stairs after rushing through a shower, I had to tell myself not to be the creeper and to stop visibly drooling. She is gorgeous. Up close, I can see that her blue eyes sometimes flicker with shades of green. Her blonde hair is all piled up on top of her head, with loose strands already breaking free around her face.

"I just have a quick stop to make—be one minute; stay here. I'm locking the doors to prevent people getting in, not you getting out," I say as I pull into a carpark right out front of the café I called while she was in the shower. She looks at me like I need a shrink but smiles and agrees to stay put.

I'm in and out of the café within two minutes and back in the car. "I'm not sure how you take your coffee yet. I went for the safe bet and ordered you a flat white." I hand her the coffee cup, which she takes hesitantly.

"Thank you. You really didn't need to do this, but I appreciate it. I love flat whites; also, vanilla lattes are a regular for me."

I hand her the bag with the two muffins. "One's blueberry; the other's chocolate chip. Eat."

She looks at me like I've lost my head now, her face scrunched up and brows furrowed. "What?" I ask.

"I can't eat this in your car. I'll make a mess. You'll end up with crumbs all over the place; you will need to get a detail. I don't know how much a car like this cost to get detailed, but I know I can't afford that. So, thank you for the muffin, but I can't possibly eat in the Batmobile." She's trying to hand the paper bag back to me, and all I can think is: wow, she is cute when she gets nervous and worked up.

"Sunshine, you are eating the muffin; you will eat in this car. I don't care if you get crumbs everywhere —that's nothing a vacuum can't fix. What I care about is the fact that you were planning on going to work for god knows how many hours without even eating breakfast. You know breakfast is the most important meal of the day, right?" She's still holding the bag out to me. I ignore her and pull back out onto the road.

It takes a moment, and she's quiet when she speaks again. "Thank you." She's not looking at me when she says it, head down while looking at the paper bag like she can will it away.

Eventually she opens the bag and takes a small chunk of the chocolate chip muffin, popping it into her mouth. Almost as soon as it hits her tongue, she lets out a pleasurable moan. I look over. Her eyes are closed and her head's leaning back; it's a good look on her, a damn good look. I have to will myself to look back at the road and subtly adjust my jeans to allow for my growing cock.

Fuck me, I don't know what it is about this girl, but she ticks every one of my ideal woman list items —a list I didn't know I even had until I saw her. I don't even care that I can see crumbs dropping in my car. I've never let anyone so much as have a coffee in this car before, let alone eat a savoury. Bray would not let me hear the end of it if he found out I let a girl eat in this beast. But the thought of her not eating just pissed me off.

We're almost at the hospital. I don't want to drop her off and not know when I will see her again. My brain is scrambling for ideas on how I'm going to make that happen. I need to see her again. Attempting to not look like the arse I have probably been portraying, I try to make small talk, covertly trying to find out more about this woman who has consumed my mind from the moment she walked through the doors of my club last night.

"Do you work all weekend?" I try to sound casual, like it doesn't matter to me either way, but it does. I don't want her working tomorrow. If she works tomorrow, that's another day I'll have to wait to see her.

She turns and looks at me, inspecting my profile. She must be happy with what she finds because there is a smile to her voice when she replies, "No. I work today and then have two days off. How about you? Do you work all weekend?" She smiles as she asks me the question, like she's already predicted the answer.

"I work every day, sunshine." I send her a wink. She smiles big now, and I swear I would do anything to keep seeing that smile. It makes me feel something good. I can't put a label on the feeling, but I just know it's good. It's not a feeling I've ever had before.

"Okay, well, not all of us are… whatever it is you are." She waves her hand up and down at me. "Some of us, namely me, have normal jobs, average jobs, stable jobs. Jobs that mean I know I will have enough money to eat every week. If I turn up to work on time and don't get myself fired…"

The way she talks about knowing she will have enough money to eat every week bothers me. Was there a time she didn't have enough food, money, or stability? The way she talks about her job is kind of sad. She doesn't sound like she likes her job, but turns up every week for the paycheck—which is fine. It's what most of the population does to survive.

"Well, I for one think you have an outstanding job. What other job could you have where you get to wear those scrubs, looking cute as hell all day anyway?"

She spins her head so quickly towards me, mouth hanging open. She hides her shock just as quickly as she showed it. "There is nothing cute about these scrubs. They're blue… blue." She repeats the colour like I don't know what the colour blue is.

"It doesn't matter if they're blue, green, or orange; they are cute on *you*." I add emphasis to the you because I've been in hospitals. I know that not everyone can pull off a pair of scrubs. But Alyssa? Damn, can she pull that shit off.

"Blue is not cute; blue is literally the colour for depression. Blue is the colour people use to represent being sad. Wearing blue scrubs is not cute." She really doesn't seem to like the colour blue.

"We can agree to disagree. Why did you choose nursing?" I surprise myself with the fact that I honestly want to know the answer.

"That's a conversation for another time. We're here. You can just stop anywhere near that door and I'll jump out. Thank you so much for the ride. You don't know how much I appreciate it, really, and the coffee and the muffin. Sorry for the mess, but I told you so." Alyssa rushes out her thanks like it will get her out of the car quicker.

It's ten minutes to eleven—she's not late, *yet*. I park the car and I'm around at her door before she can figure out how the door opens from the inside. I reach a hand in and pull her out, almost pulling her flush against me. Every bone in my body wants to pull her in and kiss her like my life depends on it. Shit, maybe my life does depend on it? No, I don't want to scare her off, especially with what happened to her last night fresh in her head.

I show a lot of fucking restraint when I take a step back. "What time do you finish?"

She squints at me. I'm not sure if it's the sun that's shining in her eyes, or if she's trying to figure out if she wants to tell me. "I finish at eleven tonight. I'm doing a twelve-hour shift today. Why?"

She's smart; she seems to know I don't ask questions for the fun of it. "I'll pick you up from this same spot at eleven tonight."

Before she has time to argue with me, I walk back around the car and jump in, leaving her standing there gaping at me as I pull away.

WALKING INTO MY PENTHOUSE, the first thing I notice is Bray, Dean and Ella sitting in the living room. All at once, they lift their heads, looking at me expectantly.

"What the fuck are you all doing here?" I ask, annoyed that they're in my fucking house. All I want to do is strip off and get into bed and sleep. Well, there is one other thing I wouldn't mind doing, and that's jerking one out to the image of sweet, beautiful Alyssa.

Alyssa, who has had my cock straining within the confines of my jeans ever since she moaned around that first bite of the muffin this morning. Okay, if I'm being honest, it's been fucking hard since she walked through the doors of my club.

Bray seems to be the only brave one out of the group. Well, it's either bravery or stupidity. I haven't decided which one yet. "Where the fuck have you been?" he shouts.

Raising my eyebrows at him, I don't bother answering his question. I repeat mine first. "What the fuck are you all doing here?"

This time, it's Ella who pipes up, "Last I checked, I live here, but I'll leave you two with the grouch."

I watch as she walks down the hall, not even a minute later hearing the tell-tale sound of the door being slammed, and I cringe at the damage she's doing to the doors. Ella has never been able to shut a door quietly.

I turn back towards Bray and Dean, who are still lounging on my damn sofa and looking like they don't have a care in the world. "She's right; she lives here. You two fuckers, however, do not." I reach into my pocket and pull out the keys for the McLaren, throwing them in Bray's direction. He catches them with ease. "Make yourself useful and take the McLaren to the detailers. I'm going to get a few hours' sleep. I'll see the both of you at the club around seven tonight." I start towards my bedroom, thinking I can make a quick escape.

"Wait, you had it detailed two days ago. Why do you need it cleaned again so soon?" Bray and his nosey bastard questions... I turn back around to see him waiting for an explanation with raised eyebrows.

"Because I ate a muffin in it this morning and made a fucking mess of it. Besides, it's my fucking car. If I want to get the damn thing detailed every other day, I bloody well will." I can't help the frustrated tone; after sitting up all night watching Alyssa as she slept on the couch in my office, I'm too damn tired to care.

"You don't even like muffins," Dean unhelpfully adds.

"Remind me again why you're here?" I give him a death glare that would make most men shit themselves. Not him though. Dean has been one of my best mates since the beginning of high school. I may employ him as my head of security, but he's more than that—he's family.

"I'm here, arsehole, because someone had to give Ella a ride home from the club last night when I realised you weren't coming home. Bray wasn't here either, so I stayed the night so she wouldn't be left here by herself." At my raised eyebrows, he quickly adds, "On the couch, I slept on the fucking couch." He points towards the pillow and blankets that are still spilled out on the couch.

"Thanks for that, but that doesn't explain why you're still here?" I run my hands through my hair, not even sure I care why they're here. "That's easy," he says with a huge-ass smile on his face. "Bray here rocked up this morning. When we noticed you didn't come home last night and still weren't home this morning, we got busy figuring out where someone would have buried your sorry ass, so we could go dig it up and give you the burial we thought you deserved. Seeing as though we couldn't for the life of us think of any other reason you wouldn't have come home, or answered any of our thousand calls or texts."

He's right. I have ignored their calls and texts all morning. Not wanting to explain myself, I just grunt out, "Last I checked, I'm a grown-ass twenty-eight-year-old man, and I sure as hell don't have a fucking curfew. I'll see both you fuckers after I've had some damn sleep." Without looking back, I make my way to my room before locking my door behind me.

I strip off and climb into bed. I almost moan at the thought of getting a few hours' sleep and close my eyes. After lying there for fifteen minutes with thoughts of Alyssa stuck in my head, I realise that sleep is the last thing on the mind of my cock. I reach into the bedside table and pull out a tub of lube. Squeezing some onto my hand, I reach down and give my cock a tight, slow pull. Just this simple touch sends shivers down my spine.

With thoughts of Alyssa, I pull a few more times, thinking of her on her knees, those blue eyes looking up at me as she slowly takes my cock all the way into her mouth, right to the back of her throat, sucking as she shallows her cheeks on her way back up. At this, I moan out loud. With a few more tugs and her name on my lips, I come hard, all over the fucking place.

Shaking my head at the thought of how quickly I just came to the thought of Alyssa, like I'm fucking fifteen years old again, I get up and have a quick shower before climbing back into bed and crashing.

LOOKING AT MY WATCH, I see it's nine thirty. I've been sitting here, stuck in my office with Dean and Bray, since seven o'clock. Let's just say the fact that the muffin crumbs in the McLaren were all over the passenger's side did not escape Bray's notice. For at least thirty minutes, I had to listen to both him and

Dean give me shit about letting some chick, as they called her, eat in my car. I let it slide and refused to give them any more ammunition against me.

Now we're going over tonight's plans. We have a new, up-and-coming band called Cyrus coming in to play live for the first time tonight. I've given them a thirty-minute time slot. On a Saturday night, one of the busiest nights at my club, that's a fucking generous amount of time.

Dean and Bray are arguing over how many bouncers we will need to surround the stage to prevent chaos tonight, when a knock at the door stops their argument. "Come in," I call out.

Caitlyn, my PR manager, struts in and looks me up and down before pasting a smile across her fake-ass lips. "Zac, it will be a great night. We've had a lot of positive feedback from the Cyrus promotions. We're expecting a packed house by ten thirty tonight." She looks at me expectantly.

Does she expect a fucking gold sticker for doing her job? Ignoring her, I turn to Dean. "Have you briefed the security team on the band? I don't want any issues tonight. If we have a full house by ten thirty, security needs to be on point. I want the boys at the door double checking IDs. We had a group of three underage girls make it through last Saturday night. That shit does not happen again."

Dean stands up, ready to head out. "Sure thing, boss. They've all been briefed—no one makes it close to the band."

Before he makes it to the door, I stop him. "I have an errand to run; I'm leaving at 10:30, and should be about an hour give or take. I want you to double check everything. Bray will help," I provide, pointing at Bray.

All three look at me like I've lost my head, probably because I have. I've never left the club to run any errands on a busy Saturday night before. Caitlyn walks over to me, running her hand down my arm as she tries to purr.

"I've set the band up with a table on the VIP floor before and after the show." Looking down at her hand on my arm, I back away from her reach. It has always irked me whenever she tries to touch me, but tonight it just feels wrong.

I shake the feeling off before I dismiss her to get her out of my fucking office. "That's great. I want you out there to greet and meet, mingle for a bit, and make sure they're comfortable but not too bloody comfortable. They're here to do a job, not have a free party." I walk over to the door, holding it open for her. Looking pointedly at her, I clear my throat.

She eventually gets the hint before attempting to recover. "Sure thing, boss. I'll see you out on the floor later," she says as she passes through the open door. I don't reply before shutting it right behind her.

Bray and Dean are both still standing there with shocked expressions stuck on their faces. "What?" I demand, looking from one to the other.

Bray responds first. "What the fuck kind of errand

you got to run on a Saturday night, bro?" He raises his eyebrows in question.

"Not that it's any of your fucking business, but I'm picking Alyssa up from work and giving her a lift home."

They both physically gasp before pissing themselves laughing. Once they've recovered, Dean inquires, "What kinda job does this chick have that she's working till eleven o'clock at night? Don't tell me you fell in love with a stripper, man."

I know he's joking, but that doesn't prevent the pissed off feeling boiling up inside me. "First," I say pointing at him, "her name is Alyssa ... Alyssa." I repeat her name for emphasis; sometimes these dicks can be daft. "She is not just some chick. She has a name—next time, fucking use it. Second, she's a goddamn nurse. You know, a professional—smart and uses her brains, not her banging body, to make a buck. And third, I sure as fuck have not fallen in love with anyone." I almost gag at the word. I've never been in love and don't think I ever want to be. Fuck that, I've seen that shit and it never ends well for folk like me.

Bray looks at me, shaking his head like he can't believe what he's hearing. "Okay, bro, whatever you say, but just answer me this one thing." He pauses, thinking he can add dramatic suspense. I wait him out, not giving him the response he's seeking; he eventually asks anyway, "Why are you picking up *Alyssa* and driving her home?" He adds a lot of emphasis to her name and I can't help but smile when I hear it.

I pick up my wallet and keys from my desk, pocketing them before turning back around and making my way to the door. Just before I open the door, I reply, "Because if I don't pick her up, she will catch a bloody train home, and I don't want her catching a fucking train at eleven o'clock at night." I hold the door open for them to follow me out and lock the door behind me.

Just as I'm thinking they're both going to drop the topic and get on with their jobs, Dean smirks at me. "And why do you think it is that you don't want some girl—sorry, Alyssa—you don't want Alyssa catching a train at eleven o'clock at night?" he questions as he notices the pissed off look I'm sending his way.

Shaking my head, I don't answer him as I walk away, yelling at both of them, "I'll be back. Try not to burn the place down while I'm gone, will ya?"

With that, I make my way out the back to the carpark. I want to make sure I have enough time to pick Alyssa up something to eat. I have a feeling she hasn't eaten much, if anything, since that muffin this morning.

Five

ALYSSA

I AUDIBLY SIGH as I take a seat at the nurses' station. I feel like I've been on my feet for ten hours straight, probably because I have been. Saturday shifts are always the busiest in our ER; it seems everyone saves their injuries and illnesses for Saturdays. Today, the ER has been packed with a range of cases, easy and boring cases, but busy all the same.

I've seen at least twenty kids ranging from babies to seven-year-olds with a series of really superficial boo-boos, alongside mothers who don't seem to know how to work a Band-Aid. It seems I studied for four years to apply ointment and bandages to kids' boo-boos while ensuring their mothers that their child does not have a broken bone and does not require stitching.

In a way, I guess it's sweet and nice to know that there are mothers out there who care a lot about their child's wellbeing. But a child having a scraped knee, bruised arm, or small scratches from falling over does not mean you need to rush them to emergency because their life is in danger or their bones are broken. Yeah, they should go to their regular doctor and stop running down to the hospital's emergency room.

On top of the kids with boo-boos, there were five kids who came in with actual broken bones. Those I liked, not because their bones were broken, but because the parents were usually thankful once their child was doped up enough to stop crying out in pain. These cases were straightforward—keep the patient comfortable until the doctor can see them. Send them for x-rays, send them to the orthopaedist to get a cast put on, and send them home. See? *Simple.* Boring, but still simple.

Finally, having five minutes to sit down, my mind drifts to Zac. Hot, sexy, all male Zac, otherwise known as Mr. GQ—well, in my head that is. What I wouldn't do to get him on a bed. I mentally curse myself for where I've let my thoughts go. It will never happen I tell myself; men like Zac do not go for girls like me, your everyday, girl-next-door type.

I've never had a man take such good care of me. No one has ever walked around the car to open the door for me before—not that I could figure out how to open the contraption he calls a car, anyway. I think about the way he leaned over to put my seat belt on for me, the way he stopped to buy me breakfast…

Men like Zac did not exist in the real world. There has to be a flaw; no man can be that perfect. As hard as I try to identify any flaws in Zac, I'm coming up blank. There is nothing, literally nothing, I would want to change about him.

I wonder what he got up to today… I wonder who he's with… *No, Lyssa, stop it*, I scold myself. No good will come from daydreaming of the "never going to happen" Zac.

Trying to clear my mind, I take a deep breath and take stock of my surroundings. The smell of antiseptic and sanitizer assaults my nose. The sound of machines beeping, kids crying, the synchronised sounds of coughing, the elevator doors opening and closing, feet shuffling. I can see the rows of beds separated by blue curtains, colleagues putting on and taking off gloves as they enter and leave each patient's section. Yep, I'm at work. No time to dwell on hot AF Zac.

Needing a distraction, I pull my phone to check for any missed calls or messages. It's the first time I've looked at it all day. I open my text message thread from Sarah—she's sent me five messages today.

SARAH: **I can't believe you're stuck in the hospital. The sun is out and the water is awesome today.**

. . .

SHE ATTACHED a photo of the beach. It looks inviting, however, keeping my job and eating is more appealing at the moment. Scrolling down, I read the next text.

SARAH: **It's hot out here today, and I don't mean the temperature. Although, I may need some urgent medical attention as I'm about to suffer from heat stroke. You can suffer heat stroke from being surrounded by hot, and I mean fire hot, men, right?**

THIS ONE MAKES me laugh out loud a little. Picking my head up, I see that no one is paying me any attention. I scroll through the few photos she attached of the scenery—topless men of all colours and sizes. The only thought that comes to mind when I see these men is: *they don't hold a candle to Zac.*

I really need to get my mind off this guy. I mean, I can't even enjoy the pictures of topless, hot guys at the beach. I should be able to appreciate that view, even if I am living through Sarah. Giving up on trying to see anything else in the photos, I scroll to her next message.

·   ·   ·

SARAH: **As hot as the view is here, the view in our living room this morning was ten times better.**

SHE ADDS A WINKY FACE EMOJI. I could have gone without the reminder of just how unattainable Mr. GQ was. Choosing not to dwell on that message, I go to her last message, sent about thirty minutes ago.

SARAH: **I won't be home tonight. I'm picking up some cucumber.**

PICKING up a cucumber is Sarah's not-so-subtle code that she's getting laid tonight. Having the townhouse to myself doesn't seem so bad. I could use the quiet. I won't make it home until at least midnight anyway, and that's if the trains are running on time. I send Sarah a quick text back. I should get back to the charts I was doing.

ME: **Enjoy, be safe and save the deets for brunch tomorrow.**

KNOWING I probably won't hear from her until I see her at our regular Sunday brunch meet with Holly and Reilly, I put my phone away and look back at the charts I have to get done before I can leave in an hour.

I'm halfway through the pile of charts, with forty minutes left of my shift, when I see a cup landing on the desk in front of me. Dr. Mark Allen leans on the counter, smiling at me. "Thought you could use a pick me up. Skinny cap, right?"

Nope, not right, but how many times can you correct someone. "How did you know? Thank you, doctor. I appreciate it." Picking the cup up, I take a huge gulp. It may not be a vanilla latte, but coffee is coffee.

"You know you can call me Mark, right? You don't have to call me doctor all the time." Dr. Allen winks at me.

I can't find it in myself to even contemplate putting up with his flirting today. Dr. Allen is known as a serial dater around the ER, always looking for a new nurse to sink his teeth into. Well, this nurse is not on the menu—well, not on Dr. Allen's menu. Zac's menu, however, that's a menu I could handle being on.

I smile up at Dr. Allen and do my best to get us back into the professional territory. "I think I'd prefer to stick with doctor—we are in a workplace after all. Thanks for the coffee but I really need to get these charts done." I point at the pile of folders in front of me.

His smile drops before he says, "Sure thing,

Alyssa, see you around." He turns and walks away, hopefully getting the clue that this nurse is most certainly off his menu.

After finishing my charts, I change out of my scrubs. It's almost eleven fifteen as I make my way out of the building. Just as I'm about to walk out the door, Dr. Allen catches up to me, placing a hand on my arm.

"Do you need a ride home?" He looks hopeful.

I keep walking, making my way out the exit as I say, "*Umm*, no, it's okay. Thanks, I've got a ride." I lie. I'm planning on catching the train but I'm not about to tell him that. Attempting to change the topic, I thank him again for the coffee and then look around, searching for a way to get away from him without being outright rude.

That's when I spot him, Mr. GQ, leaning up against a black Range Rover and wearing a suit, a freaking suit—dark blue with a white button-up shirt and no tie. The first few buttons on his shirt are undone, giving me just a glimpse of his chest. How is it he always looks this good? It shouldn't be legal for men to walk around looking like this. I mean, this is how accidents are caused, women stunned by the beauty and all that. It's just plain dangerous. Danger-ously beautiful is what he is.

His eyes zone in on the spot of my arm where Dr. Allen still seems to have his hand. He looks up at my face before staring straight at Dr. Allen. GQ does not look happy. I'm stuck, literally stuck in place, stunned.

He's here… I know he said he would be back to pick me up, but why on earth would he do that? Not for one second did I entertain the idea that he would actually be here when I finished work.

Zac must realise that I'm in a state of shock. He pushes off the car and stalks towards us, stopping in front of me, removing my gym bag off my shoulder and hiking it up onto his own. He holds his hand out and smirks at me. "Sunshine, your chariot awaits." He's waiting for me to slide my hand into his. I smile, taking the offering, momentarily shocked by the electric heat that comes with the contact. When I meet his eyes, I can see he felt it too.

It's clear he doesn't care to be introduced to Dr. Allen; he is totally ignoring the doctor's presence. I introduce them anyway, because I'm polite like that. "Zac, thanks for coming. This is Dr. Allen. Dr. Allen, Zac." I wave my free arm between the two, making the introduction quick.

Dr. Allen looks between our joined hands, and asks, "Zac, how do you know Alyssa?"

Before Zac can answer, I respond, "We're friends." Looking up at Zac, I can tell he doesn't look like he likes my response. He looks me up and down before giving his own, "Good friends." Zac then turns to me. "Are you ready to get out of here? The night is young, sunshine," he hints, raising his eyebrows suggestively. I laugh a little and nod my head. Zac leads me towards his car as I glance over my shoulder and give a brief goodbye to Dr. Allen; I do have to work with him.

Zac opens my door for me again. He either thinks I don't know how to open my own doors, or he's the last true gentlemen on this place called Earth. Once I'm sitting in the seat, I expect him to close my door, but he shocks me once again when he pulls the seat belt over me and buckles me in.

Smirking, he says, "Need to make sure you're securely in place." I'm assaulted with his mix of woodsy citrus scent that seems to be unique to him alone; his scent travels through my nose and straight to my core. I'm still wondering if it's normal to be so turned on from the way someone smells when Zac jumps into the driver's side.

He reaches over the back of my seat, pulling out a take-away bag from my favourite Thai restaurant. He looks at me a moment then, placing the bag on my lap, says, "I figured you probably haven't eaten properly today, so I picked you up something. It's chicken Pad Thai. There's a fork in the bag; you can eat while we drive."

I'm stunned speechless and left wondering if maybe he has some weird food fetish. "That's twice today you've brought me food. I don't know if you have some kind of weird food fetish or not, but right now I'm starving so I don't really care." Taking the take-away container out and pulling the lid off, I inhale the smell of the Thai dish.

"Thank you, this is my favourite Thai food," I add before digging in, not even caring if I'm making a mess of myself.

"I know it is." He smirks at me.

"Wait, how do you know this is my favourite? You don't even know me." I turn to look at him, secretly praying that he's not some secret, crazy, murdery stalker I didn't know I had.

He laughs at my obvious distress. "Relax, I swear I'm not a stalker. I sent Sarah a message before I picked you up and asked her what you would eat. She told me the restaurant and meal to order, so really all credit should be pointed at her."

He sent Sarah a message. This is what my brain focuses on from his response. "How do you know Sarah? And how do you have her number?" It comes out sounding much harsher than I intended, but something irrational happened when I heard: *I sent Sarah a message.* I got jealous—well, at least I think it's jealousy. I've never been jealous before so it's hard to tell.

Zac stops at a red light, and turns to look at me. I don't know what he sees on my face because he doesn't say anything for a good minute. Suddenly, he smiles, picks up my hand and kisses me on the inside of my wrist before resting our joined hands on his thigh. Well, okay then, if that hasn't put the green-eyed monster to bed a little, I don't know what would. I'm so focused on trying to breathe, and not show just how much that simple gesture has affected me, I startle a little when he talks again.

"Sunshine, you can put the claws away. I have Sarah's number, because I asked her for it this morning when you were in the shower." At this, I try to tug my hand away from him. It doesn't work; he just holds on tighter. "I asked her for her number, because I knew your phone was dead this morning and I didn't know if you would have had the chance to charge it while at work. I didn't have your number, and I wanted a way of reaching you, so I asked for Sarah's."

I can still feel the green-eyed monster wanting to come out a little. "Okay, well, thank you for the ride and the meal," I lamely get out. I use my free hand to pick the fork back up and start eating. I let out a little moan around a mouthful of noodles, and the hand that Zac is holding gets a little tighter. I look over at him to see his jaw tensed and his eyes hyper-focused on the road.

I have no idea whatever storm has rolled up within him again. I really can't keep up with this man's intense moods. I try for some light conversation.

"So, no Batmobile tonight?" I question.

He looks over and smiles slightly, his eyes lighting

up. "No, it's at the detailers; someone left muffin crumbs all through it."

I audibly gasp and drop my fork. The fork drops to the floor of the car with a pile of noodles on it. "Oh my gosh, I'm so sorry. I can pay for the detailing of the Batmobile and this one, but to be fair, I did prewarn you I'm a messy eater. Oh god, who's car is this? Now I've messed someone else's car too. That has to be a record, two cars ruined in one day."

He's full on laughing by the time I finish my little freak-out. I turn and glare at him. "It's not funny. That Batmobile obviously isn't a cheap car and I ruined it."

"Sunshine, I was joking about the muffin crumbs.

It's fine. You didn't ruin any car, and this car is one of mine, so don't worry about putting noodles everywhere." He raises my hand back to his lips and kisses the inside of my wrist again. It's confusing how much this move both calms me and makes me hot and bothered at the same time.

Placing the lid on the Pad Thai and leaning down to pick up the fork, I put it all back in the plastic bag. Zac looks over; he's not impressed. "You need to eat, Alyssa, so eat."

"I'll eat it when I get home. Besides, it's not easy eating noodles in a car." I place the bag on the floor beside my feet and lean my head back on the head-rest. "This is a really nice car. I think I like this one better than the Batmobile." I close my eyes a little. I'm so damn tired.

"You look exhausted. I knew I should have made you take the day off today."

My eyes pop back open, glaring at him. "I'm sorry if I look exhausted and am not up to your level of expectations of how one should look, but I just finished a twelve-hour shift in the emergency depart-ment. I didn't even get a proper lunch break. And just so you know, there is nothing you could have done to make me take a day off. You don't own me, and I certainly don't answer to anyone!"

Zac looks over and smirks at me. Dammit, I'm mad at him, and it's really hard to stay mad at him when he looks at me like that. "Yet," he mumbles under his breath, almost like he's telling himself something. "Sunshine, I wouldn't have to *force* you to take a day off. I can be very persuasive when I want something, and sunshine, I will stop at nothing to get what I want, even if that's you taking a day off to rest when you need it." I'm gobsmacked, my mouth hanging open. I don't even know how to respond to that and before I can even contemplate a half intelligent thought, he adds, "And as for how you look, you could wear a hessian sack and still be the most beautiful woman I've ever seen."

I just stare at him. Who is this man? And where the hell has he been all my life? I pinch my leg. Yep, definitely awake, and *this* Zac far surpasses anything I could dream up. I'm racking my brain for something to say to him when his phone rings over the speaker system in the car.

The screen reads: Bray calling. Zac looks over at me and says, "Sorry," before answering the call. "Be careful with your words." That's how he answers the call. As I'm contemplating why not a simple hello, a rough voice fills the car.

"Zac, man, you gotta get to the club, NOW!" The guy on the other end sounds like he's yelling.

"Bray, for the love of god, tell me you haven't burnt down my club in the hour I've been gone?" Zac demands.

"No, it's Ella."

Zac's entire body tenses. Who is Ella? Whoever she is, she must be important to both men, as I can see the worry overtake Zac's features and can hear it in the man's voice on the phone.

"What happened? Where is she, Bray?" Zac's voice is strained as he grits out the demands.

"Bro, you have to fucking get back here now. She was in the VIP section, went to go to the bathroom and the drummer from the band fucking attacked her —the about to be dead fucking drummer."

Zac's body vibrates as he listens. He spins the car around going faster than what is probably safe. I stay quiet, not sure what's going on. Whatever it is, whoever this Ella is, he cares about her.

"I'm ten minutes away, Bray. What do you mean he fucking attacked her? What the fuck did he do?"

I can vaguely hear the sounds of someone crying in the background when Bray speaks again. "She's okay, Zac. I'm with her in your office. Dean has the fucker downstairs; he's only keeping him on ice until you get here. I had to make him promise not to go lethal until you got here, man. I've never seen Dean like this. He's a caged lion at the moment, bro. But Ella, she's banged up, cut on her head, black eye. From what I can see, bruises on her arms and legs. She's not speaking, won't talk to anyone. When Dean found her in the bathroom, she clung to him. She wouldn't even let me fucking take her from him and carry her up here. I don't know what to do, Zac. Tell me I can finish this. I don't think I can wait for you to get here."

"Bray, stay with Ella. Don't let anyone in the office who isn't Dean until I get there. I'm going as fast as I can. Just stay with Ella, okay?" Zac sounds like he's trying to calm Bray with his words—whatever he says must do something because Bray agrees.

"Okay, I'll wait for you to get here, but then the gloves come off. I'm going to fucking kill him." With that, the phone disconnects.

Zac turns to look at me; he looks torn. "I'm sorry, sunshine. I have to make a detour. I promise I will get you home. I can have one of the security guys drive you once we get to the club if you want."

I don't really know what's going on back at the club, but I know right now, Zac is struggling and I don't want to add any stress to his night. "Whatever you want me to do, I'll do. If you want me to wait for you, I'll wait. If you'd rather I go home and let you deal with whatever it is you have to do, I'll do that too," I say, giving his hand a squeeze.

"What I want right now is to get my hands on the fucker who thought he could touch my baby sister!" Looking across at me as we pull into a carpark, he says, "I want you to stay. Wait for me. I want to take you home tonight. I *will* take you home tonight."

Six

ZAC

*P*ULLING into the carpark at the club, I look over at Alyssa and take a deep breath, attempting to calm my rage. I should get someone to take her home. I shouldn't want her to be here when I may just kill someone in the underground cellar of my club. I shouldn't want her to see the other side of me, the side that will hunt and kill to protect those close to me.

I know I should let her go now, try to forget her and not bring her down with my level of shit. I know I should, but I don't. I don't want to let her go. I don't care if I have to spend the next month grovelling and apologising for whatever she is about to witness tonight, because right now, I need her. I can't explain it or put a label on what it is, but having her next to me feels right.

"Wait there," I instruct her as I jump out of the car and go around to her side. Opening her door, I reach in for her hand to help her out. Although every bone in my body is screaming at me to run up to my office to make sure Ella is okay, I don't. I take another deep breath and silently count to ten in my head.

Gripping Alyssa's hand, I walk as calmly as I can muster. When I notice that Alyssa is struggling to keep up with my pace, I slow a little. We stop at the elevator; stabbing at the button over and over does not make it open any quicker. Alyssa gives my hand a squeeze and looks up at me with those grey-blue eyes of hers. The doors open and I pull her in. As soon as the doors close, my arms go around her. I hold her tight, probably too tight.

"I'm sorry for whatever you're about to see, for whatever I have to do tonight. Know that no matter how much I may want you here, how much I need you here, if at any time you want to leave and go home, you tell me and I will have someone take you."

She rests her head against my chest, wrapping her arms around me. She hugs me back but it's what she says that has me holding her tight and not wanting to let her go. "I want to be wherever you are, but I also don't want to be in the way. So, you need to tell me if I am."

Damn, I think I could be losing my mind. I can't ever recall wanting... no, *needing*... a woman as much as I need Alyssa right now. "Sunshine, you could never be in the way. You are right where you belong." As the doors open, I grab her hand and pull her along the hall to my office.

Nothing could have prepared me for the sight that greeted me as I walked into my office. Ella is curled up on the corner of the couch. She's rocking slightly, crying silent tears that I can see run down her cheeks. She's bleeding from a gash on her forehead, an enormous bruise is forming on her right eye, and her arms are covered in marks. My world is tumbling; the anger I thought I had controlled comes barrelling back full force.

Bray is pacing back and forward throughout the office. He stops as soon as he notices me. "Zac, thank god you're here. She won't let me touch her. She keeps asking for fucking Dean. Where the fuck is Dean?" He looks like he's about to lose it.

Alyssa squeezes my hand before walking slowly over to Ella. She takes a seat on the couch next to her, not touching her and speaking softly. "Ella, my name's Alyssa, but you can call me Lyssa—all my friends call me Lyssa. I'm a nurse. I can help you. Would you like me to help get you cleaned up a bit?"

Bray and I both watch in shock as Ella picks her head up and gives a slight nod. I let out a breath I didn't know I was holding before going over to Ella and crouching in front of her.

"Ella, sweetheart, I need to know…" Swallowing, I try again. "I need you to tell me what happened, please."

Ella looks at me. "Zac?" she questions like she doesn't believe it's actually me.

"Yeah, honey, it's me Zac. Can you tell me what happened?"

"I… I was so scared, Zac. I didn't know what to do. I screamed for help. I kicked, scratched and hit wherever I could, just like you told me to, but he was too big." Her sobs get louder. This is killing me. I can feel my body vibrate with rage.

Alyssa must sense something in me; she touches my shoulder. "Zac, I'm going to take her through there." She points to the bathroom. "I need you to get me a first aid kit. I can help her. The cut on her head is not bad; it looks it because head wounds bleed a lot. It doesn't look too deep." She turns to Ella. "Ella, honey, I'm going to take you to the shower and help you get cleaned." I watch as Alyssa grabs Ella's hand to help her up. Ella follows Alyssa blindly through to the bathroom attached to my office.

Bray watches them go through, then he looks at me. "I'm going downstairs. I can't stand this, Zac. I feel helpless. I should have been there. This shouldn't have happened to her. This won't happen again. I will make sure every asshole out there knows what will happen to them if they even think about touching her," he says, pointing towards the bathroom door.

"Give me five minutes. I'll get the first aid kit for Alyssa and meet you down there. Don't finish without me," I demand. I need this… I need this fucker's blood on my hands. I need to watch the life drain out of him. I dig a first aid kit out of the cabinet and knock on the bathroom door.

Alyssa cracks the door open slightly, not enough for me to see in. "Is she okay?" I ask, almost pleading that she is.

"She will be." She takes the first aid kit before stopping me from entering. "Zac, I'll take care of her. You can trust me to do this for you, for her."

Nodding in agreement, I let out a breath. "I know... I just need to know how bad it is."

She reads between the lines and nods her head. "I'll find out."

"Thank you. I'm going downstairs for a bit. I won't be too long, but I'm locking the office door. Don't open it for anyone. Everyone that needs to be in here has a key, okay?"

She gives a small smile and says, "Okay, I'll be here when you get back." I place a kiss on her forehead. Turning, I walk out the door, looking forward to getting all my rage out on this fucker.

WALKING INTO THE BASEMENT, I can hear the tell-tale signs of skin meeting skin. I can hear Bray telling the fucker the mistakes he made tonight.

"You think you can come into our club, touch our sister and get away with it? You just signed your own death certificate, fucker."

I walk through the room they're in and see they have the drummer hooked up to chains; his face is already unrecognisable. Turning to Dean, who is pacing the back wall, I ask, "Did you have to start without me? You know how much I enjoy the start of the show."

Dean looks up but doesn't greet me with his usual devious smirk—the one he usually saves for these situations. He's hanging on by a thread.

"Zac, just let me take him out. I need to take him out." I look at him, really look at him, for a moment.

"This isn't just some random fucker who wronged me, Dean. He thought he could touch my sister, my fucking sister!" I yell. Dean bends his head, running his hands through his hair. He lets out an anguished grunt and continues pacing the back wall.

Looking back over, I see Bray hasn't given up on this fucker. I walk over and tap him out. He looks at me, nods his head, and goes to stand in front of the door. Leaning his back against the door, he focuses his eyes on the drummer as he says, "You think Dean was bad? You think I was hard on you? Well, now you're about to wish for death to greet you." Bray laughs a little.

I take my time rolling the sleeves of my shirt up. I look the drummer in the face, although I suspect he's having a hard time seeing me, seeing as though both of his eyes are pretty much swollen shut already. I stand in front of him.

"So, I hear you thought you could put your grubby little hands on my little sister. You know you shouldn't touch things that don't belong to you, don't you? Especially when those things don't want to be touched," I say, oddly calm.

Now that I'm in this space, I can feel my rage simmering. I'm always calm once I get into this zone. It's like a drug—a rush of endorphins runs through me. What can I say? I fucking enjoy teaching fuckers like this a lesson. It's sick… I'm sure I'm a perfect candidate for the nuthouse, but I don't fucking care. What I care about right now is that this fucker put his hands on my sister, hurt my sister.

I look over to Dean. "Pass me the sheers," I say, holding my hand out.

Dean picks up the sheers and walks over to hand them to me, giving me his trademark devious smirk. He knows what I have planned and is one hundred percent on board with it. I make a show of opening and closing the sheers a few times before lining them up with a pinkie.

The fucker must realise what I have planned because he attempts to back up and move his hand away. He can't though; those chains have no give in them.

As I cut through his pinkie, I say, "This little piggy…" and revel in the scream he lets out. I continue until all of his fingers have gone, and the drummer is about to lose consciousness.

Grabbing him by the throat, I say, "I would love to stay and play, but I have more pressing matters." I don't let go until I know he's no longer breathing. Turning to Dean and Bray, I growl, "Deal with this. I need to get back upstairs to Ella."

They don't say anything, knowing better than to question me right now. I walk out of the room, feeling only slightly better than when I walked in.

I stop at a bathroom to get cleaned up a bit. Looking at my reflection, I can see blood splattered over my white dress shirt, up my arms and even on my face. I strip the shirt off and scrub my arms and face the best I can in a fucking sink with hand soap. Deciding it's an improvement, I make my way up to my office.

I find Ella curled up on the couch, asleep. She looks better, her face cleaned and not covered in blood; some butterfly stitches have been placed along the cut on her forehead. Alyssa is sitting on the chair opposite Ella, looking down at her phone. She looks up and turns her head towards me, gasping a little when she sees me. She looks back to Ella before standing and walking over to me. She doesn't say anything as she grabs my hand and leads me into the bathroom.

Alyssa slightly closes the door but leaves it ajar

enough so she can still see into the office. She's quiet as she turns the water on in the shower, testing its warmth. Once she seems satisfied, she turns to me. "I'm not going to ask, and you don't have to say anything. What you do need to do is shower, get cleaned. Ella does not need to see you like this."

I'm speechless. How have I stumbled across what is the absolute most perfect woman? I must have done something right in my life, because Alyssa seems like a gift—one I will gladly accept without ever giving back. I take too long staring at her in amazement because she reaches for my belt, undoing it before undoing my pants and letting them drop.

Just as I'm about to tell her I can do this myself, that I'm okay, she lowers herself to the ground to untie my shoes, slipping one off at a time. Seeing her on her knees before me is a sight I want to burn into my memory—one I can recall over and over again. Once my shoes, socks and pants are removed, she stands back up, looking at me. She smiles, like she knows what I'm thinking. And judging by the erection currently residing in my boxers, I'm sure she knows just what seeing her down there did to me.

"Do you need help with the rest?" she asks, pointing to my boxers.

"More than you know right now," I say as I pull my boxers down myself and step into the shower. I expect her to walk out and leave me to it. She doesn't; she hikes herself up onto the basin and sits there watching me shower. Her sitting there, openly ogling me and not even trying to hide the fact that she's watching... let's just say it's not helping the hard situation I have going on.

As I'm washing my hair out, she says, "You know, I see naked bodies all the time. It's part of the job, but I can't say I've ever seen one as spectacularly built as yours." I think I actually fucking blush a little at her compliment.

"You've never looked in the mirror then," I reply, to which she scoffs. I will have to work on her self-esteem at a later time; right now, I'm tired. I need to get Ella home and I need to get into bed, preferably with Alyssa next to me.

Stepping out of the shower, Alyssa holds a towel out to me. "Thanks," I get out gruffly as I make quick work of drying myself so I can wrap the towel around my waist.

"I would say you're welcome, but really, the pleasure's been all mine," she says, blushing a little.

I step up closer to her, grabbing her knees so I can open her legs and step between them. "Trust me, sunshine, I plan to give you the kind of pleasure you haven't even dreamt about yet, over and over again. But right now, I'm going to do something completely selfish, something that is going to give me an unbelievable amount of pleasure." I tuck a strand of hair behind her ear and twirl the end around my finger.

"What's that?" She's breathless. It's good to know I have the same effect on her that she's having on me.

"This." I lean in and kiss her lips, softly at first,

seeking, giving her plenty of time to pull back. When she doesn't pull back, that's all the signal I need to go full steam ahead. Grabbing the back of her head, I tilt it to just the right angle before using my tongue, seeking entrance into the haven that is her mouth. Alyssa doesn't disappoint; she opens for me and greedily matches me stroke for stroke. I'm so lost in this kiss... I could kiss her forever and not get enough of this mouth.

Alyssa pulls back. I outright groan in disappointment. "As much as I would love to sit here and do this all night, I think you should get your sister home. She's had a rough night."

Shit, she's right. I can't believe I was so caught up in all that is Alyssa that I briefly forgot why we were even in my office in the first place. "You're right. I need to take her home, but I'm also taking you home with me, with us. Let me get changed and we can head out."

I reach into the small wardrobe, where I keep spare sets of clothes, and pull out a pair of jeans and a t-shirt. Turning, I see Alyssa hasn't moved. She's chewing on her bottom lip, lost in her own thoughts.

"Don't overthink it, Alyssa. I'm taking you home to sleep. Nothing will happen that you don't want to happen. But I really fucking want you in my bed tonight, please." Well shit, that's a first for me. I've never taken a woman home to my actual apartment before, and I've never wanted to sleep next to any woman all fucking night, let alone practically begged one to sleep in my bed.

"I get the feeling that you don't say please often," she says, looking straight into my eyes. "Okay, I'll come home with you, but just to sleep and only because I'm really freaking tired." I feel like I just won the lottery.

"Thank you."

Just before I'm about to walk out of the bathroom, I stop, turn back around to Alyssa and ask the one question that's been nagging at me ever since Bray called me back to the club.

"How… Did…" Taking a breath, I try again. "How hurt is she?" I ask, pointing my thumb back in the direction of the office.

Alyssa grabs my hand and squeezes. "She wasn't raped. He didn't get the chance to get that far before some guy named Dean found her."

"Thank fuck for that. Remind me to give Dean a fucking pay raise." I lead her out to the office.

Crouching down in front of Ella, I reach out and stroke her hair. She doesn't flinch at my touch and I take this as a good sign. "Ella, sweetheart, we're going to take you home."

She nods and lets me pick her up. With that, I walk out of my office with the two most important women in my life.

STEPPING out of the elevator into my apartment, I've got Ella in my arms and Alyssa right beside me. I'm greeted by a very antsy Dean and Bray waiting in my living room. Dean is up and moving—probably the quickest I've ever seen the man move.

"Here, let me take her to her room." Dean holds his hands out to take Ella. I don't move for a moment, shocked by my friend's actions. I'm about to say that I'll do it myself when I look over to Bray, who subtly shakes his head no at me. I relent and hand Ella over to Dean; he doesn't say anything as he walks down the hall to her room.

Looking over at Bray, I ask, "Do I even want to know?" I gesture down the hall to where Dean just disappeared into Ella's bedroom.

"No, you really don't, not tonight anyway." Bray stands up from the lounge he was sprawled across and walks towards me. Knowing he probably has some smart-ass shit to say about the fact that I've got a woman here, I attempt to escape his shit.

Grabbing Alyssa's hand, I say, "I'll catch you

tomorrow. I'm going to bed." I walk towards the hall, pulling Alyssa behind me.

Bray moves lightning quick, like the fighter he is. I don't even see him move before he's standing in front of me. He holds a hand out for Alyssa. "Since my brother has the manners of a goat, I'll do the introductions myself. I'm Bray, obviously the good-looking brother." Alyssa smiles and takes his hand. I'm quick to pull her hand out of Bray's grasp and get a raised eyebrow from him in return.

Alyssa looks up at me before turning to Bray. "I'm Alyssa. It's nice to meet you. We will have to agree to disagree on who's the more handsome brother though."

Bray laughs. "I think I like you, Alyssa, if he…" He points a finger at my chest. "…messes up, you know where to find me." The bastard smirks at her.

I don't give Alyssa a chance to respond. I shoulder barge past Bray and lead her towards my bedroom, calling behind me, "Don't be a dick. This one's sticking."

He laughs and then I hear the front door open and close. Closing my bedroom door behind me, I walk over to the dresser and pull out a t-shirt for Alyssa to sleep in, before holding it out to her. "You can sleep in this. The bathroom's through that door." I point to the en suite.

"Thank you," she says ever so quietly as she takes the shirt, shutting the en suite door behind her.

I make quick work of stripping down to my boxers

and climb into bed, pulling the covers back on her side and waiting for her to return while mentally repeating to myself: *Don't stuff this up. Don't stuff this up.*

All thoughts come to a halt when Alyssa walks out of the bathroom wearing my shirt. Holy shit, I did not think this through. I thought I could keep my hands to myself, but fuck... After seeing her look like this, it's taking every ounce of my self-control to not sink my cock into her and claim her, mark her as mine.

I'm lost for words—whatever game I thought I had just went out the window. I'm sitting here staring at her as she makes her way to the bed. She looks a little unsure, and I know I need to put her at ease, but how?

"Do I have something on my face?" she asks. All I can do is shake my head no. "Then why are you looking at me like that?"

I don't know how honest to be. I don't want to scare her away, but I also want to let her know exactly what my intentions are. I'm momentarily speechless.

"I don't think I've ever seen anyone look as fucking hot as you do right now, wearing my shirt. Fuck, I can't even think straight right now, sunshine. All I can think about is getting a taste of you, how you're going to feel when I finally sink my cock into your pussy and have your walls tighten around me." I shake my head, attempting to clear those thoughts.

Alyssa is blushing hard and is frozen at the side of the bed. Maybe I was a little too honest. "Don't worry, sunshine. I gave you my word; it's not happening tonight. All I'm going to do tonight is hold on to you, so I know you'll still be here when I wake in the morning."

She nods. "Okay, but since we're being honest and all here, I've seen what you're packing and if you think that…" She waves her hand in the general direction of my cock. "…is ever going to fit into me, you are surely mistaken."

I laugh a little, tugging her closer to me. Wrapping my arm around her body, I hold her tight. Kissing her forehead, I speak into her ear, "Baby, it'll fit. You might not know this yet, but you were made for me." I settle onto the pillow behind her, breathing in her scent. *Huh*, I never thought I would be one for spooning and cuddling. Right now, I can't think of a better feeling than how it feels to hold her close to me.

"I can hear you thinking, sunshine. Go to sleep. There is always tomorrow," I tell her as she squirms around a little more before settling into me, into my arms.

"Goodnight, Zac. I really hope we always have a tomorrow," she whispers.

Her words have slayed me. I can't even respond, so I just hold her, and that's how I fall asleep, having the best fucking sleep I've ever had.

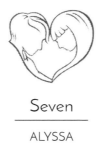

Seven

ALYSSA

"*ARGH*," I groan and slap my hand out to reach the buzzing sound that's coming from next to my head somewhere. "Shut up," I say, slapping aimlessly.

A mix of a moan and a laugh comes from behind me and I freeze, my body tensing as I abruptly become aware of the body that's right up against my back, the heavy arm draped over my waist. I breathe in through my nose and inhale that scent, that woodsy and citrus mixture—the scent I know belongs to Zac. With this knowledge, my body relaxes and I sink back into his embrace.

"I'm taking it you're not a morning person, sunshine?" His deep voice vibrates behind me.

The buzzing next to my head starts up and I groan again, turning over and burying my face into his chest. "Make it stop," I plead as I snuggle into his chest, and what a chest it is. If I wasn't trying to fall back asleep, I would have the energy to give this chest the attention it so deserves. It's smooth, wide, solid and smells of him. I inhale deep, not even caring if he can tell I'm sniffing him.

I feel his arm reach across me before he settles back down. "That buzzing you're so intent on stopping is your phone. I don't think it's going to stop until you answer it." He kisses the top of my head. I've never had anyone kiss the top of my head before. I've seen it in movies, read about it in books a lot, but never experienced it, until now. The simple act brings out a feeling of being cherished, a feeling I'm coming to really, really like having.

"Just turn it off. I'm sleeping. Can't they tell I'm sleeping?" I mumble.

Zac laughs and the damn phone starts up again; he's holding it in his hand. "It's Sarah," he says. "Do you want me to answer it for you?"

Peeking my head up with one eye open, I grab the phone and hit the power button. Handing it back to him, I proudly proclaim, "That's how you answer a phone while you're sleeping." With that, I snuggle back into his chest; his arms wrap around me tight as he pulls me closer.

"For future reference, sunshine, if you ever turn your phone off when I'm calling, I will show up on your doorstep, no matter what time it is."

Shrugging, I look up at him. "All I heard just then was: sunshine, if you ever want to see me in person and not just have a phone convo, switch your phone and I'll be there." I give the most serene smile I can muster this early in the morning. "I'm okay with that."

Zac smiles and leans down. He kisses my forehead, then the tip of my nose, before landing on my lips. His kisses start off soft. I tilt my head up, seeking more of him. Raising my arm, I reach up to his neck and pull him closer. He doesn't let me have control for long. He takes over, swiping his tongue out and seeking entrance. I don't deny him. I moan into his kiss. I need more. Trailing my hand down his chest, I feel the ridges and grooves of well-defined muscles. This has me moaning into his mouth even louder. Just then, a horrible high-pitched ringtone blares. I jump at the sound, pulling away from him.

Zac has an indescribable look on his face. I can't tell what he's thinking, but I don't have to guess for long before he offers his thoughts. "Damn, sunshine, I could get used to waking up like this." He smirks.

"Me too, but definitely without the blaring noise coming from what must be your phone, because I did the responsible thing and turned mine off." I'm sure I sound a little pissed off, because frankly, that phone interrupted a really freaking good moment for me.

Rolling over, Zac picks up his phone, which starts blaring again. His face scrunches up as he looks at the screen. "It's Sarah. Maybe you should answer it. She kinda scares me a little—plus, she's not going to stop calling."

Taking the phone from him to press the green

answer button, I give him the best death glare I can, while he just shakes his head and laughs. I need to work on that glare.

"Sarah, why are you calling my—" I stop mid-sentence, avoiding a colossal clingy girl mistake as I was about to say *boyfriend* without even thinking twice about it. Instead, I correct myself. "Zac. Why are you calling Zac's phone at some ungodly hour in the morning? Are you dead or close to being dead?" Sarah knows I'm not keen on being woken up, so she deserves my wrath right now.

"Soooo, he's your Zac now, is he?" Her singsong voice carries through the phone. "Do tell. When in the last twenty-four hours did this development happen?" She's laughing now.

"Shut up. You're obviously not dead or close to being dead, so I'm hanging up now. Have a nice life." I wait, rather than hanging up, because I know she will only call back if I do.

"Wait, I called your Zac," she says with fake sweetness to her voice, "because you switched your phone off, and now I know why you're ignoring me. But you need to get up. I don't care if you're in the middle of purchasing a cucumber, get up and get dressed. We have brunch in forty-five minutes and if you're not there, I will enjoy telling the twins all about your Zac without you."

I look up at Zac, who can hear every damn word Sarah has said. She has a habit of yelling down the bloody phone. He looks puzzled and mouths the word *cucumber?* in question to me. I just shake my head no, in a kind of *don't ask* motion.

"Okay, don't do anything drastic, and just so you know, the cucumber is still at the store. I'll meet you there." Hanging up, I hand the phone back to Zac.

Turning my phone back on, I wait for it to start up. "Shit, I have to go. Sorry, but it's Sunday and Sunday is girls' brunch day. I have to get to the café. Wait, where exactly are we? I need to figure out how to get to the station." I'm rushing around the room, looking for my things, before remembering I left my clothes in the bathroom. I head in there and don't bother shutting the door before I strip Zac's shirt off and put my jeans back on. As I'm doing up my bra, I look up into the mirror. I can see Zac's reflection. He's still sitting on the bed and staring straight at me—well, at my breasts that is.

He slowly lifts his head and meets my gaze in the mirror. Clearing his throat, he says, "I'll drive you. You're not catching the damn train." He gets out of bed and saunters (yes, saunters) into the bathroom. Wrapping his arms around my waist, he whispers into my ear, "Although if you'd rather stay here in bed, I can make sure Sarah won't be able to find you."

I place my hands on his chest as I turn into him— on his rock-hard chest that has me running those same hands up and down the plains of his abs, exploring all the dips and curves that I just want to run my tongue across. "As much as I want to stay here and jump back into bed with you…" I pause for a second when he moans. "I'm not the kind of friend that bails on plans, especially the longstanding traditional plans."

Looking down at my breasts, he moans again. "Okay, but you need to cover these beauties up before I devour them. Once I start, there will be no stopping."

He steps back and walks out of the bathroom. Watching him walk away from me in nothing but his black boxer briefs is a sight I won't be forgetting in a hurry. I stare at his tanned, sculpted back with muscles so defined that anyone would think this man was carved from stone. Then there's his ass. Once my eyes make their way to that perfection, I finally understand the saying *an ass you can bounce a quarter off*, because damn… I'm still staring at his retreating form when he walks into what must be a wardrobe. He looks back over his shoulder at me and smirks. The bastard knew I was checking him out. I feel the blush creep up from my neck.

After putting my top back on, I dig a hairbrush out of my bag and go to work on attacking the bird's nest that has taken over my hair. Zac stands at the doorway and I think I have drool dripping down my open mouth. Wearing a pair of faded denim jeans, a black long sleeve Henley, and black boots, he is sex on a stick.

"How is it you spend two minutes getting dressed and look like the GQ cover model for January through to December?" I ask, not expecting an answer as I go back to detangling the bird's nest.

"Good to know you like what you see." He smirks. His eyes follow my body down my back, stopping on my ass. "Are you sure this brunch has to be a girls only thing?"

I nod my head yes. "You'd be bored to death. All we do is eat, drink mimosas and talk about boys, clothes and shoes."

He narrows his eyes at me. "You talk about boys? And just how many boys will you have to discuss at this week's brunch, sunshine?" I look at his clenched face in the mirror. Is he jealous? It's ludicrous if he is.

Deciding to play on this a bit, I scrunch my face up. "I don't have any boys to talk about." I pause, thinking for a moment. "Oh wait, there was that one guy. Oh, and then that lawyer I met on the train a few days ago." I continue to put on my thinking face.

Zac's jaw tightens even more. "I think we need to get something straight, sunshine. You haven't known me for long so I'll give you that concession. But one thing you need to know is I don't share." He annunci-ates the three words *I don't share* slowly.

I blink up at him. "Okay, well, I won't ask to have a sip of your coffee this morning." I know full well that that's not what he was referring to.

"Maybe I wasn't very clear, so let me try again." Turning me around so I'm facing him, Zac tilts my chin until our eyes meet before he says, "I will share anything with you; what I will not share, under any circumstances, is you." His stare is so intense, sincere. I think he actually means what he is saying—well, he has me believing, anyway.

"Okay, look, I don't know what this is," I say, pointing between the both of us, "but if you won't share, then I won't be sharing either. So, wherever your little black book of women is, Mr. GQ…" I turn my voice sugary sweet before adding, "…do us both a favour and lose it now, otherwise you might just have more bodies to bury."

"Where the hell have you been all my life, sunshine? You might not know what this is, me and you, and that's okay, because I know. This is us always having a tomorrow, together." He kisses my lips ever so lightly before stepping back. "Finish getting ready. I'm going to check on Ella before we head out."

ZAC PULLS UP into a carpark out front of the café. I go to open the door and he grabs my hand. "Wait here," he says before jumping out and walking around the front of the car. He opens my door, but before he lets me out, he says, "You should always wait for me to open your door, sunshine."

Does he think we're living in the 1930s? "Zac, that's sweet, it really is, but I know how to open doors and I don't need anyone to do things for me. I've been looking after myself since I was five years old, even opening my own doors."

His face tenses up as he holds his hand out for me. Once my hand is in his, he helps me out. "We will come back to that statement when we have more time."

It doesn't register with me that Zac is still holding my hand and walking me into the café until I see the table with Sarah, Holly, and Reilly, all of whom have bugged out eyes pointed towards me and Zac. Stopping, I tug on Zac's hand to pull him back, so he turns and looks at me.

"Zac, you can't crash girls' brunch. I've seen you naked and you're definitely missing the parts that make you a girl. Also, I'm certain you are not gay, although you sure are pretty enough to pull that off if you wanted to."

Zac laughs. "I assure you I'm not gay, and if you want me to, I'm more than happy to prove it to you anywhere, anytime. I don't plan on staying. I just wanted to walk you to your table to make sure you got there. I'll be back to pick you up though. I programmed my number in your phone. Make sure you call me when you're ready to leave, please."

Well, that does it… I think I will do anything he wants when he adds that *please* on the end of a request. "I'll call you. I promise. Thank you." He kisses me like no one is watching, and to be honest, I get so lost the moment those lips of his meet mine, I couldn't even tell you where we were at that very moment. My only care when he's kissing me is how I can keep him kissing me longer.

Before I know it, Zac pulls away from the kiss. "See you soon, sunshine. Have fun with your friends." He gives me that panty-melting smirk and walks out. I'm left standing in the middle of the café, watching him and trying to figure out why I feel like a part of me went with him.

IF I THOUGHT my friends would be kind enough not to bring up the fact that they just watched what was one of the best kisses I've received in my life, I was sorely mistaken. The moment I sat down, I put myself in the firing line. All three of my best friends are

never spoken to any of them like this. I don't recall ever being this mad at any of them. I know I'm being irrational, but I just can't seem to help myself.

Reilly looks at me and smiles. "I think you've finally been hit with the love bug, Lyssa. I've been waiting for this day to happen. We need to celebrate. I'll get the first round of mimosas and then you can tell us all about this Zac that we," she says, pointing to the three of them, "apparently may not appreciate in any way, form, or manner that's not pure and platonic." She gets up and heads to the counter.

"I'm not in love with him!" I declare to Holly and Sarah, both of whom just look at me with disbelieving grins.

"Of course, you're not in love. Despite what my sister thinks, it takes longer than twenty-four hours or a night of good sex to fall in love." Holly doesn't sound like she believes her own words.

"You both know Reilly can't tell the difference between being in love with someone and being in love with someone's cucumber. You," Sarah says, pointing at me to drive her point further, "are most definitely in love with the man. I can tell."

"I like him, maybe even like him a lot, but it's not love!" I defend myself.

Reilly comes back with eight mimosa glasses. "You know there are only four of us, right? And it's only like 10:30 a.m. not p.m." I raise my eyebrow at her.

"Well, we are celebrating the fact that you're in love, sorry lust, for the very first time. This is only the first round." She hands everyone a drink and then, holding hers up, she toasts, "To being in lust and not love!"

Taking a sip, I savour the flavours that hit my tongue. Just as I put my glass on the table, my phone plays the chorus of "Stuck Like Glue." I just stare at it. It stops and then plays the chorus again and the girls all start laughing and singing along at a *not so quiet* level. I can feel the redness creep up my neck as I slowly die of embarrassment.

Before my phone makes any more noise, I pick up. There are two missed messages from *my own GQ*. Instantly, I know who it is. I can't believe he programmed his name into my phone as *my own GQ* and personalised the tone. I open the messages to read what could be so important that it couldn't possibly wait a few hours. I mean, he hasn't been gone that long.

MY OWN GQ: **Sunshine, don't forget to order food to go with those mimosas. You cannot survive on liquid diets.**

HOLY SHIT, looking up, I look around the café. Is he hiding out and spying on me somewhere? I can't see him anywhere, but how else would he know I'm drinking mimosas? Looking down, I read the next message.

. . .

MY OWN GQ: **I've stopped in at the club. Got shit to do, but I will be available to pick you up whenever you're ready. Please eat something. You didn't get to eat dinner last night. xx**

OKAY, so he's not here. He's at the club, but boy is the man obsessed with food. I message him back.

ME: "STUCK LIKE GLUE," **really? Also, I'm 90% sure now that you have a food fetish. Is it your desire to feed me, sir?**

I DON'T GET the chance to silence my phone before it plays the song again. Dammit, I'm going to have to remember to change his tone back to a normal *beep beep* for a message, like a normal person would have. I open his message. If I thought I was red with embarrassment before, reading his message has me ten times redder, and wet in places I won't admit to in public.

MY OWN GQ: **Yes, it is my desire to feed you, but what I desire to put into your mouth is not food. And now you have me walking around**

the club with a fucking hard-on. Did I mention I have employees here? I'm sure they don't need to see their boss with a hard-on!

"WHATEVER THE GUY just sent you is good. Let me see!" Reilly holds her hand out.

"Not a freaking chance in hell," I tell her. "And the guy has a name—it's Zac."

"So, now's a good time to tell us all about this Zac of yours, Lyssa. You've kept us waiting long enough." Holly rests her chin on her hands, like she's getting ready to hear a juicy story.

I tell them all about how I went on the blind date, how I got roofied and how Zac looked after me. Sarah then fills in. "He drove her home the next morning, and waited for her in our living room while she had a shower, just so he could drive her to work. The boy sure is smitten." She smiles.

"One, he's not a boy. I can assure you he is all man. Two, he was just helping me get to work on time, considering I was so late. Not smitten, just a kind person."

"So, tell us, how did it go from him dropping you at the hospital to him dropping you here and playing hockey with your tonsils?" Reilly asks.

I decide not to tell them about going to the club to help his sister. Or making Zac shower when he came back into the office covered in blood—the only thought I had on *that* was: *thank god it wasn't his blood.*

Thinking logically, I know I should care about whatever it is he did that had him coming back covered in blood. But for the life of me, I can't bother to care. All I care about is that he's okay, and his sister can sleep at night knowing whoever attacked her did not get away with it, whatever happened to him.

Instead, I tell the girls how Zac was waiting for me outside the hospital when I finished my shift and saved me from the awkwardness of Dr. Mark. They've all heard about Dr. Mark before, so that bit of information is not new to them.

"So, he picked you up, took you home and fed you cucumber?" Sarah asks.

I shake my head. "No, I have not had the cucumber... yet. We slept. That's it. He held me all night."

"Sure he's not gay? Because if I had you in my bed all night, we would not just sleep—that's for sure. Although, that kiss was way too convincing for him to be gay." Reilly likes to say she's an alcohol-fuelled lesbian. Meaning if she's drunk enough, she'd be into it.

"Thanks, I think?" I hold my glass up in her direction before drinking the last of it.

It's one o'clock when we finish the last drink, and it's not until I'm dialling Zac's number that I notice how tipsy I am. "Who are you calling?" Sarah asks.

"Zac. He wants to pick me up," I say with a huge smile.

"I bet that's not all he wants to do," Reilly shouts

out. At the same time, I can hear laughing on the other side of the phone.

"Sunshine, I assure you... picking you up is not all I want to do. Are you ready to head out? I'll be there in fifteen."

I sigh. I actually sigh into the phone out loud. Oh god, maybe it's not a good idea to see Zac while I'm tipsy on mimosas.

"Zac, I can just get an Uber home. You don't have to come back here to get me."

"Sunshine, do not get in a fucking Uber. I swear..." He takes a breath. "I'm already on my way. Just wait for me." He pauses and then adds, "Please."

"Okay, I'll wait for you. You'd be a much better view than any Uber driver anyway. Oh god, I said that out loud, didn't I?" I can hear Zac laughing. "I'm hanging up. I'll see you soon."

I don't give him a chance to respond before I hang up the phone. Looking back at my friends, I watch as they all let out the laughter they were unsuccessfully attempting to hold in. It must be contagious because I join them, laughing until my eyes water.

Eight

ZAC

*W*ALKING INTO THE CAFÉ, I can hear the four women before I see them. I approach their table slowly, even though every bone in my body wants to run and grab Alyssa so I can pull her back into my arms. I stop at the table, sitting in the empty seat next to Alyssa.

Putting my arm around the back of her chair, I ask, "Sunshine, did you have a good time?"

I already know the answer to my question. I can tell by the rosy colour to her cheeks that she's had a few mimosas. She doesn't answer my question. Instead, she turns and smiles at me before practically jumping into my lap. She reaches up, pulling my head down to hers, and plants her lips against mine.

It feels like heaven, her soft, full lips on mine. Swiping my tongue out, I lick her lips, seeking entrance. She doesn't keep me waiting, and I swirl my tongue, tasting her mouth. She tastes sweet, a mixture of orange juice and what I think is chocolate. What-ever it is, she's intoxicating and I'm not talking about the obvious alcohol I can taste on her lips.

I hate to do it, but I have to pull back. If I don't, I'll have her spread across this table before I know it. She groans as I pull away, and I can't help but laugh at how damn cute she is.

"Why… why can't you just keep kissing me? I like your kisses, Zac, like really, *really* like them." She purrs a little, which has my cock harder than it was a minute ago, and it was already fucking hard.

Leaning in, I whisper in her ear so she's the only one that can hear, "Sunshine, I want nothing more right now than to keep kissing you. I want to strip you naked and kiss every part of your body from your head to your toes. I want to worship you the way you deserve to be worshiped, but that can't happen in a café full of people. I already told you *I don't share*."

Alyssa looks at me, mouth open. She eventually says, "Let's go. I'm ready."

I laugh at her eagerness. I don't remember a time I've laughed so frequently, but Alyssa seems to bring it out of me with ease. "Baby, you might want to at least say goodbye to your friends first."

I wave at the three women who are all sitting at the table and staring at us like we're an alien lifeform. Alyssa looks across at them. Before she can say anything, one of her friends speaks up, "*Uhh*, no, you don't, Mister Tall-dark-and-handsome. It's Sunday! Sunday means girls' day. You don't get to take her away from us on girls' day. We have partying to do, we have celebrating to do, and we have cucumbers to pick up."

All four women laugh when Alyssa says, "Well, I don't need to pick up any cucumbers. I have one that's just perfect already."

I have no idea what their fascination with cucumbers is and can't help with that, but the first two points I can address, and still keep Alyssa with me. "Well, it just so happens partying and celebrating are something I can help with. How about I reserve a VIP table for you at The Merge tonight? You all go home, rest, sober up and meet Alyssa at the club at ten tonight?"

The four women look from one another. It's like they're having a conversation without speaking—kind of creepy if you ask me. Sarah speaks up this time. "Will there be bottle service included with the VIP table? If so, we're in. Also, you're giving me a ride home with Alyssa."

"It wouldn't be VIP without table service. I can drop you off at your place, but I'll be taking Alyssa home with me." I leave no room for arguments.

Lucky for me, Alyssa seems onboard with my plan. "Okay, I will see you twinnies later tonight. And *you*, get up. We're going. I don't have all day."

Standing up, Alyssa grabs my hand and pulls, but she stops suddenly. "Oh wait!" She picks her purse up from the table. "I just need to go pay then we can go."

As she's trying to pull away from me, I stop her

and pull her back to my side. "I already paid for the table. Let's go."

If I thought she would be grateful for having her and her friends' meals and drinks paid for, I was wrong. She pulls away from me, crossing her arms over her chest, which only makes her breasts look like a fucking offering. I'm finding it hard to look her in her eyes and not stare at them like a creep. Again, I'm struck with the thought, *Damn, she's cute*, which makes me smile. Wrong move again.

"What the hell are you smiling for, GQ? This isn't funny. I don't need you to pay for my meals. I have a job you know. I can pay for my own things. Holly? She has a job; she's a kindergarten teacher. She can pay for her own things too. And Sarah? She's a makeup artist. She makes money. Funnily, she can pay for her own meals. Reilly…" She pauses and takes a breath. "Well, she's between jobs right now, but she's about to get one. I know it's happening for her soon. But okay, maybe you can pay for hers."

I wait to make sure she's finished with her little tirade. "Are you finished, or is there more?" I unfold her arms and pull her back into me. "I know you have a job, a stable one with stable pay if I remember correctly." She nods her head. "I didn't pay for your meal and drinks because I don't think you can. I paid because I wanted to do something nice for you. As for paying for your friends? They just happen to benefit from me doing something nice for you."

Alyssa doesn't say anything, but leans her body

into mine. I take this as a win. Reilly (I'm pretty sure it's Reilly) says, "Well, I for one am all for anyone paying for me! Until I get that next job, that is."

Looking over to Sarah, I say, "If you need a ride, let's go." I take Alyssa's hand and lead her out to the car.

Settling Alyssa into the passenger seat, I walk around and jump in the car. Looking back, I make sure Sarah has put her own seat belt on before I pull out. "Here, drink this, sunshine." She takes the water I hand over but sits it on her lap instead of opening it.

"You're so pretty, Zac. Why are you so damn pretty? I'm gonna go to jail, aren't I?" she asks so seriously.

Picking up her hand and joining it with mine, I bring her wrist to my mouth and kiss it before resting our joined hands on my thigh. I like touching her. If I had it my way, I would always be touching some part of her. I haven't even had her yet, and I'm craving her touch this badly. How is it going to be once I finally get her in my bed and naked?

I'm pulled from my thoughts when Alyssa speaks again. "I really like when you do that. It sends shivers straight through me, but the good kind, not the creepy kind."

Looking into the back seat, she says to Sarah, "I'm definitely going to jail in the near future. You'll come visit, right?"

Sarah laughs and adds, "I'll probably be your

damn cellmate. We'll have to turn lesbian; they don't serve cucumbers in jail, you know."

I have to shake my head to clear my thoughts. All I heard was: *We'll have to turn lesbian.* Usually, the thought of two women would be a major turn on for me, but the thought of Alyssa being with anyone else, even a woman, sends rage through my entire body.

"Sunshine, you are not going to jail. Whatever you did, I'll fix it for you. All you have to do is tell me. I can fix it. And Sarah, you can keep your filthy hands off my woman. Under no circumstances will you be turning her lesbian, jail or no jail. You got me?"

Both Alyssa and Sarah crack up, and laughter fills the car. I could listen to the sound of Alyssa's laugh forever; it's like the best played song I've ever heard.

Sarah mumbles, "Your woman," and then bursts out in laughter again.

This, I don't find funny. "Yes, my woman, my Alyssa, and I don't share."

"*Aw*, you called her my Alyssa, and this morning she called you her Zac." Tapping Alyssa on the shoulder, she says seriously, "Jail is most certainly in your future, my friend."

"Alyssa, baby, what the hell have you done that you think you're going to end up in jail?" Both women laugh again. I'm not impressed. All this talk of jail, after what I just did last night... Fuck me, does she know what I did? Does she think whatever I do will come back on her? The thought that she would be worried about that has me feeling nauseous.

Alyssa must notice a change in me. Squeezing my hand, she says, "It's not what I've done yet. It's what I'm likely to do to all the girls who think they can get to you. Well, they will have to go through me now, because I don't share and I happen to be a very scrappy fighter. I learnt young."

It does not escape my attention that she made a comment about learning how to fight young, nor does this morning's comment about taking care of herself since she was five. Now is not the time to bring it up though, and I'm feeling relief that she isn't concerned about my actions coming back to her, not that I would ever fucking let that happen.

Pulling into the carpark out front of Alyssa's townhouse, I open her door for her. "Run in and pack an overnight bag. Or better yet, pack enough for a few days so you won't have to come back. I'll wait out here. I've got a call I need to make."

Alyssa reaches up on her tiptoes and lays a kiss onto my cheek. "Sure thing, stud-muffin." I watch in shock as she grabs Sarah's arm and they walk into their townhouse together.

"I'M JUST GOING to freshen up real quick," Alyssa says as she goes into the bathroom and shuts the door. I finally have her back in my bedroom, where I've wanted her to be since she left it this morning. Sitting on the edge of the bed, I toe my boots and socks off. I take my shirt off and start undoing my belt when the bathroom door opens. I look up and all the breath I had leaves me.

Thank you God, Jesus, Buddha and whatever other godly divinity sent this angel my way. Standing in the bathroom doorway, Alyssa is wearing matching black lace panties and a bra. I can see her nipples through the sheer lace of the bra, her hair cascading down over her shoulder.

"Holy shit, sunshine, I don't even know what to say right now."

She's a little shy. She sobered up between leaving the café and arriving here. Looking down, she says, "Well, you could either say you like what you see, or you don't like what you see. I will survive either option."

Is she fucking kidding me? "Baby, I love what I'm seeing right now. You are goddamn perfect. I couldn't even dream you up if I tried." Walking over to her, I grab the back of her head and smash my mouth to hers, devouring and getting high off the taste of her. I think she may just be my new addiction.

She wraps her arms around my neck, pulling my head down further into hers. Groaning, I pick her up from under her legs and push her against the wall. Alyssa arches and grinds against my cock. I think I might be at risk of coming in my fucking pants if she keeps that up. I kiss down her throat.

"I want to kiss and lick every inch of your body," I whisper, nipping at her ear. Her moans are getting louder. I need to get her spread out on my bed before this ends too soon. "Bed, I need you on the bed for me, baby." Still holding her, I carry her to the bed and lay her down, falling on top of her and settling between her legs.

"Zac, I need you inside me. I don't think I've ever needed anything more in my life," she purrs. *Fuck me.* How am I meant to perform when I'm ready to come just from hearing her moans and pleas?

"I plan on burying myself so far inside of you. I plan on ruining you for all time." Kissing my way down her throat, I sit her up and unclasp her bra, letting her breasts fall free. Filling both of my hands with a breast each, I squeeze her nipples. "Sunshine, you have the most perfect tits." Dipping down, I pop one into my mouth and suck, while attending to the other one with my fingers.

Alyssa arches her back up, moaning and pleading, "Zac, oh god, please."

I know what she needs, but I want to hear her ask for it. "Please what, baby? What do you need?" I move on to her other breast, sucking, licking, savouring.

"I need you in me, now, damn it." I laugh at how demanding she is.

Trailing a hand down her flat stomach, I reach my hand into her panties, stopping just above her clit. "What part of me do you need inside you, baby? Do you want my fingers, my tongue, my cock?"

I continue to lick and suck on her nipples. My fingers find their way to her clit—she's wet. I moan at how wet and responsive she is to me. "You're so fucking wet, sunshine," I growl, dipping a finger inside her before pulling it back out and swirling around her clit.

Her moans are getting louder. She's arching her back up, trying to harden the light friction I'm providing with my fingers. "Please, Zac, I need... I need... your fingers. No, your cock. *Mmm,* no, your tongue. Dammit, I want it all."

"All you had to do was ask, sunshine." I leave her breasts and trail my tongue down her stomach. Sitting up, I pull her panties down her legs. Spreading her legs wide, I settle my shoulders between them. I lay my hands on her thighs holding them open.

"I have been dreaming about tasting you since I first saw you. I bet you're sweet like sugar. Do you taste sweet, sunshine?" I ask as I kiss up and down the inside of her thighs. I can see her arousal, I can smell her arousal, and soon enough, I will taste her arousal. I growl at the thought.

"Well, how about you stop talking about it and find out for yourself," she demands breathlessly.

Laughing, I do just that. I swipe my tongue from the bottom of her slit up to the top, slowly.

"Oh god, that's so good." I can tell she's on the brink. I want to ride this out for as long as I can, but I also just really want to see her fucking come.

I go in hard, licking and sucking like my life depends on it. She's squirming underneath me, moaning out my name. I feel like I'm drunk on the smell and taste of her.

"Goddammit, you're so fucking tight. I can't wait to feel your pussy choking my cock as you come." I feel her tighten around my fingers; it seems she likes the dirty talk. *Good.* Pumping my fingers in and out, I curve them inside her until I find the spot I know will send her wild. Circling my tongue around her engorged clit, I lick and suck.

I feel her whole body tense, her pussy squeezing the fuck out of my fingers, as she screams out, "Oh god! Zac! Oh my god!"

I continue pumping my fingers and licking until

she comes down. "That was the most beautiful thing I've seen," I tell her as I stand up and remove my jeans, finally giving my cock the freedom he's been seeking. Reaching into the bedside table, I find a

condom and rip it open. I don't waste time getting it on before I settle between her legs. She's barely come down from the orgasm she just had as I push the tip inside her.

I can't think of a better feeling, slowly pushing inside. "I think this is what heaven must feel like," I say, kissing her as I slowly glide my cock further into her.

Once I'm buried to the hilt, I feel her tense. I stop moving, gritting my teeth. It takes everything in me not to fuck the fuck out of her right now. "You're so fucking tight. This pussy was made for me."

Once I feel her muscles loosen, I start to move in and out. She feels so fucking good. I don't think I'm going to last long. Reaching down between our bodies, I circle a finger around her clit. "I need you to come again. You feel so fucking good on my cock, sunshine."

I pump in and out of her faster and harder, and she matches my movements thrust for thrust. "Zac, don't stop. Oh god, don't fucking stop," she screams out.

Leaning down, I whisper in her ear, "I'm never going to stop fucking you. There will always be tomorrow for us."

Her pussy walls tighten and strangle my cock. She

tips her head back, screaming my name. This moment, as she comes on my cock for the first time, will be burned in my memory as the best fucking day of my life.

I can feel the tingling sensation up my spine; my balls tighten as I pump into her roughly until I come undone. I come hard as I continue to pump, claiming her as mine.

"Alyssa. You. Are. Fucking. Mine." Catching my weight as I fall on top of her, I roll to the side, landing next to her. We both lie there breathing heavily, basking in the orgasm afterglow, and catching our breath.

"That was… oh god, I don't even know what that was. What the hell was that, Zac?" Alyssa rolls her head, meeting my eyes.

"That, sunshine, was fucking perfection. You are perfection." She chews on her bottom lip. I've noticed she does this when she's thinking. "Hold that thought. Don't move." I go into the bathroom and dispose of the condom, wetting a washcloth before I go back out to find Alyssa right where I left her. Standing above her, I spread her legs open and use the cloth to clean between her legs.

She stares at me. "What the hell are you doing?" She looks mortified, but I don't fucking care.

"I'm wiping your pussy. Correction, I'm wiping my fucking pussy." My face is deadpan.

"I can take care of that myself. Just give me a few

minutes for my legs to not feel like Jell-O," she says, trying to shut her legs on me.

Not going to fucking happen, *ever*. "I take care of what's mine, and sunshine, this pussy…" I cup my hand over her pussy. "…is mine."

Throwing the washcloth in the laundry basket, I climb back into bed and pull Alyssa into me.

As I pull the blankets up, covering us, she looks up at me. "When I have more energy, we will revisit this concept of you thinking you have a proprietorship of my anatomy."

I don't bother arguing that I intend to own every inch of her; instead, I kiss her forehead. "Go to sleep. We can discuss who owns what after we wake up."

Just as I think she's asleep, she whispers, "Zac?"

"Yeah?" My voice is just as quiet.

Alyssa keeps her head down. "I'm scared of what this is." She's quiet, and as I'm thinking of what to say to reassure her, she continues, "Of what's happening between you and me."

Well fuck me, I never would have believed you if you told me I'd feel like this for one woman, that I would give anything and everything for just one more tomorrow with her, if that's all I could have.

"Sunshine, I'm scared too. But not of what's happening between you and me, because whatever it is, it's already happened. There's no use fighting it." Pausing, I lay kisses on the top of her head before confessing my real fear to her. "What I'm scared of is what will happen if I don't have a tomorrow with you.

If something happens or if I fuck this up and make you realise you could do one hundred times better. Not having you, that's what I'm scared of."

Alyssa picks her head up and kisses my chest, right where my heart lays. "I'll be here for as many tomorrows as you want me to be," she says before laying her head back down. That's how we drift off to sleep.

Nine

ALYSSA

I WAKE to the feel of kisses being run down my face, down my neck and back up again. Smiling, I can tell who is responsible for those kisses by his scent alone. Breathing in deeply, I inhale that woodsy and citrus scent. Wait, inhaling through my nose again, I note there is another scent that registers to my brain, *coffee*.

"I smell coffee," I mumble with my eyes still closed. "Please tell me I'm not dreaming and there is coffee in my near future."

I can feel the vibration of Zac's chuckle. "Time to wake up, sunshine. Yes, I have a vanilla latte ready and waiting." Well, that does it.

My eyes pop open and I'm greeted by a vision that has me believing I must still be dreaming. Zac, shirtless, all those tanned muscles on display right in front of me, all within reaching distance. Even better—

okay, maybe not better but definitely equal to—he's holding out a coffee cup.

"I honestly don't know what I want to reach for more, you or the coffee." I smile, taking the coffee cup and bringing it straight to my mouth. At the perfect taste of the vanilla coffee concoction, I moan, "*Mmm*, this is worth being woken up for."

"So, I lose out to coffee? Well, if that isn't a blow to the ego, I don't know what is." Zac is pouting. It's cute.

Taking my time, I take a huge gulp of coffee, slowly put the cup down onto the bedside table, and then I'm on him. Reaching up, I grab his head, pulling it closer to meet mine. He doesn't put up any struggle. Smashing my lips to his, I kiss him like it's the first and last kiss, like his lips provide the elements I need to continue breathing. I try to pour everything I'm feeling into the kiss. He doesn't let me down, returning my fever with a frantic version of his own, taking control as he tilts my head and caresses my mouth with his tongue. By the time we pull apart, I'm breathless and I can feel my lips are kiss swollen.

"It was a really, really hard choice. You came a very close second to the coffee, but it's a vanilla latte." Picking up the coffee cup, I inhale the aroma before sipping at it.

Zac shakes his head, trailing his hand up and down my leg. "I'll just have to work on it a bit more. There are things I could do that would give you a much better wake up than that sugary syrup you like to call coffee."

I highly doubt it, but I'm not about to stop him from trying. "Well, hot stuff, why don't you give it your best shot and I'll let you know how you rate." I slowly pull the blanket down to reveal the top of my breasts, stopping just before my nipples are uncovered.

"As much as it kills me right now to say this, we don't have time. You have plans with your friends, and honestly, I'm a little scared of what those women will do to my club if I don't get you there." The whole time he's speaking to my breasts, his eyes fixated on the mounds.

Trying to entice him to forget the plans, I let the blanket drop completely to my waist and with as much innocence as I can put into my voice, I say, "Well, if you're sure there's no time…" I leave the sentence hanging.

Zac licks his lips, bringing his eyes up to meet mine with a hardened stare. "That's not fair. How am I meant to walk away from an offering like that?"

He reaches his hands out and grabs hold of my breasts, one in each hand, squeezing a few times. I arch my back up towards him, moaning a little. How can his touch affect me so easily? Pulling away and standing up, he smirks that panty-melting smirk.

"You know what? I think I will wait to ravish this body when we get home. I didn't do it enough justice this afternoon, but tonight, I plan on rectifying that. Get ready. We need to leave in an hour," he demands, walking out the bedroom door.

TAKING one last look in the mirror, I decide it will have to do. I'm wearing a gold sequin mini dress; thin spaghetti straps cross over at the back down to my waist, leaving the top half of my back exposed. The dress is loose fitting. The fabric dips down between my breasts, making them look like they're being hugged. It's short, much shorter than anything I would normally wear.

Sarah threw the dress at me as I was packing a bag earlier today and said, "If you don't wear it, I will comment on your lover boy's endearing qualities all night long."

So, instead of being tempted to kill my best friend with pure, unjustified, jealousy-fuelled rage, I'm wearing the damn dress, paired with a pair of gold strappy heels. I've left my hair down in waves and attempted to give myself a subtle smoky eye, paired with bright red lips. Being best friends with a makeup artist has its perks; you pick up a thing or two over the years.

Coming to terms with the fact that I can't hide out in Zac's bathroom anymore, I take a deep breath in an attempt to calm my nerves. Why I'm nervous, I have absolutely no freaking idea. Well, it could be anxiety about what Zac's reaction to the dress will be; he's either going to hate it or love it. I remind myself on the walk down the hallway out to the living room that it doesn't matter either way. I dress for me, not for the approval of any man.

Stepping into the living room, I search for Zac. He's nowhere to be seen. Dean and Bray, however, are both lounging on the sofas with a drink in their hands. My heels click on the floor as I step further into the room, and their heads snap up and around in my direction.

"Holy fucking shit," Bray says, shaking his head at me. Well, okay then, not really sure what to make of that statement. Before I conjure up a response, Dean speaks up, "I'm guessing Zac hasn't seen her yet. This is going to be fun." He rubs his hands together and smiles wide.

"I don't recall burying bodies ever being fun, Dean, but I guess it might be worth it to see Zac lose a bit of that always calm and in control demeanour."

Having no idea what the hell they're talking about, I walk over to the floor-to-ceiling windows I didn't notice when I was in this room yesterday. The view here is breathtaking. I can see the Sydney Harbour Bridge, the city lights twinkling like fairy lights.

"This view is breathtaking," I say, still mesmerised by the city lights.

I hear a throat clear. "I agree; the view is breathtaking."

Spinning around, I see Zac. His eyes travel up my body from my feet and by the time his eyes meet mine, they are wide open, a mixture of shock and arousal crossing his face.

"Holy fucking shit," Zac grunts out.

"Yep, that's what I said." Bray smirks at me. I can feel the shades of red creeping up my neck.

Tilting my head, I inspect Bray closer. He's good looking for sure, big with obvious muscle on top of muscle. He's wearing black jeans and a grey t-shirt. I can see tattoos covering both of his arms. He has bad boy heartbreaker written all over him. No matter how good looking he is, he just doesn't do it for me. Nothing. Zilch. Not even a flicker of an ember.

When I look at Zac though, who is wearing a very well-fitted navy suit with a white dress shirt—he has a dark navy striped tie hanging loosely around his neck —forget about an ember. Getting my fill of Zac starts a bonfire within me, my panties instantly wet.

Zac walks up to Bray and slaps him across the head. "Get your greedy fucking eyes off her."

Dean and Bray both laugh as Zac continues to move until he stops directly in front of me, effectively blocking their view of me.

"Sunshine, please tell me there is more of this dress you left back in the bedroom." His fingers trail along the hem of the dress on my upper thigh.

Squinting my eyes at him, I take a step back, crossing my arms and asking, "What's wrong with my dress, Zac?"

"Nothing, I love the dress. You look stunning, baby. What I don't like is that every other asshole in a ten- mile radius will have their eyes glued to you, and I'm probably going to have to get dumbo one and dumbo two over there to bury a few bodies before the end of the night."

"I said that too." Bray laughs.

I angle my head around Zac's body and glare at him, raising my eyebrows. He holds his hands up in a surrender motion. Taking the win, I set my glare back to Zac.

"You have two choices and I strongly recommend you choose wisely. One." I hold up a finger. "You can step into the year 2020. You know, where men don't actually get to tell women what they can and can't wear out in public? And when you've come to your senses, you can take me to your club to meet my friends. I might even let you stick around, even though it's girls' night." I pause and Zac grits his teeth, jaw locked. Oh boy, he is not happy with that option.

Continuing, I hold up a second finger. "Two, you can go and do whatever it is you would normally do on a Sunday night. I will call an Uber and make my own way to your club and have a great time with my friends, without you."

"Damn, bro, didn't see that one coming. I thought she was a quiet little timid thing, but kitten's got claws." Bray laughs, coming up to me to wrap an arm around my shoulder. I look up at Zac and see him fuming. Imagine a cartoon character with smoke coming out of its ears, that's Zac right now, only no actual smoke.

"I approve by the way, Lyssa, and if this douche chooses option two, I will be more than happy to give you a ride to the club." Bray smirks down at me in what I'm guessing is a smirk that would melt the panties right off a lot of girls.

Zac actually growls, full on, out loud growls, like a bloody grizzly bear. "Because you're my brother, and you happen to make me a shitload of money with that arm, I'm going to give you five seconds to remove it from my woman before I fucking break it," he grits out.

Bray immediately removes his arm and steps a whole two steps away from me. *Huh*, maybe he thinks Zac would really break his arm. I doubt he would, but it's not worth testing the theory right now.

Thinking back on what Zac said, I question the both of them, "What do you mean he makes you a lot of money with that arm?" I have no idea what Bray does, other than live to get a rise out of his brother.

Zac looks at Bray before giving a nonanswer. "I'll tell you later."

Bray raises his eyebrows in shock, shaking his head. He picks up keys from the coffee table, throwing them at Zac. As Zac catches them, Bray smiles and says, "The McLaren's back from the detailers. You know, I never could figure out how you managed to get chocolate muffin crumbs all over the car when you've never so much as had water in the car, and you don't even like chocolate." He looks directly in my direction before adding, "I think I get it now."

My mouth hangs open and I look at Zac questioningly. I thought he was joking about the car being at the cleaners. Instead of answering, he grabs my hand and starts pulling me towards the door.

Just as we're all about to get in the elevator, I ask, "Is Ella coming tonight?"

All three men, all at the same time, say, "Not a fucking chance."

"*Huh*, you know, it's cute how you all can finish each other's sentences like that." I smile innocently, stepping inside. Turning around, I'm greeted with three very intimidating scowls; but for some reason, I've never felt safer.

SITTING in the passenger seat of the Batmobile, the guilt of making such a mess that Zac had to have his car detailed plays on my mind. "You know, I can pay you for whatever cost you had to pay to clean the car."

I look over to Zac; he's looking back at me with his brows creased. "What are you talking about?"

Rolling my eyes at him, I respond, "It was me that put chocolate muffin crumbs everywhere. If it's true you don't eat in your car, why the hell would you give me, probably the messiest eater on the continent, a bloody muffin to eat in here?"

Bringing my hand up to his mouth, he kisses the inside of my wrist. I can't help but melt a little at the action and he knows it.

"Sunshine, I eat in the car. I just don't let Bray or anyone else eat in the car. I happen to love this car way more than him."

Zac looks across to me, his eyes drifting down to my legs, where my dress has ridden up high on my thighs, before looking back at the road. "Please, tell me you are wearing underwear under that shirt you're wearing as a dress," he groans.

"So, you let me eat in the fancy-ass Batmobile but not your brother. You know, that's crazy. What if I stained the carpet or got crumbs stuck in crevices you'll never get them out of?" Staring at him expectantly, I wait for an actual answer.

"It just so happens I like you way more than I like this car, so you eating is more important to me than having a clean car." Squeezing my hand, he looks over at me. "Now answer my question. You are wearing underwear under that dress, right?"

All I heard out of that was: *I like you more than I like this car.* And I swoon. This is a really freaking nice car. Wondering how much information to give him about the underwear that I'm wearing, I give the best innocent smile I can muster.

"*Umm*, underwear?" I question.

"I swear to everything holy, sunshine, if you tell me you're not wearing underwear, I'm turning the damn car around and taking you home and handcuffing you to the fucking bed."

Well, okay then, I was not expecting that reaction. The mention of handcuffs, and what little underwear I'm wearing is becoming very wet.

"Of course I'm wearing underwear, Zac." Smiling at him, I decide to tell him exactly what kind of underwear. "I happen to be wearing a lacy white thong under this dress."

The car swerves to the side of the road, skidding to a stop. I don't even have time to think about what's happening before Zac's tormented gaze is searing into me.

"Are you fucking kidding me right now? Your ass is uncovered? You bend over and every fucker around is going to see your ass."

"Well, I don't plan on bending over, Zac, and just so you know, I've been wearing dresses for a while now. You know, considering I am a girl, and a girl who likes dresses, I know how not to show my ass to everyone when wearing one. It's a skill really, a talent some might say."

Just as he's about to say something, his phone rings over the Bluetooth of the car, announcing that the caller is Bray. "What?" Zac grunts out.

"What the fuck did you stop for? I've got plans; some of us actually want to get to the club before it fucking closes," Bray yells back. Looking in the rear-view mirror, I see the Range Rover behind us; Dean's driving and Bray's in the passenger seat.

"Oh, I can answer this one, sweetie." I turn on my sugary sweet voice and smile at Zac, who, by the way, is now frowning at me.

"Oh, this is gonna be good," I hear Dean mumble.

"Bray, it's my fault. Obviously, I should have waited until we got to the club before describing what kind of underwear I'm wearing." Laughing a little to myself, I stop when I notice that no one else is laughing.

Zac looks like he's about to burst a blood vessel in his forehead, and Dean and Bray are so damn quiet I thought they were disconnected until I hear Bray's voice again. "Lyssa, don't take this the wrong way, because I like you, like really fucking like you. But could you maybe wait until you provide me with a nephew before you give my brother a heart attack? Because I'm really fucking great uncle material. Uncle Bray has a ring to it, don't you think?"

At the mention of kids, I can feel the panic over-take me. My skin feels clammy. I'm nauseous. I need air. I need… oh god, I can't breathe in here. I need to get out of this fucking car. Searching around the car, I look for a way out, a way to wind the damn window down, something. Zac notices my distress and grabs my arms, stopping me in my place.

"Bray, we'll meet you at the club." Disconnecting the call, he doesn't wait for a response.

"Sunshine, breathe. You're okay." Although his voice is soft, I can hear the worry in it. "Alyssa, baby, breathe with me, okay? In… out… in… out."

He brings his face right up close to mine, his lips just shy of touching mine. I can feel his breath on my lips, breathing in deep as I inhale his scent.

"That's it, baby, just keep breathing with me. You're okay. I've got you. I'm never going to let anything happen to you." His voice is soothing, and he's rubbing his hands up and down my arms. I can feel myself relax, and with that, comes the embarrassment. I can't believe I just had a panic attack in front of Zac, surely now he will see just how broken I am.

Attempting to turn my head so he can't see my shame, I'm stopped as his hands cup my face. "Sunshine, you never need to be embarrassed in front of me, ever."

He's so sincere. I can't take it. My eyes well up and before I can stop it, I feel a tear drop down my cheeks. Zac uses his thumb to swipe it away.

"I'm gonna fucking kill him," he mumbles.

Confused and wanting the focus off me, I ask, "Who?"

"My fucking idiot brother. Whatever he said made you panic and cry."

Shit, I don't want to cause issues with his family.

"It's not Bray's fault, and I'm sorry. Sometimes I have panic attacks. I can't predict when they're going to happen. They don't happen often though. This is the first one in over a year."

Shaking his head, he leans in and kisses my lips ever so lightly. "I'm still going to rip him apart." He pauses and then asks, "What did he say that caused the panic? And don't try to tell me it wasn't him. I know it's something he said."

Not really having any other option, I go for the truth and if it makes him want to run far, far away from me, well, I will survive, I think.

"He wants to be an uncle," I say, looking down at my fingers.

"Why would Bray wanting to be an uncle make you panic?" he asks. He's patient and waits for me to answer.

"Because, well, because I don't think I can give you that. I don't think I want to have kids and if I can't give you that, you'll want to find someone else who will. I can't... I can't..." Shaking my head, I feel another tear escape. Zac swipes it away and kisses my lips again in an ever so light touch of his lips.

"Alyssa, Bray's a fucking idiot. That's all there is to it. He was joking, okay? But it doesn't matter anyway.

Do you know why?" he asks. I shake my head no in answer. "It doesn't matter, because I couldn't give two fucks if Bray wants to be a fucking uncle. I have raised Ella and Bray since our parents died when she was only thirteen. I'd do anything for them. But I don't need to have kids of my own. If we have kids, that's up to us to decide, not anyone else. I don't want kids if it means not having you. There is nothing you can say that is going to make me want to look for anyone else, okay?"

"Okay," I agree, not sure if I believe myself.

"Do you still want to go to the club? I can and will take you home if you want, or anywhere else you want to go."

Reaching up and kissing his lips, I say, "I don't know how I got so lucky to have you, but I'm not giving you back, so I hope you realise you're stuck now. Yes, I want to go to the club. Let's go."

Zac pulls the car back out onto the road. Picking my hand up and kissing my wrist, he says, "There's no one else I'd want to be stuck to."

Ten

ZAC

*S*ITTING in my office, attempting to get an hour's worth of work done while Alyssa is on the VIP floor of the club, wearing that fucking dress—a dress I plan on fucking burning as soon as it hits my bedroom floor tonight—is pure torture. I don't know what I was thinking. I don't think I've done anything productive since I came in here forty-five minutes ago.

My eyes drift to the flat screen on the wall, where I am viewing the security footage of the very floor Alyssa is on. I can't help but watch her; she's mesmerising. Not that she realises how goddamn beautiful she is. I've watched many men attempt to get close to her in the short time I've been up here, each time being intercepted by either Dean or James.

Before leaving Alyssa with her friends, I made sure James was the only bartender serving her table. I may have threatened his job if anything happened to her, or if any motherfucker got too close to her. It appears his job is safe with how well he runs interference on all the motherfuckers with a goddamn death wish, wanting to get closer to my woman.

I was prepared to break my own brother's bloody arm when I saw him with that arm around her. I don't know what's happening to me. I've never been so irrational before, never been so infatuated with a woman before that it feels like I can't breathe properly unless I'm with her.

When she had that panic attack in the car tonight, my heart felt like it was being ripped to shreds. I've never wanted to hold anybody together so badly; I would have done anything to take her fear away. It would be so easy for me to have Dean run a background check on her, find out all the secrets she holds and what the fuck happened to her to cause such fear.

I don't want to find out about her that way though. I want her to trust me. If I go digging around in her past and she found out, well, I don't think she'd take that very well. I just have to be patient and wait for her to open up to me, to let me in.

Patience is not something I've been known to have, but for Alyssa, I'm willing to give it a go. As I watch her on the screen, I don't think there is anything I wouldn't do for her, or die trying to do. She's laughing, dancing with Reilly or Holly—I really can't tell which is which with those two. Sarah is dancing with some random guy. Bray and Dean are sitting, nursing drinks and watching Alyssa and Reilly.

The fact that they're getting a front-row seat, watching my woman dance like that, in that fucking dress, makes me see red. It should be me getting that front-row seat, not any other fucker... even if I tasked them both with the job of watching her.

Groaning, I turn back to my computer screen. I've been trying to read over the events planned for the next few weeks. I don't know what the fuck Caitlyn was thinking when she booked the same band for two weekends in a row. The same fucking band that was now missing a drummer.

Picking up my phone, I dial Caitlyn. The call goes straight to voicemail. "Where the fuck are you? We've got a problem with Cyrus. You should know better than to book the same band two weeks in a fucking row. Fix it. Get them off next week's schedule and find a replacement act."

Hanging up the phone, I look back at the flat screen. I'm on my feet as soon as I see what's happening. Moving closer, I scan every monitor for Alyssa. I can't fucking see her anywhere. What I can see has me running out of my office and down to the VIP floor.

Down on the VIP floor, I push my way through security. Not that I have to try hard; as soon as they realise who's pushing through, they fucking move out of my way. Stopping at the section that Alyssa should be, I turn in a 360, seeking her out.

Turning back, my gaze lands on Sarah. "Where

the fuck is she?" I yell at her. She flinches but shakes her head, tears running down her cheeks.

"Fuck," I growl, turning back around.

I should be concerned with who the fucker is that Bray has pinned under him. He throws punches like his life depends on it, although whoever the fuck he's laying into is all but lifeless under him. Dean steps up and pulls him back. I still can't see her.

Charging up to Dean and Bray, I demand, "Someone needs to tell me where the fuck she is, *now*." I'm on the verge of a fucking nervous breakdown. Why the fuck can't I see her? She should be here. I'm running my hands through my hair when Dean finally speaks up, "James took her up to your office when shit hit the fan. She should be in your office, man."

"Fuck!" I'm yelling at no one in particular. I look over at Dean and quickly bite out, "Bring them up to the office. Alyssa will probably shoot me if anything happens to her friends in my club." I point back to the three women huddled together.

Throwing my office door open, I find Alyssa on the couch, holding an ice pack to her face. I feel my blood go cold. I am seething; someone fucking hurt her. As I walk towards her, I can feel my body vibrate with rage at the thought of some fucker laying hands on her.

James gets up from where he was sitting next to her. Just before I reach her, I hear Caitlyn from the other side of the office.

"Zac, thank god you're here! I tried to tell them they couldn't be in here. I told them to leave and they wouldn't listen. James should know better than to bring some floozy up to your office."

Alyssa sticks her head up. She looks back and forward from me to Caitlyn—whatever she is thinking, it's not good. "James, get her fucking out of my office," I tell him, motioning to Caitlyn. He nods and moves towards her, pulling her out by her arm.

If I thought she'd go quietly, I was mistaken. "Zac, you called me, remember? Told me you needed me? I came straight away."

I'm still staring at Alyssa; she's dropped the ice pack and I can see a large bruise forming on the side of her face. I can also see the doubt clouding over her eyes as she stares at Caitlyn, who is not so willingly being shoved out of the room. I need to fix this and set things straight. I can't have Alyssa doubting me.

"James, wait."

James turns around and halts his steps, still holding onto a now smiling Caitlyn. She won't be smiling for long. Smirking at her, I slowly articulate every word so that they are not misinterpreted.

"Caitlyn, I called you because I pay you to do a job. A job I fucking expect you to do, but since you seem more concerned with placing yourself where you don't belong, you're fired for inappropriate conduct. Don't bother coming back."

Nodding at James, I watch as he escorts her out of my office before shutting the door and leaving me alone with Alyssa. Squatting down in front of her, I grab her face in my hands. She flinches as my hands go up to her face. I hate myself instantly. I hate that she would fear my hands. Sliding my hands as gently as I can along her cheeks, I try my darndest to reassure her.

"Sunshine, I would never hurt you. I don't want you to ever be afraid of that. I would cut my own hands off before I used them to cause harm to you. Please tell me you know this, please." She looks at me and nods her head, but that's not going to work for me. "I need the words, sunshine. I need to hear the words."

In an ever so quiet voice, she says, "I know, Zac. I don't know how I know, because I hardly know you, but deep down in my bones, I know you won't hurt me."

I sit up on the couch next to her and pull her onto my lap. "Baby, I need you to tell me who hurt you. I will make sure they can never lay a hand on you again," I say, kissing her forehead.

"I don't know what happened. I was dancing with Reilly when someone came up behind me and grabbed me. I knew instantly it wasn't you, so I turned around and kneed him in the balls."

I'm so fucking proud that she stood up for herself. I can't help but smile. "Sunshine, I'm glad you kneed the fucker in the balls. I think I need to give you a gun. That way, on the very near impossible chance that any fucker ever gets close enough to touch you again, you just shoot them." I lay kisses over her hairline.

She tucks her head into my chest. "It would be dangerous to give me a gun, Zac. I was kicked out of at least ten foster homes for what the department liked to call physical misconduct."

Again, she has brought up her childhood and it sounds like a fucking nightmare, but we don't have time to hash that out right now.

"We will come back to that topic later. What happened after you kicked the fucker in the balls?" I need to know how she got that bruise on her face, so I know how painful to make this fucker's death.

"He backhanded me," she says so matter-of-factly. I feel like this is not the first time this has happened to her.

Well, never fucking again. I will not let anyone hurt her again, even if I have to be her personal fucking shield twenty-four seven.

She continues, "Then before I knew it, James was picking me up off the ground and Bray was on top of the guy laying into him. Did you know Bray can really pack a punch?" I laugh a little at her question, and she looks up at me, waiting for an explanation.

"Sunshine, Bray is a cage fighter. Underground fighting and currently undefeated. Yeah, I know he can pack a fucking punch. That right hook of his earns me a lot of fucking money."

I watch her face to try to gauge her reaction to this news. She surprises me when she laughs. "Of course he is. Do me a favour, and let's not tell Reilly that bit of information, please."

At that moment, the door swings open and the woman in question asks, "Don't tell Reilly what?" She looks at us and before either of us has a chance to reply, she's answering her own question... sort of.

"Oh, wait, let me guess... Don't tell Reilly that you're going to run off and elope and live HEA?" she questions.

"What the hell is HEA?" This comes from a very rough-voiced Bray.

Reilly spins around, facing him. "Something you're probably going to deny yourself of ever having," she says.

I can tell he still has no idea what she's referring to, but he drops it. Reilly spins back around and at my head nod, she continues her guessing game.

"I know! You've finally quit nursing and you're signing up to work the pole. I've told you, you would make a killing with those boobs."

I growl out, "Over my dead fucking body."

"So no to the stripper career? Oh, I've got it, you discovered Zac's too much man for one woman, and you want me to be your sister wife." She raises her eyebrows suggestively at Alyssa. "Just so you know, Lyssa, if there was anyone in the world I would be sister wives with, it would be you."

I can feel Alyssa's body tense. She's fucking hot when she gets her green-eyed monster on. Before she can say anything, Bray cuts in, "You're not going to be her sister wife. My brother doesn't share well. Besides, a girl like you needs more than sharing a man. You need one all for yourself. It's going to be a tough job, but I'm up for the challenge." Bray turns his full smirk on to Reilly. *Huh*, interesting. But right now, I don't care about my brother trying to get laid. I care about where I can get my hands on the fucker who hurt Alyssa.

Whispering in her ear so only she can hear, I say, "Baby, I'm going to step out the door, just for a minute. I will be right outside the door. Will you be okay here with your girls for a moment?"

Snuggling into my neck, I feel her breathe me in. I love when she does this, although I'm smart enough to not let on that I know that's what she's doing. I love that she takes comfort in me, in my body, in my hold, and even in my fucking smell.

"I'll be fine. Stop worrying so much. It's going to take more than a little slap to keep me down, Zac. I'm not some damsel in distress you have to babysit. If you have work to do, I can just go home with the girls and see you tomorrow, or whenever."

Lifting her chin so her eyes are on me, I say, "You're not going anywhere but my fucking bed tonight, sunshine. I will be right outside that fucking door."

I kiss her, claiming her lips. I pull away far too soon for my liking, but the sooner I deal with this, the sooner I can take my woman home to bed.

Standing, I grunt out to Bray and Dean, "Out." Pointing to the door, I lead the way out.

As soon as the door closes, I am on them. "What the fuck happened? How could you let some fucker get close enough to lay a fucking hand on her, let alone fucking hit her?"

I can feel my body fuming, vibrating with rage again. Now that I don't have Alyssa in my arms, I am an inferno of pure rage. It's almost like she's a balm to my soul, calming me like nothing else can. For a few minutes, in that office while I was holding her, I had forgotten how fucking angry I was.

"Bro, it was the fucking singer for Cyrus. Caitlyn gave the band fucking VIP passes again. We didn't want to draw any attention, so we let them be."

Bray looks pointedly at me. I know he's right; we can't draw unwanted attention from that band. There can't be a link between their missing drummer and our club. I know they'll never find his body, but we still don't need that headache.

"That doesn't answer how he got close to her," I say, pointing to the door.

"He was dancing with Sarah. She was into it, so we left it alone. One of the other guys at the band's table started talking shit about how their drummer was last seen here in the club and never left, started questioning where he was. Bray and I went over to dig out what they knew." Dean shakes his head and runs a hand through his hair. He's frustrated—well, good, because I'm still fucking fuming. "Look, man, I'm sorry. I shouldn't have left her. I didn't think. I shouldn't have left her."

"No, you fucking shouldn't have. She should not be sitting in there with a fucking shiner. Where the fuck is this fucker now? I can't wait to get my fucking hands on him."

Bray looks at me with concern. "Zac, you can't kill him. You killed his brother last night. You think the band won't start asking louder questions if their lead fucking singer went missing from this club right after their drummer?" He paces, running his hands through the ends of his hair. Stopping in front of me, he looks me square in the eye. "Look, man, the guy had to be taken off in a fucking ambulance. The beating I just gave him… he'd have to be fucking stupid to show his face around here again."

"I know you're right, but it doesn't do anything to help the fact that I feel like I need to kill the fucker. Fuck. Okay, you're right. We don't need anyone questioning the club in relation to missing fucking bodies." I pause and take a calming breath before I go back into the office to Alyssa. I don't want her to see me so worked up. I need to be in control. I need her to see me as someone in control. Walking in, I'm stunned at the scene that greets me: Alyssa and Reilly, drinks in hand, dancing around what I'm assuming is an imaginary pole.

Fuck me, this friend of hers is a dangerous influence. "If my girlfriend ever ends up on a real pole,

I will hunt you down, Reilly, and I won't be kind just because you're a girl."

All four women gasp and stare at me with mouths wide open. I raise an eyebrow in question at them, but they say nothing. Turning my head to the guys for help on this one, I see Dean over in the far corner, texting someone. Who the fuck he's texting, god only knows. Bray is staring at Reilly. I don't know what's going on with him there, but I'm not touching that one with a ten-foot pole. Bray will break the girl's heart if he goes near her, then Alyssa will be pissed at me, and I don't want to have to choose sides between my brother and her. It scares me to think Bray wouldn't come out on the winning side.

"Okay, I give. What'd I say?" I ask the four women but staring directly at mine, at Alyssa.

She doesn't say anything but runs towards me, jumping up into my arms. I brace myself at the very last moment, only stumbling back one step before she's plastered herself to my body, slamming her lips down onto mine. It doesn't take me long to take control of the kiss. I swipe my tongue along her lips, and she opens wide for me. I take everything she will-ingly gives. This kiss is one of ownership, of me owning her, of her owning me. In this kiss, we tell each other exactly what we don't say with words.

Pulling back from the kiss, I smirk at Alyssa. "Sun-shine, if that's the kind of greeting I'm going to get every time I leave for five minutes, I might have to find reasons to stand on the other side of the door more often."

She smiles and leans her mouth down to my ear, so that only I can hear her reply. Although, looking at the smiles on her friends' faces, I get the feeling they don't need to hear for them to know exactly what's gotten into their friend.

"That kiss isn't because you left and came back, although if it means you're always going to come back, I will gladly give you that kind of greeting kiss every time." She pauses and kisses just behind my ear briefly before continuing, "Sorry I get distracted by your... well, your everything. That kiss, that was because you just called me your girlfriend. Well, at least I think you did, you did, right? Oh god, if it was a slip of the tongue, we can totally just forget—" I cut her off, slamming my lips back onto hers.

A throat clears. "As hot as fuck as Lyssa is, it's not so hot when she's playing tonsil hockey with my fucking brother, my *older* brother, might I add. I'm out." Turning, Bray pulls his trademark smirk on Alyssa's friends. "Any of you lovely ladies need a ride? Home, that is?"

Not giving any of them a chance, I answer for them. "They all need a ride home, bro. I'm taking my girlfriend home to bed." I take extra care to annunciate the word girlfriend, letting them all, especially Alyssa, fucking know that it was not a fucking slip of the tongue. She is mine.

Eleven

ALYSSA

*S*TANDING in Zac's bathroom, looking at my reflection in the mirror, I inspect the bruise forming on my face. It's not that bad. I expected it to be a lot worse from the way Zac reacted when he saw my face. This is nothing a bit of foundation won't cover; besides, I've had worse bruises left on my face before.

Shaking my head to clear thoughts from the past, I run the water and wash my face and then strip out of my clothes. Taking one last look in the mirror, I pull my hair out of the hair tie and run my hands through it, letting the waves fall over my shoulders.

Opening the door and stepping back into the bedroom, I freeze, the breath taken out of me. I don't know how he does it, how he affects me so easily. It's almost like as soon as I lay eyes on him, I'm instantly wet and needy.

Zac is standing by the side of the bed, shirtless.

155

He's removed his shoes and socks and has the button and fly undone on his dress pants. I can see the top of his black Calvin Kleins. He just stands there with all those tanned muscles on display.

His torso is strong, with a wide chest and broad shoulders. A narrow waist with goddamn washboard abs… I always thought the term "washboard abs" was just an exaggerated saying, but I get it now… boy, do I get it now. What I wouldn't do to run my tongue over all of those ridges of his body.

Smirking at me like he knows just how much his body affects me, he asks, "See something you like, sunshine?"

As my eyes roam up and down his body again, for like the zillionth time since stepping out of the bathroom, I can see the outline of his now hard cock trying to escape the confines of his pants. Smiling up at him and fluttering my lashes, I aim for coy.

"Meh, it's not bad, but it sure looks like you're really liking what you see right now." I point to his very obvious and very impressive erection.

"I'm about ten seconds away from throwing you down on this fucking bed, tying you up, and showing you exactly just how much I fucking love what I see right now," he growls out, literally growls.

As he goes to take a step forward, I hold my hand in a stop motion. To my surprise, he stops in his spot, a concerned look crossing his features.

"Stop right there, GQ. Don't you dare move a muscle." Turning, I dig through my clutch for my phone. Finding it, I hold it up excitedly. "I need to capture all this perfectness." At his shocked look, it crosses my mind that he might not actually want me to take photos of him in a state of undress. "You don't mind, do you?"

"Baby, you can take as many pictures of me as you want. In fact, your camera roll should be filled of pictures of just me."

Smiling, I snap away. It's a perfect shot. Looking at the picture, I say, "This is fucking amazing, really." Throwing the phone back down on the dresser, I look up at Zac. "At least now, whenever I'm in my bed by myself, I can look at this picture and scream your name when I make myself come." I smile as sweetly as I can manage.

Zac's eyebrows raise and within five seconds, he has me over his shoulder and storming back towards the bed. Landing in the middle of the bed, I haven't even had time to get my bearings before he's on top of me and his lips are slammed onto mine.

Zac's hands hold my head in place, tilting it slightly, allowing him the access to my mouth he hungrily seeks. I can feel this kiss all the way down to my toes, tingles running through my body. I arch my hips up, seeking the friction that my core is desperate for. My hips meet nothing but air. I groan out loud at the disappointment and frustration of not being able to get the friction I'm desperate for.

Zac laughs into the kiss. Pulling away, he looks at me with those emerald green eyes. Mesmerising, that's what they are, his eyes. They draw you in and hold you captured. I'm lost, so lost to this man.

"Patience, sunshine. I plan on taking my time with you tonight. I rushed too much earlier, but now, now I'm going to savour you." He runs wet kisses down my neck and back up, nibbling on my ear. "I will treasure your body like it was made to be treasured."

I can feel how wet I am. I can feel the moisture dampen my centre. Wrapping my legs around his waist, I arch my hips up again, my core just grazing Zac's hardened cock. But it's not enough. Letting out a moan, I try again to arch my hips up, only to have Zac pull back. Into my ear, he whispers, "This greedy pussy of yours is going to get you into trouble, sunshine. What am I going to do with you?"

"You could start by giving me what I want, now, Zac. I need you inside me now, dammit." I moan as his cock barely grazes my pussy. "Please." I'm at the point that I don't even care that I'm begging. I mean, I don't recall ever being so wanton that I was reduced to begging.

Zac laughs. He sits up and runs his hands down the sides of my ribs and back up; my body arches up towards him. "I fucking love how responsive your body is to my touch, sunshine."

I reach my hands up to touch him, and run my hands over his pecs. He catches them before I get to those lickable fucking abs.

"*Tsk, tsk, tsk.*" Shaking his head, he puts my arms

up over my head. "Leave 'em there, or I will tie them down."

I can't help the moan that escapes me as I think about being tied down and at his mercy. I've never even considered letting any man tie me down before, but the thought of Zac tying me down, that sends tingles straight to my core.

"So, it seems my sunshine likes the thought of being tied up, served up on a platter for me to devour, to worship this body as I see fit." His stare pierces through me. I moan, raising my hips, only to groan out when they meet nothing but air. Zac stands from the bed. Staring down at me, he orders (yes, orders), "Don't fucking move."

He walks into his walk-in wardrobe, coming back out holding a long piece of thin black rope. My eyes are drawn to the rope as he gets closer, kneeling over the top of me as he watches my expression for what seems like forever.

"Do you trust me?" he asks.

Without hesitating, I look him straight in the eyes, hold my arms out towards him with my wrists together, palms facing up, and say, "Yes, without a doubt."

I feel Zac shiver at my answer. He leans down and kisses my lips softly before whispering, "Thank you."

Zac coils the black rope around both my wrists, pulling at the knot. Picking me up like I weigh nothing at all, he positions me in the centre of the bed before raising my arms and tying the rope to the head of the bed. Kneeling between my legs, he spreads my thighs as wide as they will open, staring down at my still covered pussy.

"I actually don't know where to start, what to devour first. Should I start up here?" he says, palming my breasts and tweaking my nipples. "Or…" Moving one hand down my stomach, he cups my now quivering centre. "Should I start at the promise land, and give my pussy the attention she is so greedily seeking."

"*Argh, mmm.*" I don't know whether I moan or groan, but whatever noise I make has Zac sending me his trademark panty-melting smirk. Leaning down, he takes one of my nipples into his mouth, sucking right through the lace of my bra, his other hand paying attention to my other nipple.

"Oh god, Zac, please." I'm not sure what I'm begging for… for him to stop, or for him to keep delivering this sweet torture.

Releasing my nipple, he moves to the other side. As he puts it in his mouth, he asks, "Please what, baby? All you have to do is ask, and I will happily deliver." He sucks harder, flicking his tongue.

When he finally releases my nipple and raises up, he stares down at me. "I fucking love these tits. I could drown in these tits."

"Please don't stop." I'm begging again, going out of my mind with need.

"You don't even have to ask, because I'm never going to fucking stop worshiping your body, sunshine." He unclasps my bra from my back and raises the straps up to where my wrists are tied. My breasts falling free, my nipples are hard and wanting his mouth back on them. Unconsciously, I raise my body up towards him as much as I can.

Zac grabs both of my breasts, squeezing and tweaking my nipples. Moaning out loud, I question, "Is it possible to come with you only touching my breasts, because right now, I think it's a high possibility… oh god."

He chuckles. "That's something we will have to test out one day, but not today. I'm hungry and haven't eaten dinner yet."

This both confuses me and riles me up. How dare he tease me to the brink, only to leave to eat? "You want to stop and eat food now? Are you kidding me?" I'm sure if my eyes could send daggers his way, they would be.

He looks at me, shaking his head, amused. Reaching down, he grabs the fabric of my panties in both hands and pulls. I hear the tear, the ripping sound. Why this has me turned on, I don't know, but I also don't care. Zac brings my panties up to his nose and inhales.

"I fucking love the smell of you." He throws the panties over his shoulder and onto the floor as he says, "*Mmm*, I'm not hungry for food, sunshine. I'm fucking starved for the taste of you on my lips."

That's a meal I can be down for—well, technically he would be the one that would be down. "Well, what are you waiting for?"

Trying to get him to get on with it, I remember how good he was with his tongue earlier, and I can't wait to get that tongue on me again. Zac starts kissing his way down my stomach. He skips my pussy, lifts my left leg and lays wet kisses from my knee up my inner thighs, stopping just short of where my pussy is begging for his attention. Putting that leg down, he repeats the action on the opposite leg.

By the time he rests his shoulder between my legs, I am crazy with lust, need. I can feel my body quivering. I can feel the moisture seep down my thighs. Just as I think Zac is finally going to put his mouth on my most needy parts, he leans down to my very inner thigh and bites.

"Oh god!" I scream out. The pain of the bite is quickly eased as he licks over the spot. Then he bites again, just higher than the previous bite.

"*Argh.*"

There's pain, but then there is a pleasure, a kind of pleasure I've never felt before. It's intense and I want more. As Zac is licking the bite mark, I'm relishing this mixture of pain and pleasure. He turns his head and bites my other thigh. Again, I squirm and moan, yell out loud. I expect to feel his tongue on my thigh where he bit me, but instead he licks me, from the bottom of my pussy to the top. He licks slowly and by the time he reaches my clit, it only takes one circle of his tongue to send me over the edge.

Screaming out his name, I buck as I squeeze his head between my thighs, keeping him in place. Zac continues to lick me, swirling his tongue around and around my clit, riding the wave. I think I see stars. Zac lays soft kisses on the lips of my pussy as my body relaxes into the bed.

When he raises his head to look at me, he says, "That is the sexiest fucking thing I've ever seen. Your face when you come, I could watch it over and over again."

I'm breathing heavily, still catching my breath from the orgasm of all orgasms, my chest rising and falling in fast motions. "If you're trying to kill me by orgasm, mission accomplished. I think I just died and went to heaven."

Moving up my body, he kisses my lips and I can taste myself. "I don't want to kill you by orgasm, baby, just ruin you for all other men." At the mention of other men, his face becomes hard. I'm realising he has a very strong jealous streak, but apparently so do I, so I guess we're even there.

"You ruined me for all other men from the moment our eyes connected from across the bar," I tell him honestly, and he groans. He stands up and drops his pants and briefs to the floor in one go, freeing one hell of an impressive erection. I didn't know there were such things as beautiful cocks before, but his is a freaking work of art. I'm staring. I know I am staring at it; he knows I'm staring at it.

He picks a condom up off the side table, and I have the sudden thought that I'd rather he doesn't use one. I don't dare voice this opinion, though. I watch, as he slides the condom down his shaft before he tugs a few times as he makes his way back to my bed, wishing I had a camera to capture that material.

Smirking, he settles between my legs. "I can't wait to feel your pussy choke my cock. I've been dying to get back inside you from the moment I slipped out of you today." I raise my hips, trying to reach him. He chuckles and slaps my pussy lightly. "Such a hungry, greedy pussy. What am I going to do with it?"

I don't think he's actually asking me the question, but I answer anyway. "You're going to fuck it, and you're going to fuck it hard," I demand.

I watch as his body shivers before he lines the tip of his cock up to my entrance. "That dirty mouth of yours is trouble, sunshine." He pushes into me in one hard thrust. Buried to the hilt, he steadies himself. Leaning down, he whispers into my ear, "I fucking love your dirty mouth." And with that, he pumps in and out, slowly at first and then faster.

Lifting one leg and resting my calf on his shoulder, the angle allows him to go deeper, every thrust hitting that sweet spot inside. My arms are straining. I can feel the rope burns forming on my wrists, but the pain is adding to the immense pleasure.

"Oh god, Zac, it's so good. Don't stop."

Grunting, he slows his pace as he says, "There's nothing in the world that could get me to stop fucking you, Alyssa. I'm going to be fucking you for the rest of my life." Hearing him use my name, Alyssa, instead of sunshine or baby, I know he truly believes what he says.

Zac pulls out, and I growl at him. He just laughs and spins my body over so I'm on my hands and knees. Looking over my shoulder, I see him lining himself up with my entrance. He looks up and smirks. I can feel my pussy tighten at the sight, a smirk downright dangerous to womankind. Zac groans and slaps my ass. I let out a screech, but the pain quickly becomes pleasure and I hear myself asking for more.

"Again," I say, looking back at him.

"Gladly," he replies, laying a slap on my other cheek before rubbing his hands over the sting. He's pumping so hard into me, if it weren't for his current hold on my hips, I'm pretty sure I would not be able to hold myself up right now.

He lays two more slaps on my ass before leaning over and biting my shoulder. The bite does it. I come, screaming his name. I feel Zac jerk inside me. I feel his come spurting out, filling the condom. He roars my name out so loud I wouldn't be surprised if the whole building heard it.

My lifeless body collapses on the bed. I couldn't move if I wanted to. I barely register Zac untying the rope and rubbing my wrists before pulling the blankets back up over me. I'm so tired, that I don't fight it when I hear Zac whisper into my ear, "Go to sleep, baby. We always have tomorrow."

I look up at him. "Promise?"

"I fucking swear it," he says, kissing me on the forehead, then my nose, then my lips.

I'M WOKEN by the soundtrack of Rocky, which I've come to know as Bray's ringtone. Grumbling, I make half-conscious demands. "Turn it off or I'll break it." Slapping my hand across the bed, in an attempt to make the sound stop, my hand meets a solid wall of muscle. I hear Zac's groan as he rolls over.

"What? There better be a good fucking reason for you to be calling this fucking early." There's a short silence as he listens to Bray on the other end of the phone, and then Zac's getting up out of bed. "Fuck, okay, I'll be there as soon as I can."

Rolling onto my back, I open one eye to see Zac throw his phone down on the bed he just got out of. He walks around to my side. Leaning down, he kisses my forehead and whispers, "I have to go handle something. Go back to sleep. I'll be back before you know it." Nodding my head, I close my eyes, letting sleep take me over.

The next time I wake, it's to my own phone blasting out. I really need to remember to turn these phones off when I'm sleeping. Seeing that it's my boss calling, I answer, trying not to sound like I'm asleep.

"Hello, this is Alyssa," I say in the most professional tone I can muster while also covering a yawn.

"Hello, Alyssa. It's Nicki. Thank goodness. You're the first nurse to answer my call this morning; we're short staffed. Five nurses have called in sick. If you can make it here within the next hour and a half, there is a twelve-hour overtime shift with your name on it." Nicki doesn't take a single breath as she rushes out the request.

I'm tempted to say no, to choose to stay in this bed, this comfy, warm bed that smells like Zac, over going to work in the cold and depressing hospital. Then I remember how much extra money I could make with twelve hours at overtime rates and my decision is made.

"I'll be there, Nicki."

"Thanks, see you soon." She doesn't give me the chance to say goodbye as she disconnects the call. Jumping out of bed, I order an Uber and rush through getting dressed. I'll shower once I'm home and can get into my scrubs. It's not until I'm sitting in the Uber that I get a chance to send Zac a message to let him know I'm going into work.

Alyssa: Hi, I just wanted to let you know I've been called into work, so had to leave your comfy bed, as much as I'd rather stay in it all day. Xoxo

I debate the *xoxo* added to the end of the text but decide to just send it. If he doesn't like it, too bad. I don't have long to dwell on how he will take the *xoxo* because my phone blares out "Stuck Like Glue." Groaning at the song, albeit with an enormous smile on my face, I peek up to see the Uber driver looking at me through the rear-view mirror. I silently apologise before answering the call.

"Hel—"

I don't even get the full hello out before Zac is interrupting my greeting. "Sunshine, where are you?"

"Well, hello to you too, babe. You know most people start a conversation with a greeting like *hello*, *howdy*… I'd even take a *g'day, mate*," I say in a saccharine sweet voice.

"Hello, beautiful, now tell me, where are you?"

He sounds annoyed but I have no clue what I've done to annoy him. Even an annoyed Zac is a hot Zac. Seeing how far I can push him, I say, "Well, at this very second, I'm in an Uber on my way back to my apartment."

"Take this turn, John. It's quicker," I say to the driver, pointing to my left. He swerves the car left at the last minute, resulting in the car behind us blaring their horn.

This does not go unnoticed by Zac. "Why can I

hear tires screeching and horns blaring? Please tell me you're okay, sunshine. Actually, just send me this Uber driver's details. I might need to have a word with him about how he should drive with such precious cargo."

He sounds so serious I have to laugh, which doesn't ease his distress. "You might think I'm joking, but I assure you I am not."

"Oh, I have no doubt you're not joking, but I also know I have no intentions of doing what you just requested either. I'm fine, and John here is getting me home as quickly as he safely can. I have one hour and fifteen minutes to get to work, so as much as I'd love to sit around and chat all day, I really have to go. I'm just pulling into my townhouse now. Bye, Zac. I'll talk to you later."

I hang up without letting him add anything else. Giving John a thanks and a wave, I'm out the door and running towards my townhouse.

Twelve

ZAC

*S*TUCK in the police station for two hours, waiting for my brother to be bailed out, is not how I thought I'd be spending my morning today. The mother-fucking asshole from the club last night tried to press assault charges against him. The charges were dropped as soon as Dean delivered the CCTV footage—the video showing that fucker hits Alyssa across the face before Bray pounces on him.

I get a text message from Alyssa on my way back to the penthouse, on my way back to my bed, where I left her. "Fuck!" Hitting her name, I call her rather than text her back. She's in a fucking Uber on her way back to her place. Alyssa hangs up on me though, before I can talk her into turning around and going straight back to bed.

"Dammit!" I hit the steering wheel and turn to look at Bray. "Stop fucking laughing. This is all your fault, you know."

Bray raises one eyebrow at me. "Tell me, brother, how is it my fault that your *girlfriend* is going to work, instead of waiting for you in your bed?" He uses hand quotation marks around girlfriend—that just pisses me off more.

"Because, if I didn't have to get up at the arse-crack of dawn to bail your ass out of jail, I would have been in bed still with my girlfriend. I would have been able to get up to drive her home and to work, and she wouldn't have had to get into an Uber with some fucker named John, driving like he's in *Grand Theft Auto.*"

My hands are gripping the steering wheel tight, as I drive towards Alyssa's townhouse. "There is just way too much wrong with that statement. I'm not gonna touch it with a ten-foot pole. You know you're going the wrong way, right? The penthouse is back that way." Bray smirks as he points his thumb over his shoulder.

Shaking my head, I tell him, "We're going to Alyssa's."

I see him scrunching his eyebrows together. "Why are we going to Alyssa's? You heard that she's going to work, right?"

"We're going there, because I plan on driving her to work, so she doesn't have to catch a fucking train or take an Uber." I take a deep breath, in an attempt to clear away thoughts of just what could go wrong if she caught a train.

Bray is quiet. Looking over at him, I see him

staring back at me. "You're really hung up on this girl, aren't you?" he asks earnestly.

Thinking on his question a moment, I answer honestly, "I know it's fast, but I've never felt like this. Like I don't breathe properly unless she's in the same room, like every time I have to leave her, part of me stays with her. I can't shake these feelings, but honestly, I don't want to shake them either."

I'm expecting some smart-arse response about being pussy whipped, but instead, I get the very rare, serious Bray. "Good, you deserve some good in your life, but you might have to actually tell her why you don't like her getting public transport. Otherwise, you're going to come across like even more of a controlling bastard than you already are." I know he's right, but how do I bring up a conversation I've refused to have for the last five years?

"I'll try," is all I commit to.

"You do that. I think she will be more agreeable to not using public transport if you tell her. Also, if you're in love with this girl, you should probably lock her down before she comes to her senses and realises she's with the wrong brother." He smirks.

I reach out and punch his arm, not that it affects him any. "Brother or not, I will kill you if you lay a hand on her."

"Oh, I know you would." He laughs.

I KNOCK on Alyssa's front door with Bray standing right behind me. Turning my head back towards him, I say, "You know, you can wait in the car?"

He laughs at me. "And miss this shit show you're about to get in? Never."

Just as I'm about to tell him to get the fuck back in the car, the door swings open to a dripping wet Alyssa, standing there in a fucking towel. I'm instantly hard at the sight, that is, until Bray opens his fucking mouth.

"Damn, I can see why my brother has given up his balls to you, Lyssa."

Stepping into the open doorway, I grab Alyssa's waist and walk her backwards a few steps before slamming the door in Bray's face. Alyssa stands there, staring at me like I've lost my head. I probably have. I can't believe she'd answer the door in a fucking towel. "I'll just wait in the car, kids," Bray yells through the door.

"*Umm*, hi?" Alyssa questions, holding the towel tighter around her body.

"Hi? Hi?" I question back. "Why the fuck are you answering the door with no clothes on?"

Walking her backwards, I've got her backed against the wall before she answers, "Because I just got out of the shower, and then some ass was trying to bang my bloody door down. So, I thought: *huh*, maybe if I opened it to see what the ass wanted, the door would stay intact." She's smiling up at me like butter wouldn't melt in her mouth.

"Some ass, *huh*? What if it wasn't me at the door? Do you let any random ass see you in a state of undress?" Trailing my fingertips down her arm, I watch as her skin pebbles under my touch.

"I, *ah*…" Shaking her head, she pushes me back. "I don't have time for this, Zac. I need to get dressed and get to work." She marches back up the stairs. I follow her like the lost fucking puppy I am whenever I'm around her.

Standing in her doorway, I take in her room. It suits her, matches her. She has a queen-size bed with a large cream fabric bedhead, with white covers and pink pillows in varying shades and sizes. Hearing the slamming of a drawer pulls my attention back to her. She's standing at a white dresser, holding her scrubs.

She glares at me. "Are you planning on watching me get dressed for work? Why are you here, Zac?"

"I'd much rather watch you undress."

Smirking, I roam my eyes up and down her body. Then she does the unthinkable. She drops her fucking towel and stands there, just feet away from me, naked. She smiles like she's just won an argument.

"If you want to actually make it to work in time, sunshine, I suggest you cover that delectable body of yours up, now," I grunt out.

Alyssa tilts her head, her eyes roaming up and down my body. I can't help the erection that is painfully trying to escape the confines of my jeans. It seems I just have to be in the same room as her, and I'm instantly fucking hard; but being in a room with her naked takes it to next-level fucking hard. As her eyes linger on my straining erection, I groan and read-just myself. I remind her of what she should be doing. "Sunshine, if you want him to come out and play, he's more than willing. But if I get my hands on you, we won't be leaving this bedroom for the rest of the day. Your choice."

She dresses quickly. I watch every move, every curve of her body being covered up by those damn scrubs. When she turns her back to me, I adjust my cock again. He's not getting the message that it's not playtime. Alyssa turns back around and I'm stunned. She looks like a fucking wet dream. I never got the whole nurse roleplay thing before, but fuck me, she can give me a sponge bath any fucking day.

My eyes roam over her. It's like they can't decide which part of her body they want to take in; it's all just that damn good. She stands there in blue scrubs. Her hair is piled up on top of her head and a stetho-scope hangs around her neck. Rubbing a hand over my jaw, I try not to let out the moan that wants to escape.

"Dammit, I thought covering your body would give my cock the message it's not playtime. But damn, sunshine, you look like a fucking wet dream in those scrubs." Shaking my head, my eyes continue to roam up and down her body.

She saunters up to me. Laying a hand on my chest, she looks up and asks, "Did you bring the Batmobile?" Confused at her question and with the blood currently all being directed to my cock, I grunt out, "*Uh-huh*."

Then she does something that blows my mind. Her hand slides down my chest. She has my belt and jeans undone before my brain can catch up with what she's doing. Reaching into my boxers, she frees my cock, stroking up and down softly.

My cock is already fucking hard, pre-cum leaking from my tip. Alyssa drops to her knees and looks up at me. I swear I could fucking come just from seeing her in front of me on her knees. She swipes her tongue, licking my shaft from my balls up to the tip before swirling her tongue around the tip. She repeats this action two more times before she takes me into her mouth fully.

It takes everything in me not to come as soon as I hit the back of her throat. Alyssa moans around my cock, sending vibrations right down to my balls, before swallowing.

"Fuck me."

She looks up and smiles around my cock before sliding her mouth right up to the tip and back down again. I'm not going to last long. The wet, warm feel of her mouth, her eyes peering up at me, it's too much. I can feel my balls start to tighten, tingling sensations running down my spine. Grabbing the sides of her face, I hold her still as I pump my cock in and out of her.

"I'm gonna come," I warn her, giving her the chance to pull back.

She grabs my ass and pulls me into her mouth, sucking harder. I come in long, hot spurts down her throat and she swallows every last drop. She licks my cock clean before I lift her up, holding her chin as I claim her mouth with my own. I can taste myself on her, but I couldn't fucking care.

"That was the best damn blowjob I've ever had," I praise her, using my thumb to rub her now swollen bottom lip.

She pulls away, creasing her eyebrows. "If you ever want to receive another of those, from me…" She pauses to point to herself dramatically. "…you'd be best not to mention previous blowjobs from other women."

I can't help but smile. I love that she gets jealous. It goes both ways.

"Sunshine, you did know I wasn't a virgin, right?" I ask her just to tease.

The question backfires on me when she answers,

"Oh, I know you weren't, but guess what? Neither was I."

She smirks and pushes past me through the doorway, making her way downstairs. It takes me a while to clear my head of the rage I encounter at thoughts of her with another man.

WALKING OUT TO THE CAR, after making sure Alyssa's front door was locked, I'm stopped in my tracks when I see Alyssa hugging Bray, who notices my approach and smirks as he wraps his arms around her waist.

"What the fuck?" I yell as I approach, ripping her away from him and holding her against my chest.

As Bray laughs and dodges my right hook, Alyssa turns in my arms and smiles as she says, "Relax, Zac. I was just thanking him for last night. You know, for saving me from getting more than just a light bruise on my face."

At the mention of the bruise on her face, my eyes

zone into her cheek and my rage only heightens. "You couldn't do that, without having his arms wrapped around you?" I sulk. I know I'm sulking, but I can't seem to help it.

Alyssa wraps her arms around me. Standing on her tiptoes, she whispers in my ear, "It was your cock that was literally in my mouth not five minutes ago. I don't think you need to be jealous of your own brother." She smiles and turns to Bray. "Wipe the smile off your face, before I let him unleash on you. Now, are you driving me to work, or do I need to call an Uber? Because I'm too late for the train now."

The thought of her getting on the train sends my blood cold, I grunt out, "You're not catching a fucking train."

Bray goes to climb into the passenger seat.

"Not a fucking chance. Get in the back." Pushing him out of the way, I hold the door open for Alyssa to climb in. Pulling out of the driveway, I grab her hand and bring her wrist to my mouth before resting our joined hands on my thigh. The first time I did this, I noticed how much she melted and relaxed into her seat, just like she does now.

Nearing the hospital, I ask her, "What time do you finish? I'll pick you up."

She looks over at me. "I finish at midnight, but you don't have to pick me up. I can get a train or an Uber. It's fine, really."

I can't help the rage that comes over me. "Like fuck you will get a fucking train at midnight. Are you crazy? It doesn't matter. I'll be here to take you home."

I hear Bray clear his throat in the back seat as he pretends to be busy on his phone. Alyssa doesn't miss it either.

"You're either a control freak, or have serious issues with people catching trains. I'm good with either option right now, because I really freaking like your cars and appreciate the ride."

Bray clears his throat again, unsuccessfully disguising a laugh. Alyssa turns around in her seat, facing him.

"Care to share why you got arrested this morning, and had to drag Zac out of bed to bail you out?"

The fact that she knew why I had to go and help Bray both surprises and confuses me. How the hell did she know that he got arrested? As I'm racking my brain trying to figure out how she knew, Bray slaps the back of my head.

"You told her? What happened to the bro code, man? Bros before—"

I cut in, not letting him finish his sentence. "I swear to god, Bray, if you finish that sentence, you'll find yourself walking home." He wisely shuts his mouth.

"He didn't have to tell me. Reilly sent me a message this morning, worried about you and the fact you got taken away in handcuffs." Turning back to face the front, Alyssa continues, "So why did you get arrested, Bray?"

"It's on a need-to-know basis, and you, dearie, do not need to worry your pretty little head about it," Bray says so matter-of-factly.

Alyssa turns back and shoots daggers at him. "That's fine. I don't need to know, but there is something you need to know." She waits for him to acknowledge her.

"And what's that?" he asks.

"Oh, you know, just that if you hurt my friend, I will rip your balls off, cook them in spaghetti and feed them to you. I'd hate to have to tell Zac that I deformed his one and only brother." She thinks about this for a second before looking at me. "Wait, there aren't any more of you, right?"

"Nope, just me, Bray, and Ella," I say.

Deciding it's best to change the subject before she questions any further into the family, I ask Bray, "I need you to put feelers out for a new PR manager."

He grumbles that he's on it, but Alyssa suddenly gets excited. "Wait, you're looking for a new PR manager? For the club?"

Her excitement is contagious, and I can't help but smile at her. "If you want the job, sunshine, it's yours." Bray coughs in the back seat, and I shoot him a glare that he catches through the rear-view mirror. Alyssa's laugh fills the car. It's a laugh that I could listen to all day, a laugh I want to hear a lot more of.

"I don't think I'm qualified to be your PR manager, Zac, but I do happen to be very good friends with someone who does have a degree in public relations and is currently between jobs."

I would have given her the job whether she could do it or not, just because it would mean I would see more of her. Curious to know which friend she is referring to, I ask, "Who's your friend?"

Alyssa looks at me a moment before she rushes out, "Reilly." Noticing my screwed-up face, she adds, "I know what you're thinking, but she really is good at what she does."

"Not a fucking chance," Bray grunts from the back seat.

It's a good thing it's not his club, and just to rub that fact home, I tell Alyssa, "Tell Reilly she's got the job and to meet me at the club in two hours." I wait for her squeal and happy dance to stop before I finish my thought, "On a one-month trial basis, but no promises, sunshine."

Bray curses to himself in the back seat. Alyssa looks back at him but decides not to say anything.

"I'm going to text her now. I promise you won't be disappointed." Alyssa texts back and forward with who I assume is Reilly for the rest of the trip.

Pulling up in front of the hospital, I hop out and walk around to the passenger door. Reaching a hand in, I help her out and pull her straight into me. Stepping back and away from the car, I slam my lips down on hers, claiming her, not caring if anyone is watching.

Pulling back, I brush her swollen lip with my

thumb. "I love these lips. I don't think I've ever enjoyed kissing someone so much before."

Raising an eyebrow at me, she says, "Really? You're going to ruin this moment by comparing me to past conquests?"

"Sunshine, you are anything but a conquest. You're my tomorrow." Pulling her in and hugging her tight, I bury my head into her neck, inhaling the strawberry-vanilla scent I can't seem to get enough of.

"*Mmm*, and you're a charmer, GQ, but I really do need to get in there."

I reluctantly let her go. "Make sure you're free tomorrow. I'm taking you on a date. No friends, no annoying siblings. Just you and me, sunshine."

"Sounds like a plan," she says as she walks away. "I'll see you at twelve," I call out to remind her I'll be picking her up.

I HAVE GONE THROUGH ALL the tasks I need Reilly to get done before the weekend. I'm a little surprised at the difference I'm seeing in Reilly today. She's the utmost professional and nothing like the drunk girl I saw last night—the one attempting to teach my girlfriend how to fucking pole dance. I'm about to show her to her office when my phone pings with the song "My Girl" by The Temptations.

Smiling, because I know it's Alyssa, I answer her call. "Sunshine, I assure you, your friend is gainfully employed."

Hearing her laugh brightens my smile even further. I don't recall a time when I've smiled so damn much before, but I think I like it.

"That's good to know, but it's not the reason I called." She giggles.

"Not that I don't love hearing your voice, but do you care to share with me why you called?"

I notice Reilly looking down at her phone, busying herself and attempting to hide the fact that her eyebrows just shot up to her hairline.

I'm making my way out of the office before what Alyssa says next stops me in my tracks. "I called to thank you for the roses, of course. They are beautiful, Zac. Thank you."

Hearing the joy in her voice makes me wish I did send her flowers.

"Sunshine, as much as I would like to say those roses are from me, they're not," I grunt out. Whoever the fuck is sending my woman roses is a fucking dead man walking.

"Well, if you didn't send them, who did?" she asks

quietly. I don't miss the shake in her voice. Is she scared? She has no reason to be scared.

"Is there a card with the flowers, Alyssa?" I ask, desperate to know who just made it to my hit list.

Reilly's eyes go wide as she shakes her head no. My eyebrows draw together, confusion over her reaction taking over.

Alyssa replies in a shaky voice, "Y... yes, there is. I didn't open it because I thought you sent them, Zac."

Her reaction to receiving flowers from an unknown sender sends chills down my spine. Why is she so fucking scared? Attempting to calm her, I tell her, "Sunshine, it's okay. Read the card to me. What does it say?"

Now, Reilly is getting up, rushing towards me. She snatches the phone right out of my hand, puts the call on speaker and pushes me out of the office and towards the elevator.

"Lyssa, it's Reilly. You are okay. You are safe. You're in the hospital. Nothing can happen to you in the hospital." Reilly speaks calmly into the phone while pushing me into the lift and pressing the button for the ground floor. "Lyssa, listen to me. Do not open that card. Don't touch it. We are on our way to you, okay? Zac and I, we're coming to get you, okay?"

Alyssa's voice is so quiet as she agrees with Reilly. "I want you to stay on the phone with me until we get there. Go and tell whoever you need to tell that you're sick and you need to go home, okay?"

Reilly's calm tone is doing nothing to calm my

racing heart. What the fuck is going on? Reilly continues to talk to Lyssa, while I stare at the phone like it can give me the answers I fucking need right now.

"Lyssa, don't hang up just put the phone in your pocket while you talk to your boss," she instructs and, looking briefly at me, she says quietly, "Lyssa, it's not him, okay. It can't be. He's still in jail. It's not him."

"It's not him," Alyssa repeats quietly. "I'm going to put the phone in my pocket and tell the registrar I have to go." All I can hear on the line is the shuffling of fabric.

Following Reilly out to the back carpark, I'm quiet when I voice all the questions currently storming through my head. "What the fuck is going on, Reilly? Why is she so fucking freaked out, and who the fuck is *he*?"

Reilly puts her finger to her lips as she whispers, "You need to drive. If you care about Alyssa at all, you need to get to the hospital now. Just know that she needs us. I can't tell you why. It's not my story to tell."

Cursing, I jump into the car. Reilly barely has the passenger door shut before I have the car screaming out of the carpark in the direction of the hospital.

Thirteen

ALYSSA

I CAN'T BELIEVE this is happening right now, just when I thought my life was heading in the right direction. I finally met a guy who I actually like, like really freaking like. If I could admit it to myself, I might actually even love him.

This cannot be happening again. I barely survived the last time. I don't think I could survive this. Not to mention the fact that Zac would run at the first sight of just how much crazy I come packaged with. I mean, why would he stick around with a freaked-out nutcase, who can't even get a bunch of flowers without having a full-blown panic attack?

Well, that's not entirely true. I got excited and swooned when I thought the roses came from Zac. I was so excited I called him to thank him without checking the card first. As soon as he said they weren't from him, the panic kicked in, the flashbacks started, and I was back to that place from two years ago.

I'm now sitting in a locked bathroom stall, the roses tossed on the ground, staring at me, taunting me. It can't be him again. I know he's still in jail, at least I thought he was still in jail.

Oh god, what if he got out? What if he's not in jail anymore?

I spent six months of my life being tortured by him, all the while not even knowing who it was that was torturing me.

I can't stop the shaking. I know I'm in the midst of a panic attack, but I can't seem to do anything to stop it. How did Zac manage to calm me so easily during my panic attack in his car? This situation is much worse, with the possibility that I will have to spend my time locked in my apartment again because I fear what's waiting for me on the outside. It took me two months after he was sentenced to go outside again, and that was with Sarah, Reilly and Holly all holding my hand the whole time.

Remembering Reilly was still on the phone, I pull my phone out of my pocket.

"Reilly, I can't survive this again. I just can't. Make it stop... please make it stop," I plead with one of my best friends.

"Lyssa, it's not happening again, okay? Listen to me. This is just a misunderstanding. Zac and I are on our way. We're almost there, just hold on." Her voice is calm, the total opposite of how I'm feeling.

Just then, the thought of Zac seeing me like this, this mess of a person, hits me. He's going to run. I will lose him before I even really got a chance to have him.

"Reilly, he can't see me like this. I can't let him see me like this." My breathing is heavy and uneven.

"Who?" Reilly asks.

"Zac, he can't see me like this, Reilly. He's going to get one look at me and run. I'm going to lose him, aren't I?"

There's a loud bang and a growl that comes through the phone before Reilly clears her throat.

"Lyssa, *umm*, you most certainly are not going to lose him. And if he leaves you just because you had a little panic attack, I'm going to find him and feed him his own balls," she says in her ever-sweet voice.

"I really like this one, Reilly, like really, *really* like. I don't want to lose him. Oh god, why is this happening again? Just when I thought I could be happy, that I found my happy."

"We're just pulling into the hospital now. Where are you, Lyssa? I'll come get you," Reilly asks.

"I… I've locked myself in the ladies, just inside the emergency entrance. I didn't know what to do," I confess.

"Fuck!" I hear him loud and clear on the phone, in that deep and gravelly voice.

Then I hear Reilly yelling out, "Zac, wait up. It's the ladies. You can't just waltz in there, you know."

Reilly sounds like she's running. Before I can contemplate what's happening, the door to the ladies bangs against the wall. The first thing I think is *they're going to be too late. He's found me already.* I see a pair of dress shoes stop at the stall door I'm locked behind.

"Sunshine, I need you to open the door, please." It's Zac's voice. Is it really him, or have I somehow conjured his voice in my mind?

"Zac?" I ask so quietly I didn't think he would even hear me.

"Yeah, sunshine. It's me. Please open the door." His voice sounds strained.

Timidly reaching up for the lock, I slide the latch across and step back to pull the door open. There he stands, on the other side of the door. I don't even have the door open all the way before he's pulling me into his arms. I can feel my body shaking. I can feel the tears running down my face.

Clinging to him as tight as I can, I beg, "Please don't leave me. I'm sorry. So sorry. I'm not always like this, I swear, just… please don't leave."

Zac picks me up, walking to the far side of the bathroom. He sits on the floor with me and I crawl into his lap. I bury my face into his chest; my fingers hurt from how tightly they are clinging to the fabric of his shirt, but I can't loosen them. Zac strokes my hair while planting gentle kisses on the top of my head.

"Alyssa, there is nothing in this world that will make me leave you. We will always have tomorrow, remember?" he says so soothingly.

"Promise?" I ask.

"Promise," he says while he continues to stroke my hair.

Just then, Reilly bursts through the door. "Jesus Christ, Zac, how the hell can you run so freaking fast?"

She's kneeling down beside me, rubbing my arm. "Lyssa, honey, I'm here. It's going to be okay." Nodding my head, I don't attempt to lift it off Zac's chest. "We need to get you out of here. Come on, honey. Let's go home."

I lift my head to look at her. "Okay," I get out.

Zac shoos away Reilly's hand as he lifts my chin so our eyes meet. "Sunshine, let's go home." He stands up, guiding me to my feet, my hands still clinging so tightly to his shirt. "It's okay. I've got you," he says before lifting me into his arms and carrying me out of the hospital.

Stopping at the passenger side of his door, he looks down at me, still in his arms, still clinging to his shirt. Shaking his head, he mumbles, "Fuck it," before reaching into his pocket with one hand and handing a key fob to Reilly. "You drive," he demands before climbing into the back seat and settling me on his lap.

Moments later, I hear Reilly climb into the driver's side of the car. A few minutes later, she turns and looks back at Zac.

"You're sure you want me to drive this car, this very, very expensive car?"

"Reilly, for the love of god, just press *home* on the

GPS and follow the fucking directions. It's not rocket science. It's a bloody car."

Reilly starts the car and then turns to face the back again, this time to me. "Lyssa, do you want to go to Zac's, or your place? You tell me where you want to go?" she asks.

Zac growls and answers before I can put together a sentence. "Reilly, I'm your fucking boss and gave you a direction. It's your job to fucking follow it. Drive to my place, now."

"You've been my boss for two minutes, Zac. She's been my best friend for five years. My loyalty is to her, not you. You'd be best to remember that. Lyssa, tell me where you want to go before your beast here rips my head off."

Looking between the two of them, I'm confused. Are they really arguing over me?

Staring into Zac's eyes, I tell Reilly, "I want to go to Zac's. Please take me to Zac's."

Maintaining eye contact like he can see into my soul, Zac whispers, "Home, we're going home, sunshine."

The drive to Zac's was a blur. I buried my head in his chest the whole way, and when we got there, he picked me up and carried me. He held me tight as the elevator lifted to the top floor. When the doors opened, he walked me straight into his room with Reilly following suit.

Standing at the door to his room, he turns and

looks at her. "Call Bray. Tell him I want him and Dean here now," he orders, before shutting the door.

ZAC WALKS with me into the en suite bathroom, turns the shower on and sits me on the vanity. My fingers curl around his shirt as he steps back. I'm not ready to let go yet. When I'm in his arms, it's like nothing can touch me. I feel the safest I've ever felt when wrapped up in him. Putting his hands over the top of mine, he holds them there. We stay like that for minutes, the room filling up with steam before he says, "Sunshine, I'm not going anywhere. I will wait for as long as you need to feel comfortable to let go, but I'm not going anywhere."

After a minute, I slowly unfurl my fingers from his shirt. Zac pulls my top up and over my head before reaching around and unclasping my bra. Bending to his knees, he undoes my laces, removing my shoes and socks. Pulling me to a standing position, he pulls down my pants and panties in one go. The whole time, I stand as close as I can to him.

Zac's eyes travel up and down my body slowly, before he strips his own clothing off. Grabbing my hand, he leads me into the shower and under the spray of the water. I stand still. I can feel my body begin to relax. Zac reaches behind me and picks up a loofah and squirts some bodywash onto it. He slowly works the loofah over my shoulders; his movements are slow. He moves the loofah down my right arm and back up again, across my collarbone and down my left arm.

The scents of vanilla and raspberry fill the shower as Zac works the loofah over my body. He pays extra attention to my breasts, and I can't help but squirm with the sensations currently running through my body. He works the soap down my stomach then kneels, running the soapy loofah down each leg. When he reaches the apex of my thighs, I can't help the moan that escapes my mouth as I feel the scratchy, soapy fabric rub against the lips of my pussy.

Zac looks up at me as though he is about to say something; instead, he shakes his head and stands. I audibly grunt, at which he fails to hide a chuckle.

I tilt my head back as he runs his fingers through my hair. Zac reaches behind me, squirting shampoo onto his hands before rubbing his fingers through my hair. Massaging my scalp, he watches as I lean my head into him, the fruity smell of the shampoo filling the air.

I have never had anyone wash my hair before, other than at the salon. I don't recall a time since my mother died that I have felt so cherished and loved. I wouldn't say that Zac loves me. I mean, how can he? We've only known each other a few days, but the feelings I have for him are deep and unlike anything I've ever felt before.

I tilt my head back again, and he rinses out the shampoo before repeating the process with conditioner. Zac reaches around and turns off the shower. I have completely submitted my body to his will by now.

Grabbing some fluffy white towels off the shelf, he wraps one around himself, and I can't help but notice the impressive erection he is currently sporting. Drying me just as thoroughly as he washed me, he bends down and lifts one foot, resting it on his thigh. He drags the soft fabric of the towel from my ankle to my thigh, stopping right before the spot that I'm now aching for him to touch.

Smirking up at me, he puts my foot down and brings my other leg up, repeating the process. This time, he does rub the towel between my thighs. As I let out a moan, he pulls the towel away and stands up. He knows what he's doing to me. He knows I'm aching for his touch there. His fingers, his mouth, his cock... right now, I'd take any of them. I'm not picky.

Picking up a clean towel, he wraps my hair up before guiding me out of the bathroom and straight into his walk-in wardrobe. I can't help but let out a frustrated groan. Zac looks back at me and chuckles.

Chuckles. The asshole chuckles at me. As I'm standing there, slightly fuming, yet still very turned on, he hands me a shirt and a pair of sweats.

Looking me straight in the eye, he says, "Get dressed. We need to talk."

Arghh, what the hell? He expects me to get dressed and talk? I'm so worked up I'm surprised I'm not combusting. Holding the clothes out to the side, I look up at him.

"Either you are going to get me off right now, or I will march my naked self out to your bed and use my own fingers to finish what you started in there," I huff, pointing in the direction of the shower.

Zac's eyebrows raise towards his hairline. He tilts his head, slowly perusing my body from my feet to my head. Before I know it, he comes towards me, bends at the waist, and has me draped over his shoulder, storming towards what I can only hope is his bed. He slaps my ass, the sting registering the same time I'm floating and landing on the cloud-like mattress of his bed.

Yes, this I can work with. Just as the thought crosses my mind, Zac is hovering over me. He has one hand around my neck, squeezing, but not tight enough that I struggle to breathe. His other hand is cupping my pussy.

Bending down, he growls into my ear, "This pussy is mine. It's mine to play with. It's mine to pleasure."

He dips a finger in and out of me slowly and nibbles on my neck. "Sunshine, the only way this pussy is getting off is from my hands, my cock, or my mouth. Do you understand?"

I can't help but shiver at his words, my core clenching around his finger.

"Oh, god." Moaning, I attempt to lift my hips, anything to get that extra friction my core is desperate for. Zac continues to tease me, slowly inserting just the one finger.

"Please." I'm reduced to begging.

"You need more, sunshine?" Lifting his head, he looks directly into my eyes.

"Yes, more. Please, Zac," I beg, attempting to lift my hips again.

"I'll get you there, but first you have to tell me…" Bending, he sucks a nipple into his mouth.

"*Ah*, god. Tell you what?"

Letting go of my nipple with an audible pop, he lifts his head up, smirking at me. "That this pussy belongs to me and only me."

I'm just about to tell him anything to reach the orgasm that's floating on the horizon. "It's yours, all yours. Now please, let me come."

My body feels like there are thousands of live wires circuiting throughout, goosebumps coating my skin and a light sweat covering the surface. Zac withdraws his finger and begins circling it around my clit.

Leaning down to whisper in my ear, he says, "I can't wait to watch you come, to watch you fall apart from my fingers. There's just one more thing I need from you before I can let that happen."

"Oh my god, Zac, I don't care. Whatever you need, it's yours, just please." I don't even care what I'm agreeing to.

"After I give you the pleasure you need, you and I, we are going to talk," he demands. "Tell me you understand that is what's going to happen, sunshine."

"Okay… Yes, god… Okay… Talk… we will talk after." I'm reduced to a babbling mess I'm so worked up.

Chuckling, Zac lowers his head to my nipple again. Licking it once, he says, "Glad we can agree on things so easily," then proceeds to suck on my nipple, while roughly inserting two fingers inside me with increasing speed.

My back arches off the bed. "Yes! Oh god. Yes! Please don't stop."

Zac circles his thumb around my clit while thrusting his fingers inside me. He moves his mouth to my other breast, squeezing tighter around my throat, and I see stars. My body starts to involuntarily shake, my core clenching around his fingers, as I scream out his name through my release.

Zac draws every inch of pleasure from me as I slowly come down from my orgasmic high. He lifts his head to meet my eyes, raising one eyebrow.

"Better?" he questions with the cockiest grin plastered on his face—like he doesn't know how good he is at that.

"*Mmhmm,*" I mumble, feeling completely relaxed. Zac raises off the bed and walks back into his wardrobe, only to reappear moments later wearing a pair of dark denim jeans and a black shirt. He must notice the disappointment on my face at him being clothed, as he laughs.

Roaming his eyes up and down my sprawled-out body, he says, "Babe, we can either have this talk with you dressed, or as naked and spread out as you are now. I don't mind either way."

"Or you could strip those jeans off and let me return the favour," I suggest.

"Oh, you will definitely get a chance to return the favour, but first, we are having that talk." He smirks.

Realising I'm not going to get out of this, I grunt as I get off the bed. "Fine, but I'm getting dressed first."

Fourteen

ZAC

*S*ITTING on the bed with Alyssa across from me, I wait for her to speak. This is uncharted territory for me. I'm not the one who usually digs and pries into a girl's life, but Alyssa is different. I want to know everything, but right now, the one thing I want to know is why she had a fucking panic attack after receiving flowers. I also want to know who the *he* is that she seemed so fucking scared of.

When I got to her in that bathroom, I felt like my world was tipped on its axis. She looked so fucking broken and scared; all I wanted to do was hold her and put her back together. When she clung to me and wouldn't let go, it destroyed me to see her so frightened. I never want to see that again.

"Sunshine, I need to know why you had a panic attack about the flowers."

Keeping my voice soft, I try to reassure her that

she's safe here, that I would never let anything happen to her. As she looks me in the eye, I can see the tears starting to form. Her entire body shakes as she takes a deep breath in. It's fucking killing me, seeing her like this.

Reaching forward, I lift her by her hips, placing her on my lap so she is straddling me. Cupping her face, I wipe away the tears that are freely falling and wait for her to speak.

Taking a few deep breaths, she looks me in the eye, pleading, "I can't lose you. What if I tell you and you decide it's too much, that I'm too damaged?"

I don't know how to reassure her I'm not going anywhere. I try to show in my actions just how much she means to me. I kiss her under each eye, kissing away her tears before lightly pressing my lips to hers.

"Alyssa, I'm not going anywhere, and you are not fucking damaged. Understand?" My voice is getting gruffer as I continue to rein in my anger at whatever the fuck made her think she was damaged.

Nodding her head, she says, "Okay." She takes another big breath in before she finally lets me in. "I grew up in foster care, many foster care homes actually. My mum died when I was five. She didn't have any family; it was always just my mum and me. I don't remember much about her, but I do remember that she was sick, like all the time. I found out later that she died from breast cancer."

Alyssa pauses, looking for something on my face. She must not find the reaction that she expects, as she continues. "It's why I don't want kids; breast cancer can be hereditary and I can't think of anything worse than leaving a child behind with no one to love them, like I was."

I understand her reasons for not wanting children, however, I don't agree with her that her kids would be left alone, or that she is destined to have the same fate as her mother.

"Sunshine, if you had kids, they sure as fuck wouldn't be left with no one. They would have me. Because, if you decided you wanted kids, I'm the only person you're going to have them with." She opens her mouth to argue but I'm not finished yet. Placing my finger over her mouth, I add, "Also, you don't know that you will have the same fate as your mother. I'm sure I don't have to tell you that the medical industry has advanced a lot since you were five."

"I know. I haven't even had the gene test done yet to see if I have the inherited gene mutation linked to breast cancer." She looks down at her lap, twisting her fingers together. "I figured if I don't know, then I won't stress about it as much. Five to ten percent of breast cancers are thought to be hereditary. What if I'm in that five to ten percent?"

"Sunshine, you can't live with that fear. You should get the test, and we will deal with whatever comes our way, together."

I rub my hands up and down her legs, not sure if it's reassuring her or me at this point.

"Promise?" she asks, looking so insecure.

"I swear we will always have a tomorrow together." Leaning in, I meet her lips ever so lightly then sit back and wait for her to continue.

Shaking her head, she says, "Anyway. One foster home I lived in when I was fifteen, they had five other kids living there too. There was one guy—he was seventeen—always gave me the creepy kind of vibe, you know? His name was Steven. I did everything I could to stay clear of him, but he was always there, always staring at me. I knew I had to get out of that house, so I..." She trails off, looking away.

"You what?"

"I slapped the foster mum across the face, wasn't my finest moment, but I knew it would be my ticket out. I was moved to a different home the next day, but not before her husband returned the favour and slapped me around a bit."

I'm doing everything I can to not show the rage rolling through my body at the thought of a grown-ass man slapping around a fifteen-year-old Alyssa. I know my face must tell my anger as I clench my jaw. Alyssa takes in my face, placing her hands on my shoulders.

"I swear I'm not that child anymore, Zac. I don't go around hitting people, really. I became a nurse because I wanted to help people."

Shaking my head, I consider what she must have been like at fifteen. "Sunshine, I couldn't care less if you went around slaughtering people. I'd have Dean and Bray bury the bodies for you. I'd only ask that you don't slaughter me in my sleep." I smirk at her, in an attempt to lighten the mood, even if what I say is one hundred percent truth.

The thought scares the crap out of me. I don't think there is anything this girl could do that would sway my opinion of her. She doesn't even realise the amount of control she has over me.

Smiling, she says, "Of course I would spare you. Have you seen you? I mean, if I slaughtered you, I might as well turn it into a murder-suicide, because life would not be worth living if I don't get a daily dose of the orgasms you dish out."

I'm laughing again. When was the last time I laughed so damn much?

"I will give you as many orgasms as you like," I promise as I lean in and kiss her lightly. "As soon as we're done with this talk, that is."

"*Argh.* Okay. Well, I ran into Steven again at college, two and a half years ago. He asked me out, I declined, and I thought that was that." And the rage is back. I'm grinding my teeth in an attempt to hold it in. "Anyway, he stalked me for six months before the police could catch who it was. It was Steven, my stalker was Steven."

"What do you mean stalked you? What the fuck did he do?" I don't think I can hold in this rage much longer; I want to find the motherfucker and bury him. "It started with roses. He would send roses. At first, without cards. No messages, just bunches of roses."

Shit, her eyes are tearing up again, but I need to

hear this. I need the rest. Squeezing her thighs, I encourage her to continue. "Then it was the messages. H… he would send me text messages from random numbers, but always describing what I was wearing and where I was at that time. Like he wanted me to know I was being watched. I never knew who it was. I guess he got bored with that, because the roses started coming with the same message each time."

"What did the message say?" I ask, unsure if I want to know.

"It always said *SLUT* in bold letters. Then the text messages described what he was planning on doing to me in very detailed descriptions, right down to how he would choke the life out of me because, according to him, sluts like me were not worth the air they breathe."

I take a shaky breath in, waiting for her to continue.

"One time, he broke into my house, stole every pair of underwear I had, and left a note on my bed." She shivers, her fingers gripping the fabric of my shirt.

"It got to the point that I couldn't leave the house. I locked myself in the house for two months before he was caught. The girls took turns staying with me, so I was never alone. Then it came time for my practical placement at the hospital. I had to go in. I knew I had to do my placement. I had worked too damn hard to get

to that point in my degree; I decided I would not

lose everything I worked for because some psycho had a hard-on for me."

"And then what happened?" I ask.

"Hospital security caught him when he had me cornered in the hallway of emergency, his hands around my throat… attempting to do just what he said he would."

Shit.

"Sunshine, I didn't know. You should tell me if anything I do is a trigger for you. I just had my hand around your throat and you didn't say anything. Shit, baby, I'm so sorry."

"Zac, stop. That was not the same. Maybe it should have triggered me somehow, but it didn't. Quite the opposite, I freaking loved it. I can't explain why some things trigger a panic attack and others don't. You are the first guy I've been with since Steven was arrested. Even though that date Sarah pushed me to go on didn't pan out, it did lead me to you."

Taking my hands into her own, she takes a breath, bringing her gaze to meet mine. "I can't explain what it is, but I feel safe with you. I feel like nothing can get to me when I'm with you. I'm sorry, and I will understand if it's too much too soon for you. I've never been this clingy type before. I don't know what's come over me."

I can tell she's nervous because she's rambling. "Sunshine, cling away, because I'm not letting go. In fact, you should stay with me for a while. We can go pack some of your stuff, and I'll clear out some space in the wardrobe, or I can just order you new stuff."

Alyssa laughs like I'm joking, but she stops when she notices I'm not laughing with her.

"Wait, oh god, you're serious, aren't you?" she asks.

"Deadly serious, babe."

She shakes her head. "I'm not moving in with you. We just met like two days ago."

Her argument is weak if you ask me. "So? And it's not moving in, if it's just a few things and called staying with me." I smirk as I place my hands under her shirt, rubbing my fingers up and down the sides of her stomach. "Besides, think of how many more orgasms we could create together if you stayed here, in this bed, with me."

"*Mmm*, that has merit. But, no, I'm not staying here." Just then her stomach rumbles.

"Hungry?" I ask.

"A little," she says, shyly.

How is it she can be as daring as they come when it's about sex and then shy because she's hungry? It's fucking cute. Lifting her off my lap, I settle her on the bed.

"I'll go fetch you something to eat," I tell her. Just as I'm getting off the bed, she reaches out, gripping my shirt, fear written all over her face. "Sunshine, I'm just going to the kitchen. I'm not leaving the apartment."

I don't make a move to remove her hands. I'll wait as long as she needs me.

"O-Okay, sorry. I just…" She casts her eyes down. I lift her chin with my finger, so I can see those beautiful blue eyes.

"Babe, it's fine. You don't need to apologise to me."

Settling back down, I reach for her and pull her into my arms, kissing the top of her head. I reach over and pick up my phone, dialling Reilly's number.

"Hello, Zac? What's wrong? How is she? I swear I will—" I don't let her finish her tirade.

"Reilly, she's fine. I need you to bring in some food, something that she likes. Check the fridge." I don't wait for her response before I hang up the phone.

"Oh my god, I'm being ridiculous, aren't I?" Alyssa looks up at me, insecurity written all over her face.

"No, you're not. I don't want you to ever be embarrassed to feel how you feel, not with me. I've got you, always." I kiss the top of her head and rub my hands down her back.

"Thank you," she says, wrapping her arms around my waist.

We stay like that for a few minutes, soaking up each other in peace, until the door bursts open and three females push at each other to get in.

"What the fuck, Reilly. I said for you to bring

food, not people," I grunt at the redhead in front holding a plate of food.

"How did you all get up here anyway?" I ask, looking at Holly and Sarah.

I feel Alyssa's body tense. Looking down at her, I silently ask her what's wrong with my eyes.

"I'm sorry, Zac. I can leave. I'll take them with me. I swear I didn't ask them to come here."

Leave? Like fuck, she can leave. "Sunshine, I don't care that your friends are here; you need them. I am, however, curious how they got up here, considering you need a key pass to reach the penthouse."

At this, Reilly pipes up triumphantly, "Oh, I went down and rode back up with them. I used your card thingy." I'm speechless. Reilly, however, is not. "I also called your brother. He's currently sulking in the living room. Dean was already here, so there's that. I also introduced myself to Ella. She was a little stunned to see a random redhead in your apartment because, according to her, and I quote: *If you're one of Zac's floozies, you're too late. He's found his forever girl.* I think I might love her already. Here, Ella made you food," she says as she places the plate on the bed next to Alyssa.

Reilly takes it upon herself to sit on the bed next to Alyssa. Raising my eyebrows at her, I say, "Please, have a seat."

At this, Holly and Sarah both stalk forward and sit on the bed. Jesus Christ, what the fuck is going on in here? I look over to see Alyssa smiling. Damn, she's fucking smiling and it's like the sunshine is back within her. I decide her friends can sit wherever the fuck they want if it makes her smile.

"Babe, I'm gonna go see Bray and Dean for a few. Will you be all right in here with your girls, or do you want to come with?" I ask, hoping like fuck she wants to stay with the girls, because she does not need to hear what I have to say.

"*Umm*, I'll be okay in here, if you're sure you don't mind us all being in your room."

Leaning down, I kiss her gently. "I don't mind." I lean further into her, so only she can hear me whisper, "Besides, soon enough, you'll be calling it *our* room." Standing up, I look pointedly at Reilly, who is eyeing the open walk-in wardrobe. "Stay out of the fucking wardrobe, Reilly, unless you want to get fired on your first day."

"*Pfft*, please, as if I would want to see your designer wardrobe," she says while shaking her head.

The other three laugh as they all say in unison, "You so would." Picking up my phone, I send Reilly a text. I don't want Alyssa to know what I have to ask her friend.

Me: Meet me in the kitchen now!

I wait for Reilly's phone to beep before I shut the door. Walking through the living room, I see Bray and Dean both look up at me expectantly.

"Wait there a sec," I say as I continue to the kitchen.

Putting a mug under the expresso machine, I touch the icon labelled: *sunshine*. I may have already stored her preferred coffee method into the machine. I grab the bottle of vanilla flavouring and pour a good dose of it into the cup.

"You summoned me, boss?" Reilly says as she strolls into the kitchen.

Stirring the coffee, I hand it to her. "Give this to Alyssa for me."

"You made her a vanilla latte?" she questions, scrunching her eyebrows together. Why the fuck she's questioning this, I don't know.

"It's her favourite," I say as a way of explanation. "Oh, I know that, but how do you know that already?" She looks at me scrutinizingly.

"I pay attention when she tells me things," I say. As she reaches for the cup, I don't release it straight away. Looking her dead in the eye, I say, "I'm going to need a last name for Steven and what facility he was locked up in."

"Why? He's still in jail. I just called and checked. He isn't the one who sent those flowers. Besides, it wasn't his calling card. This one is different," she says.

"Humour me and text me through those details. What do you mean this one is different?" I question.

"The card, it said: *Dear Alyssa, Condolences on your future loss.* I don't get it, but it freaks me out, Zac. Alyssa can't go through this again. It took her two months before she would even leave the house by herself, and that was after Steven was locked away."

"Nobody will be getting to her. I won't let it happen," I say as I make my way out of the kitchen.

By the time I reach Bray and Dean in the living room, I have a text message with the details I requested from Reilly.

Reilly: Steven Johnson, sentenced to five years at Silverwater Correctional Facility.

"Who do we know on the inside at Silverwater?" I ask Bray and Dean as Reilly walks by us back towards the bedroom.

I don't miss the smile that appears when she pretends not to overhear. I look at Bray, who is currently staring at Reilly's retreating form.

Slapping him across the back of the head, I say, "No, she's an employee and a friend of Alyssa's. For the love of god, just don't."

"You're a bit late with your warning." He smirks at me.

"Why, for the love of god, can't you just keep your dick in your fucking pants for once in your life?"

"What can I say? I'm doing the female breed a kindness by letting them on my dick. The thing is a masterpiece, after all." He laughs. Dean and I both shake our heads at him.

"Do not let this affect the club, or Alyssa. I won't save you from her if you hurt her friend."

At this, Dean laughs. "I don't think Reilly's heart is the one breaking," he says, looking pointedly at Bray.

"Shut up, my heart's not broken. If she doesn't want a go on the Bray train again, well, that's her bad luck. There are plenty of other hot redheads out there more than willing to take her spot."

"Whatever you say, man," Dean says while shaking his head. Well, that's an interesting development I will delve into at a later date. Bray being turned down? I don't think I've ever seen that happen. "Anyway, Silverwater, who do we know?" I ask again.

"A few, why?" Bray says. I tell them about Alyssa being stalked, about what that motherfucker did to her, how scared she was. "Get the few we know a message for me. I will make weekly deposits into their funds account for the rest of their time if they make the fucker bleed."

"On it," Dean says, tapping away at his phone.

I look over at Bray, noticing him deep in thought. "You good, man?" I ask.

"Yeah." Shaking his head, he then says, "I don't know. How can you have one of the best experiences of your life, and then nothing? I mean, I get it might have freaked her out with me getting arrested the next morning and all. But that was for a fucking good cause if you ask me."

"I can't thank you enough for what you did for Alyssa at the club when that asshole slapped her. Have you told Reilly that they arrested you because the jerk pressed charges?"

He shakes his head, pulling at his hair. "If I tell her, she will tell Alyssa, and I don't want Alyssa to feel responsible or some shit."

"I get you not wanting to tell her, but if she asks me flat out, I can't lie to her, man," I declare.

"I know. I don't expect you to. What do you think all that's about?" Bray asks, pointing at the squashed bunch of roses on the coffee table. I pick up the card lying next to it.

Dear Alyssa,

Condolences on your future loss.

xxx

"FUCK, I don't know, man, but I intend to find out. God help the fucker who thinks he can fuck with what's mine." I throw the card down, running my hands through my hair. "You should have seen her… She was so fucking scared. I felt like a part of my soul was breaking as she clung to me."

"Well, considering you let Reilly drive the fucking McLaren, I thought you must have lost your damn mind."

Hearing footsteps come down the hall, I look up

to see Ella. Her face, bruised and battered, makes me want to murder the fucker who hurt her again. Standing, I walk to her and wrap her in my arms, kissing her temple.

"How are you feeling, sweetheart? Do you need anything?"

Wrapping her arms around me, she looks up. "I'm good, Zac, really. I just want to forget everything and get ready to leave for Uni in a few months."

"Don't remind me you're growing up, dammit." I let her go, and then her words repeat in my head: *Leave for Uni*. "Wait, what the hell do you mean leave for Uni? I thought you chose to go to ACU here in Sydney?" I ask.

"I am, but I thought it would be good to live on campus, get the total experience," she says with a hitch to her voice.

Bray and Dean both speak up. "No."

Ella stomps her foot, staring them down. "What do you mean no? Don't answer that, because it's not up to you two baboons. I can make my own damn decisions."

"Ella, honey, wouldn't you be more comfortable living here, in your home, while you study?" I plead. I'm not ready for her to leave. I've been raising her since she was thirteen. Even if I was only twenty at the time, I had to step up and go from brother to guardian.

"Please, Zac, I've thought about this a lot. I really, really want to live on campus. You can come check the place out; it's an all-girls dorm, with high security and everything. I'll come back on weekends and semester breaks. You won't even notice I'm gone. Please don't take this away from me."

Dammit, she's pleading with teary eyes. She knows I can't say no to her when she looks at me like that.

"Don't cave, man. Don't look at that angelic face and give in. You're stronger than that, bro," Bray says. I can't do it. Pulling Ella back into my arms gently, I answer, "Okay, I'll check out the dorm building, and you will come home every weekend and semester break. I know things are changing around here, but this is your home, Ella. You will always belong here."

"Thank you, Zac," she whispers. "Whipped," Dean and Bray say.

The fuckers would not have been able to say no either. I've seen Ella work her magic on both of them before. I flip them off. "Shut the fuck up. If she wants the full experience, she will get it."

"How's Alyssa?" Ella changes the subject so well. "She'll be okay. Thank you for making her food. I know she appreciates it. *I* appreciate it."

She looks up to me. "You know, she's a lucky girl to have you. I hope I find a guy as great as you one day."

"I'm the lucky one, Ella, and there is no guy out there good enough for you. I pity any fool who thinks he is."

Ella flinches in my arms and Dean gets up, mumbling something about things to do, and leaves.

I raise my eyebrows at Bray and ask, "What the fuck is that about?"

He raises his shoulders up and down. "No idea, man, but I gotta run also. You good?" he asks.

"Yeah, I'm not going to make it into the club tonight. Can you take over for me?" I ask, eliciting surprised looks from both Ella and Bray.

"Are you sure you're okay?" Bray says as he places his hand to my forehead.

I swipe his hand away. "I'm fine. I just can't leave Alyssa tonight. It's one night, Bray. I'm sure the club will survive."

With that, I walk back to my bedroom, ready to kick three feisty females out of it.

Fifteen

ALYSSA

"*Y*OU REALLY THINK they're going to be able to pull it off?" I ask Sarah, pointing to the bathroom door where Holly and Reilly have just switched clothes with each other.

Reilly says she needs a quick escape from the building to avoid, in her words, *all that is Bray*. She wouldn't elaborate on why she was avoiding him, just that it was for the greater good.

"It works on everyone but us—it will work. Not sure why she wants to avoid that piece of delicious cucumber though. I mean, are they just breeding them tall, dark and handsome in this family? If so, please tell me there is another brother hiding somewhere." Sarah looks hopefully towards me.

Laughing, I give her the bad news. "Nope, only two brothers. Sorry you were too late to the party."

We're both laughing as the door opens and Zac

strolls in, eyes locked straight to mine. The intense look in his eyes has both Sarah and I suddenly quiet, waiting in anticipation for his next move. He walks straight up to me. Bending down, he cups my face in both of his hands before bringing his lips to mine. I can't help the moan that escapes my lips. Just as I wrap my arms around his neck, pulling him closer to get more of him, Holly and Reilly step out of the bathroom door, not so quietly.

Zac immediately sits up, looking behind him towards the bathroom. Squinting back and forth between Reilly and Holly, he asks, "Why have you switched clothes?"

I watch as both of their jaws drop. No one has ever been able to tell when they pretend to be each other. Sarah is gobsmacked, pointing at Zac as she questions, "Wait, how the hell can you tell they switched? It took me three months of knowing them before I could tell when they did that."

Zac shrugs his shoulders. "I'm observant. They also have very different mannerisms."

Holly looks petrified. Pointing a finger at Reilly, she says, "It's not going to work. Oh god, why did I let you talk me into this?"

Reilly grabs Holly's hand, tugging her towards the door. "It will work; it always works. Let's just go."

On her way out, Reilly says, "Lyssa, call me if you need anything."

I nod my head and thank her.

Once Holly and Reilly are gone, Sarah looks

between Zac and me. "Well, I know when I'm the third wheel. I'm out too. Will you be okay?"

I look over at Zac. He tenses, holding my hand a little tighter. Nodding my head, I tell Sarah, "I'll be fine here. I'll head home a bit later when Zac goes to work."

Zac then declares, "She'll be staying here. I've taken the night off. I'll be here all night."

Sarah raises an eyebrow at me in question. I just shake my head. "I'll be fine. Thanks for coming. I will call you tomorrow."

"Okay, but if there's anything else—"

I cut her off before she can finish the sentence. "Sarah, go. I'll be fine."

With a nod, she walks out the door. Before the door even closes, Zac has me wrapped up in his arms. This feels like the safest place on earth.

"*Mmm*, I could get used to this," I say as I snuggle into his chest further.

He chuckles. "I sure hope you do, sunshine, because there ain't no way I'm letting go."

Why does he always know what to say to reassure my racing thoughts? Breathing in his scent, I bury my nose closer and sniff. Yep, all Zac, woodsy with a mix of citrus.

"You always smell so damn good, GQ."

I feel the vibration of his silent laugh. Kissing the top of my forehead, he says, "I'm sure you'd think otherwise if you got a whiff just after I did a gym workout."

Of course he works out. How else would one get a body like this? "You really took the night off work. Can you do that? You know I can always just go home if you need to be there?" As much as I would hate to leave this spot right now, I also don't want to be a nuisance to him.

"Sunshine, I own the place. I can do whatever the fuck I want. And you are staying put. We're going to play a game."

"A game, like a board game, cards?" I look up at him with questions. He shakes his head no.

"I was thinking a getting to know each other game. Let's start with twenty questions, shall we?"

Oh, that actually sounds fun. I'm hungry for all things that are Zac. I can't wait to know more about him.

That's how we spend the night and the whole of the next day and night. In his bed, in his bathtub, in his kitchen. Getting to know each other, both inside and out.

Our game of twenty questions turned into twenty positions. I, for one, did not know I could contort my body in so many ways. Zac ended up taking another night off work to stay in with me. If it wasn't for me insisting that I was, in fact, going into work and he should do the same, we would still be tangled up with each other in his bed.

IT'S BEEN two weeks since I received the roses. As much as he didn't want to, Zac finally told me the cryptic message that was written on the card. Neither of us could figure out what it meant. I've tried hard to put it out of my mind, but the whole thing freaks me out. What future loss could I possibly be facing, and who would be planning this loss?

I have that feeling of being watched again and I don't like it. I was doing so much better... I *am* doing much better. I stopped looking over my shoulder a while ago; to be reduced back to the skittish scared woman I was two years ago is nerve-wracking. So far, I've held it together. I have Zac to thank for that. He has been there for me in ways I could never have imagined.

Whenever I needed to go into work, he would drive me, then he would pick me up and take me back to his place. The one night I put my foot down and said I was sleeping in my own bedroom, he relented.

He then showed up on my doorstep at two a.m., begging me to let him stay with me. Because, according to Zac, he *wouldn't get a wink of sleep if I wasn't beside him*. I had to admit I was tossing and turning in my bed alone, until he turned up. Once I had his arms wrapped around me, I slept like a log.

I can't think of anything better than climbing into bed and sleeping for a solid ten hours. I've just finished a twelve-hour shift and am waiting out front of the hospital for Zac. It's the first time that he hasn't been there before I walk out. I pull my phone out of my bag and double check that I haven't had any missed calls from him.

Just as I unlock my phone, I hear his car pull in. A huge grin plastered to my face, I start towards the car, only for my smile and steps to falter when it's Bray who steps out of the driver's side and walks around to the passenger door. Immediately, I think of all the worst-case scenarios: Zac was in an accident. He was hurt. Where the hell was he? I needed to get to him.

"What's wrong? Where is he?" My voice comes out panicky as I try to slow my racing heart. Bray squints his eyes at me before coming up and wrapping an arm around me.

"He's fine, Lyssa, just stuck at the club. I am under strict orders to deliver you to him, without a scratch or hair on this pretty little head out of place. His words, not mine." He opens the door and does a sweeping motion with his arm. "Your chariot awaits."

"He's okay, really?" I ask, still not moving.

"Yes, you can call him if you want. I'm sure no

matter how busy he is, he will always answer your call."

Shaking my head, I hop into the car. "No, it's fine. I just… I don't know what came over me. I'm sorry."

Bray shuts my door and walks around to the driver's side. Looking over at me, he says, "Lyssa, you don't need to apologise to me for being worried about my brother. It's endearing, really. I'm glad he has you. Just wish I had seen you first."

I laugh. Bray has that effect on people, always able to get a laugh. "No, you don't," I tell him.

Starting the car, he pulls away from the hospital. "You're right. I just wish every woman was as willing to own their damn feelings like you do."

I suspect he's referring to Reilly. I know he likes her and has been trying to get her to agree to a date. Reilly, however, is not having it, which means she likes him a lot more than she's letting on. I haven't managed to get Bray to talk about her with me though. Anytime I try to bring it up, he changes the topic.

"Anyone I know?" I pry.

"Yep," he says, looking out at the road. "Care to share who she is?"

"Nope."

"Want to talk about it?" I give it one last try before I drop it.

Bray shakes his head and says, "Nope."

Well, okay then, subject dropped. I spend the rest of the trip zoned out and eager to see Zac. I know I only worked twelve hours, but twelve hours is a long damn time without his arms around me. We get to the club at 1:30 a.m. It's a Friday night, so I'm assuming it will be crowded.

"Is it busy in there?" I ask Bray as he opens my door, a little nervous about having to walk through the crowd and a nightclub in my damn scrubs.

"A little, but don't stress, sweetheart. You're walking through with me. You're about to make every woman in there wish they could be you." He winks.

I raise my hand to knock on Zac's office door. Bray laughs, grabbing my hand away from the door, before he opens the door and lets us in.

"You don't need to bloody knock, Lyssa." He laughs.

I swat him in the arm. "Well, it's polite to knock on a closed door," I say, defending my actions.

Bray rubs his arm like my swat actually hurt him. "Ouch, I thought we were friends, sweetheart. You know I need to fight with this arm. In about thirty minutes, actually. I might have to forfeit the fight now," he pouts at me.

I'm about to respond when I hear that deep rumbly voice wash over me. "Are you done being a moron?" Zac asks Bray as he walks up to me, engulfing me in his arms before planting his lips against mine. I vaguely notice Bray say something before I hear the door close.

Zac breaks the kiss. "Hi, sunshine."

"Hi," I respond breathlessly. But that's what he

does to me. He literally takes my breath away with each kiss.

Zac leads me over to the couch. Sitting down, he pulls me onto his lap so I'm straddling him. "I'm so sorry I couldn't pick you up, baby. I had issues to sort out with tonight's fight."

I'm lost in the feel of his hands rubbing up and down my thighs. Damn, that feels good.

"It's okay. I understand you are not my personal Uber. You really don't need to send Bray to get me either. I can get an actual Uber home if you're busy."

The look I've come to learn as Zac's *don't argue with me* look crosses his face. "You are not getting a fucking Uber, Lyssa. If I can't personally pick you up, I will send Bray or Dean to get you." He must realise that his tone is harsh as he quickly follows up with, "Sorry, sunshine, just please let me have this. I need to know that you have a safe way of getting back to me."

"Okay, but you need to tell me why you are so against public transportation, Zac."

Every time I've broached the topic, he has either distracted me with sex or very effectively changed the subject. Looking off in the distance for a while, his body tense, he appears as though he's not going to answer. And then he looks me in the eye. I can see emotions reflected in his gaze.

"My parents were killed at a train station, waiting for a train. It was a mugging gone wrong. Some bastard tried to do a run and grab of my mother's purse. She ended up tripping and falling onto the track.

My father climbed down to help her get back up, but it was too late. The train couldn't stop in time." His voice cracks at the end.

"Oh, my god, Zac, I'm so sorry." I pull him tightly into my arms.

"I was twenty. I had to all of a sudden grieve the loss of both my parents, and take on the custodial role of a thirteen and a seventeen-year-old. But I sure as fuck was not letting my siblings end up in care." He winces. "Sorry, sunshine."

Why is he apologising to me? "No, I'm sorry that you had to endure that. But I'm also proud of how you overcame such adversities and became the man you are today. One, I'm proud I get to call mine."

Leaning in, I gently kiss his lips. My heart is breaking for this beautiful man, who has had to endure so much pain and take on so much responsibility at such a young age.

Knowing it took a lot for him to share that with me, I say, "Thank you for sharing that with me."

We haven't exchanged the L word with each other yet, but I know I feel it—it's on the tip of my tongue to tell him just how much I think I love him. Fearing what his reaction would be to me saying those words, I change the subject instead.

"Who is Bray fighting tonight? Can we watch? I haven't even seen inside this Batcave you guys keep locked up tight."

Zac groans. "Why would you want to see that? I mean, I have to make an appearance now and then.

This is the last fight before we break for the holidays. But you don't need to be there, sunshine. It's dirty down there, and the cage—well, it can get really rough. There are times I even have to look away when Bray is in there."

Leaning in, I let my lips swipe across his before pulling back. "Well, if you're going to be there tonight, then I'll just tag along behind you. You won't even notice I'm there. I promise not to get in your way while you're doing your thing. Please, Zac. Please let me come and watch."

Pleading my case, I pout my bottom lip out and give my best version of puppy-dog eyes. Running his hands through his hair, he appears as though he is going to relent and take me down to the cage fight.

"First, you could never be in my way, sunshine. No matter where and what I am doing, you will always be my priority. Second, you just have to be in the same vicinity as me for me to notice you're there, and when you're not around, I notice your absence. Third, you can come, but you do not, under any circumstances, leave my side, okay?"

Nodding my head enthusiastically, I say, "Yes, okay, I won't leave your side. And just so you know, whenever I'm not with you, your absence does not go unnoticed by me."

That makes him smile. He has the most beautiful smile and I've noticed he reserves it for moments like these, when it's just us in our little cocoon. Just as I'm about to lean in and kiss him again, the door opens.

"Jesus, does nobody knock around this joint?" Zac mumbles as he turns to see who just walked into his office.

"*Umm,* I knock," I say.

Zac turns back to face me. "You are the only one not expected to, babe." That makes me smile.

"What do you want, Reilly? It better be fucking good," Zac growls.

It's not until that moment that I look over and notice that Reilly has come into the office. Squealing with delight, I jump off Zac and run over to her. I haven't seen much of my friends these last few weeks. I pull her into a deep hug.

"Oh my god, it's so good to see you, girl." Leaning into whisper in her ear, I add, "Your little avoidance method is not working. That boy is so wound up with thoughts of you, it's comical."

She just grunts. "It's good to see you too, Lyssa. How've you been?"

I don't miss that she doesn't acknowledge my little dig about Bray. "I'm good, really good actually."

I feel Zac's presence behind me as he pulls me back against his chest, wrapping an arm around my waist. "Do you have a reason to be here?"

"Yes, I do actually have a reason to be here. I work here, remember?" she sasses back. "Also, here." Reilly holds out a garment bag and shoebox I didn't even notice she was holding. "I got the dress and shoes you wanted for Lyssa, but just for future reference, you hired me as your **PR** manager, not your personal shopper. If you wanted me to pick up clothing for anyone other than Lyssa, I'd quit." Reilly finishes her tirade with a sweet smile.

"You work for me. That means you do whatever the fuck I need you to do if you want to continue working for me. And who the fuck else do you think I'd buy clothes for anyway?" Zac shakes his head as he walks towards the bathroom with the garment bag and shoebox.

I watch the back and forth between my boyfriend and my best friend. *Sigh*. I can't help but get butterflies whenever I think of Zac as my boyfriend. Anyway, as I watch how Zac and Reilly interact, I realise that they seem to have a love-hate thing going on.

I know from conversations with both of them, they do actually like the other. Neither would admit that in front of the other, though.

Reilly's voice snaps me out of my thoughts. "You have ten minutes to get changed. I'll see you downstairs," she says as she walks out of the office.

Spinning around, I cock a hand on my hip and tilt my head, staring down Zac. He smirks like he sees something amusing.

"You bought me a dress to wear tonight?" I question with a raised eyebrow.

Zac doesn't move, just nods his head. "And shoes, I bought you a dress and shoes. As sexy as those scrubs are on you, I thought you might want to change before we go downstairs." His eyes roam up and down my body.

"So, you knew all along that you were going to be taking me downstairs to watch the fight tonight?"

"Well, I sure as fuck wasn't leaving you up here alone, now was I, sunshine?"

"You just made me beg you to take me to the fight, when you were already planning on taking me." I try to brush past him to enter the bathroom, but the man has reflexes like a freaking cat. Before I know it, he has his arms wrapped around me, pulling me into him. He leans down to my ear, nibbling, before he says, "What can I say? I like hearing you beg."

My whole body heats and shivers at his words. Zac pulls away and playfully taps my butt. "Get changed, babe."

I close the door behind me and then make quick work of undressing. Staring at my reflection in the mirror, I note that the dress is gorgeous and a perfect fit. I'm not convinced that Zac had anything to do with picking it, though.

It's made of thin, black, shimmery material. The dress has a halter neck with a very spacious gap in the front, going from my belly button up. My whole back is exposed. The skirt of the dress frills out and lands halfway down my thighs. It's most definitely not a dress I would ever choose for myself, but now that it's on and I'm thinking of the reaction Zac will have, I think I'm loving it.

Being short on time, I leave my hair up in a high

ponytail. Stepping out of the bathroom door, I see Zac has his back to me, putting his suit jacket on. I hold my breath as he turns; his eyes bulge as they travel up and down my body.

"She's fucking fired," he says. I laugh, knowing full well he's not going to fire Reilly.

"So, not the dress you picked, I'm gathering?" Walking towards him, I paste on the sweetest smile.

"Not even fucking close. You can't go down there in that, sunshine. Not that you don't look good, it's just that, well, you look too fucking good. Every damn guy down there is going to be drooling at the sight of you."

He hasn't even seen the back of the dress yet. "Well, it's a good thing you've already snagged me then, huh? You have nothing to worry about, Zac. Trust me, I'm all yours and only yours." Grabbing his hand, I continue, "Let's go. I don't want to be late."

As I drag him behind me out of the office, he gets a look at the back of the dress. I hear him groan and mutter under his breath.

Sixteen

ZAC

*S*TANDING in the front row, near the cage, I hold Alyssa in front of me. Partly to cover her exposed back from prying eyes and partly to cover the erection straining in my pants. I glide my hands up and down the exposed areas on her stomach, which again is a fucking lot of exposed skin.

I've lost count of how many daggers I've shot at fuckers who think they can look at her. I'm on edge, ready to rip the heads off anyone who even thinks to look her way. Dean senses my edginess and has planted himself right beside me, constantly looking my way to see if I will explode while aiding in blocking people's view of Alyssa.

Reilly, fucking Reilly. If she wasn't so good at her job… There's also the little thing with Bray being bloody obsessed with her and her being one of Alyssa's best friends. If it wasn't for all of those things, I would fire her ass for buying this dress for Alyssa.

She knows too. Standing next to Alyssa, she looks over her shoulder and smirks at my unease. I glare back at her, but she just laughs it off.

I won't admit it to anyone—well, anyone other than my sunshine—but I think I like Reilly. I like that she can give as good as she gets. The fact that she gets her job done, and done well, without trying to find ways to flirt or touch me, like the last fucking PR manager, was a bonus.

We've watched three fights; Bray's is always the last. He is yet to be defeated. When our parents died, he had so much pent-up anger. Being a hormonal seventeen-year-old didn't help. He started getting into fights at school constantly. I didn't know what to do with him, so I ended up putting him in MMA classes. I figured if he was going to fight, he might as well do it properly and in a contained environment.

He hasn't stopped fighting since. Although we both make a lot of money off his fights, I know he's not doing it for the money. It's almost like he needs it, needs the adrenaline of being in the cage. The six-week break over the holidays that's coming up will make him crazy if he doesn't find another outlet for his energy, or a really good sparring partner.

My phone vibrates in my pocket, pulling me out of my thoughts. As I reach for it, I realise it's not my phone that vibrates; it's Alyssa's. She holds her phone out in front of her to see she has messages.

Alyssa's body tenses and freezes as she reads the text message. She drops the phone and starts looking around the underground basement wildly, like she's looking for someone. Dean bends down and picks up her phone, stepping in closer to her. Reilly turns towards Alyssa, asking her what's wrong but Alyssa doesn't say anything, just holds onto my arm that's around her waist and looks around the crowd.

She's trembling. I turn her around in my arms and bury her head in my chest. Whispering in her ear, I say, "Babe, you're okay. I've got you."

I look up at Dean. I can tell whatever he read on that phone has him raging. His jaw is tensed, and he is now looking across the cage to the crowd on the other side. He hands me the phone, before speaking to his security team through his earpiece. All I hear him say is, "Nobody gets out of this fucking basement without me knowing. Lock the entrances, single file out. I want to see every fucking face that exits this room."

I'm gripping the phone in my hand, surprised it's not breaking under my grasp. The text has my blood boiling. There is a grainy picture of Alyssa with my arms wrapped around her, standing exactly where we are now. The picture was taken from the other side of the cage. The message reads:

Unknown: You shouldn't touch things that don't belong to you! He was mine first. I saw him first! I won't warn you again, bitch. He is *MINE*. *He will be with me again, even if I have to take you out myself. xxx*

I'm holding onto Alyssa so damn tight now that she winces.

"Shit." I loosen my grip slightly. "Sorry, sunshine, you are okay. I'm never going to let anyone get to you."

Reilly is almost in hysterics beside me, demanding to know what's going on. I hand her the phone and see her face go white as a ghost as she reads the message. Her hands tremble. I need to get both Alyssa and Reilly out of this damn basement now.

I look up to the cage and hear the announcer call the start of Bray's fight. He's standing in the cage, looking over at us while staring intently at Reilly. He squints his eyes, mouthing the words, "What's wrong?"

I shake my head and hold up one finger. It's our signal for me needing him to finish the fight in one round. He looks back to Reilly, and I swear I see something pass over him as his face hardens. Bray nods his head and turns as the announcer starts the countdown. As soon as he yells out *one*, Bray lands a solid punch to his opponent's jaw, knocking him out cold.

Jumping from the cage, he storms over to us and pulls Reilly into his arms, rubbing his hands up and down her back and whispering something in her ear. For once, she doesn't fight off his touch. She hands him Alyssa's phone, and I watch as his face hardens before we all walk out of the basement together. Dean leading the way with Alyssa and Reilly between Bray and me.

I'M STANDING in the bathroom of my office, Alyssa sitting on the vanity and clinging to me. My heart is racing, blood boiling. Someone's head is going to roll for putting her through this. Dean and Bray are in the office. I can hear them shuffling around. I'm sure, by now, they are scanning through the security footage, trying to find the fucker who was stupid enough to mess with what's mine.

Rubbing my hands up and down Alyssa's back, I instruct her to breathe, attempting to calm both her and myself. "Babe, breathe, just take big breaths with me, okay? Count them with me: one, in… out; two, in… out." By the time we get to number ten, she has calmed. She lets go of her grip on my shirt and is wiping at her face.

"I'm sorry, Zac. I'm so sorry I'm bringing so much drama into your world. I don't know why this is happening again."

The tears keep rolling down her face. I wipe them off with the pad of my thumb.

"Sunshine, this is not your fault. We will find

whoever sent you that message, and they will pay for putting you through this. I promise nothing will hurt you."

Shaking her head, she pushes me back and jumps down. Turning towards the sink, I watch as she runs her hands under the water and then splashes the water over her face. I hand her a hand towel and she dries her face. Looking up into the mirror, she straightens her back and squares her shoulders back.

Turning around, she says, "You know what? You're right. I will not let someone do this to me again."

I'm so fucking proud of how strong she is, how much she can endure. What she says next floors me.

"Plus, I don't care what anyone says or thinks. You are mine, Zac. I love you too damn much to let anyone take you from me. So, if some psycho-bitch thinks she will get you, well, she will have one hell of a fight on her hands."

I'm stuck on the words *I love you* that she just threw at me. I can't wipe the huge-ass grin from my face.

"What?" she says with scrunched up eyebrows.

"You love me, *huh*?" I say with a smirk while grabbing her around the waist.

"I... *umm*... well..." she grunts and then relents, "Yes, okay. I love you, and you're just going to have to deal with that. I don't care if you're not ready to hear those words or if you don't feel the same way about—"

Placing my finger over her lips, I stop her right

there. "Sunshine, I think I've been in love with you from the moment you stepped through the doors of my club." She doesn't say anything, just stares at me, so I continue, "I love you so damn much it scares the shit out of me sometimes." This brings a smile to her face.

"You love me too?" she asks.

"So much," I say as I lean in and kiss her. Breaking the kiss, she looks up and says, "Good, because you are so stuck with me now." Stepping back, she looks up and continues, "Let's go figure out who thinks they can take my man." I can't help but smile. I'm so fucking proud of how determined she is. Just before she opens the door, I get another look at her dress.

"Wait," I say as I take off my jacket, "put this on." I don't wait for her to accept or argue before I have her draped in my jacket. She brings the collar of the jacket up to her nose and inhales.

"*Mmm*, god, you smell good," she mumbles as we make our way out of the bathroom.

Dean has the flat screen monitors that line one wall of my office on, playing the video feed from the basement and scanning through each section from the time I entered with Alyssa. Bray is pacing up and down the office with a drink in one hand and an ice pack wrapped around the other. Reilly is sitting on the couch, texting furiously on her phone. They all stop what they're doing and turn to look at us. Reilly is the first to speak.

"Sarah and Holly are on the way. We're having a slumber party tonight." She pauses and looks at me. "Girls only."

I just smirk. If she thinks she is going to get me away from Alyssa, she has another thing coming.

I'm about to say as much to her when Alyssa speaks up excitedly, "Yes, that is exactly what I need right now," as she walks over and sits with Reilly on the couch.

I know I'm pouting, but I don't care. Reilly looks over to me and laughs. "I'm sure you will survive one night without her, Romeo."

I don't think I actually would, but we're not about to find out either. Ignoring Reilly, I walk over to the screens where Dean has a shot paused, zooming in on someone.

"Have you found anything yet?"

Just as my eyes focus on the person he has zoomed in on, Bray stands behind us. "What the fuck? I always knew that chick was a bloody psychopath."

My body vibrates with rage, pure, hot rage directed at the person in that image. I always felt a weird vibe from her, but I didn't think she would be this level of crazy. I knew she had a crush on me, but damn, this, I did not fucking expect. I don't know how far she's willing to go, but I do know there is no hole deep enough for her to hide in from me. I will hunt her down, and when I find her, I'll make sure she fucking regrets the day she thought she could threaten what's mine.

"Who is it?" Reilly and Alyssa ask at the same time.

Running my hands through my hair, my frustration showing, I look at Alyssa apologetically. "Caitlyn, the PR manager I had working here just a few weeks ago."

Alyssa comes up, wraps her arms around me and buries her head into my chest. Just her touch, and being able to touch her in return, calms the raging beast within me.

Looking back over to Dean, I command, "Pull her employee records and send someone over to her house. I want to be certain it's her before we do anything."

Nodding his head, he walks towards the door. "On it. I'll check back in with you in a few hours. You guys going home?" he asks.

"We'll be back at the penthouse in about thirty," I tell him.

I feel Alyssa tense as I say the words. I already know she is going to argue about coming back to the penthouse.

"*Umm*, Zac, I need you to help me in the bathroom for a minute," she says, waltzing back into the bathroom.

I smirk at her. "Sunshine, lead the way."

Once we are locked into the bathroom with the door shut, she doesn't waste any time. "Zac, I can't come back to the penthouse tonight. I haven't seen the girls in a while and I really like the sound of lounging out with my friends right now. I'm tired, I've worked all day, and all I want to do is go home and veg for a few hours, and then sleep. And have all my girls with me for breakfast when I wake up."

I kiss her to get her to stop talking. "Sunshine, if you want to have your girls' night, you can have them all come to the penthouse and make use of the theatre room. I can have whatever you want set up there."

Her eyes well up. "Really? You would let me bring my crazy friends to your place all night? You know they will be there when you wake up, right? They won't leave until you kick them out."

Nodding, I know this. "Babe, if you want them there, I'm okay with it. Besides, I want you to start thinking of it as *our* place, not just my place."

Reaching up, she gently kisses me. "Thank you, I don't know what I did in life to deserve someone as sweet as you, but I'm not about to look a gift horse in the mouth." She kisses me again. "I'm still not moving in though." Laughing, she walks out the door.

"Yet," I tell her; she just shakes her head.

I'VE SPENT the last couple of hours listening to the shrills and laughter coming out of my theatre room. If it wasn't making Alyssa so happy, that much noise at four in the morning would annoy the shit out of me. Ella woke up from the commotion at one point. I was about to go and tell them all to get out of my fucking house for waking up my baby sister—well, all of them bar Alyssa—until Ella joined them.

I'm sitting in the living room, looking through the printed images that Dean took at Caitlyn's house. Bray is sitting opposite me, nursing a glass of whisky. Every few minutes, his lingering eyes pass down the hall towards the theatre room.

Pointing at the coffee table that has the printed photographs sprawled across it, he says, "Maybe you should put those away before one of those girls sees them."

He's right. I don't want any of them to see these images. They are disturbing and it's making me sick to my stomach, just looking at them. Caitlyn had an entire wall covered in pictures of me. Some were recent pictures of me with Alyssa, all with a big red X drawn across Alyssa's face. The thought of whisking Alyssa away to some deserted island has crossed my mind.

When I voiced this to Bray, he laughed and said, "Good luck getting her on board with that plan."

After packing the images away, I look over at Bray. "I'm assuming you'll still be here in the morning? I'm going to bed. I'm fucking tired."

Rising, I don't wait for his response. He still has a bedroom here. I will always make sure Bray and Ella have a place they can think of as home. This is that place for them.

I walk into the theatre and, without a word, pick Alyssa up and throw her over my shoulder. She squeals as I walk out with her, her friends calling out random things and Ella groaning while throwing in a, "Gross! That's my brother, girls." I laugh, heading towards my bedroom at the end of the hall.

Putting Alyssa down on the bed, I'm quick to lay my body over top of hers. She's still wearing that fucking dress. "*Mmm*, I've been waiting all night to rip this dress off your body, sunshine."

I trail kisses up and down her throat. Her body shutters, and a few quiet moans escape her.

"Have you now? Well, what are you waiting for? You have me here in your room at your mercy. Whatever are you going to do with me?"

Alyssa unbuttons my shirt, her actions painstakingly slow. "That depends. Are you tired, baby? Because if you want to curl up and sleep, then that's what we'll do. If you want to play, then I'm more than ready to play this body of yours." Grinding my hard cock into her core, I show her just how ready I am.

"*Mmm*, I pick play," she moans.

Sitting up slightly, I smirk down at her and rake my eyes slowly up and down her body. "Stay right here. Do not move an inch," I instruct her as I make my way into the walk-in wardrobe.

After finding the toys I want for tonight, I walk back into the room to see she is still in the same position I left her. She tilts her head up, her eyes going wide when she sees what I have in store for tonight. I watch as she licks her lips and her breathing becomes shallow. She's excited. *Good.*

Placing everything on the bed next to her, I pick up the pair of scissors and cut from the bottom of her dress up to her waist. Alyssa just stares, mouth open, when I cut away the fabric at the back of her neck and push the material off her body.

I smile down at her, taking in all of her beautiful, creamy, white skin. Mouth-watering breasts with the most perfect nipples—nipples I can't wait any longer to have in my mouth. I suck on one nipple while rolling the other between my fingers.

"*Mmm*, I love the taste of you. I could suck on these all day, baby, and still not have enough."

Alyssa holds my head against her chest, like I would willingly leave this spot.

"Oh my god, Zac, that feels so good," she moans. I know she has sensitive nipples. I remember making her come just from sucking and playing with them the other night.

Releasing her nipple with a plop, I sit up to reposition her to the middle of the bed, just where I want her. We have had a lot of sex the last few weeks, but we haven't played like this, the way I intend to play with her tonight. I know she gets off on a little pain. I know she's experimentative and submissive in the bedroom.

"Sunshine, if you need me to stop at all, just tell me, okay? I'll stop at any time you want."

She looks up at me. "Okay."

"I need you to know that I won't ever do anything to hurt you. All I want to do is bring you to extreme pleasure. You know that, right?"

She nods her head. "Zac, I trust you wholeheartedly. Now fuck me already, would you?"

Well shit, since she put it like that. "With pleasure, sunshine."

Picking up two sets of handcuffs, I place one on each of her wrists before securing them to the bedhead. I smirk when I see her pull at them, testing their strength. I trail my fingertips down her arms, slowly down the side of her breasts, right down to her hips and back up again. I can feel her legs tense as she attempts to close them. Too bad, I happen to be sitting between them, keeping them spread.

"You are so fucking sexy, all spread out for me like this. It's like I'm at an all you can eat buffet and I don't know which dish I want to start in on."

Picking up a set of nipple clamps, I hold them up to show her.

"Wh… what are they for?" she asks. "Nervous, baby?" I smirk.

She shakes her head and licks her lips. "No, not nervous, excited."

"Damn, you are the perfect woman, sunshine.

These," I say as I place one on her nipple, "are nipple clamps."

I watch her reaction the whole time, the way her breath hitches, her body arching off the bed. The way her face flushes...

"*Mmm*, I think someone may be a fan of the nipple clamps." I chuckle as I lean down to lick and suck at each nipple now that they have been clamped. "Oh god, Zac," Alyssa is screaming. "I will come if you keep doing that. Oh gosh, don't stop."

I keep nipping and sucking while kneading her breasts, moving from one breast to the other. Alyssa is thrashing beneath me, trying with all her might to close her legs, lift her core, seeking friction between her legs that she so desperately wants.

"I love how your body responds to me," I murmur as I trail a hand up and down her thigh, stopping each time just before I reach her centre.

"Zac, please, please, please make me come. I need... need..." She trails off.

Lifting my head, I respond, "I know what you need, sunshine, and I'm about to give it to you. You need to learn to be patient. I think this pussy of ours is a little greedy, wouldn't you say?"

I trail kisses down her body. Licking, sucking and biting on all of her creamy skin. I know she will be left with my marks all over her for the days to come. Inhaling her scent when I reach her centre, I look up to see her watching me.

"You smell fucking delicious, sunshine. I can't wait to feast on this hungry pussy."

She throws her head back, moaning. I know she gets turned on by my dirty mouth; she's admitted that to me before. I grab onto the inside of her thigh and bite down. I can taste her leaking juices covering her thighs. Turning my head, I give her other thigh the same treatment.

"*Ah*, oh god, Zac," Alyssa is moaning incoherently, loudly. I wouldn't be surprised if the whole building hears her screaming my name. Reaching my hands up to her breasts, I release the clamps at the same time my mouth sucks on her clit. She loses it, bucking wildly beneath me, screaming out a mixture of obscenities and my name. I continue to drink from her until she comes down, bringing her back to me with slow, languid licks.

Lifting up, I crawl back over her body and kiss her greedily, her tongue meeting mine hungrily, stroke for stroke. Slowing the kiss, I rise up, looking her in the eye.

"You okay, sunshine?"

She smiles up at me and I swear I see my future in that smile.

"Never been better."

"You want to stop or keep going?" I ask her, giving her full control, even though she's the one currently in handcuffs.

"*Mmm*, don't you dare stop now, Zac," she

demands, attempting to look stern. All it does is make her look cute as hell.

"Wouldn't dream of it," I say as I place a blindfold over her eyes. Picking up the riding crop, I lightly trail the tip from her lips, down her throat all the way down to her core, where I lightly tap it against her clit. I watch as her body arches, and listen to the moans she makes. Trailing the tip of the crop back up, I tap each breast slightly harder.

"Your creamy skin looks good with my markings all over it, baby. Want more?" I ask her.

"*Mmm*, more, Zac. Give me all you got," she demands.

I chuckle, knowing damn well I would never whip her with all my strength. I'm not a fucking sadist. I get off from seeing her pleasure, not seeing her in pain.

I tap the crop against her stomach, then along each thigh a few times. By the time I throw the crop to the floor and climb between her legs, she is a squirming mess. Lifting the blindfold, I want to be able to see those blue eyes as I thrust into her. I lower my head and kiss her slowly, which is the total opposite of how much my cock is aching to be buried inside of her right now.

"I need to be inside you," I say as I trail kisses down the side of her neck.

"Yes, Zac. I want you in me, now!"

Guiding my cock to her entrance, I slam into her. Alyssa brings her legs up and wraps them around me. Her hips meet me thrust for thrust.

"You feel fucking amazing, Alyssa. I don't know how much longer I can last." Reaching between our bodies, I slide my thumb around her clit.

"*Ah*, yes! Zac! I'm coming!"

Alyssa's body convulses, her pussy clenching around my cock. I feel my balls tighten, the tingling in my spine, and then I'm coming hard, spilling into her. Calling out her name…

It takes a few minutes for us to come down from our high. I fall next to her so I don't squash her, our breathing heavy. I get up and walk to the bathroom; it's only then that I realise my mistake. I didn't use a condom and I came inside her. Fuck, wetting a washer, I walk back out to see she hasn't moved.

Using the washer, I wipe between her legs. I love how she doesn't stop me from doing this anymore. But I'm about to ruin her blissful moment when I tell her what I just did.

"Sunshine, I, *umm*, I have to tell you something, but you have to promise not to get mad or hate me," I plead with her.

"Zac, I could never possibly hate you."

Taking a deep breath in, I let it out. "I forgot to use a condom," I spit out really quickly, "and I came inside you."

I hold my breath, watching her reaction. She's looking at me, her expression frozen in place.

"I'm clean, I swear. I can show you my test results from just last month." Great, now I'm blubbering.

The next thing I know, Alyssa is laughing—she's

laughing so damn hard there are tears in her eyes. I think I might have broken her. I wait for her to stop laughing.

"Something funny?" I ask.

"Yes, do you really think I couldn't tell the difference?"

Thinking this over, I just shrug.

"Zac, it's fine. You don't need to worry. I'm on birth control and I'm as clean as you can get."

Lying down, I pull her into my arms, the place where she belongs. She sighs as she settles into the nook of my shoulder.

Kissing the top of her head, I muse, "Sunshine, I'm not worried about you getting knocked up. I was worried you would hate me if you did, though. And I sure as shit was not thinking you weren't clean."

"I'm not saying I'd be stoked if I got pregnant, but I wouldn't hate you for it, Zac. I don't hate kids. I'm just petrified at the thought of leaving a child in this world like I was." She's so quiet as she tells me this.

I squeeze her a little tighter. "Alyssa, you are not alone anymore. You have a family now. And whether or not you want us, Bray and Ella, even Dean, we are your family now. I love you. I know Ella adores you and Bray and Dean, well, I feel a little sorry for you, getting lopped in with those two morons. But we love you, and when we make children together, all of our family will love them unconditionally."

Looking up at me, she says, "I love you too. And Bray and Dean are not morons, Zac." She thinks on this a bit before adding, "Well, Bray might be a little, but I'll deny it till I'm blue in the face if you tell him I said that."

Chuckling, I reach over to turn out the light. "You need to get some sleep, baby."

"Good night, Zac. I love you so damn much." "Goodnight, sunshine. I love you too. Now go to sleep. I've kept you awake long enough."

Seventeen

ALYSSA

I WAKE up alone in Zac's bed. Reaching over, I feel his side of the bed is cold. He must have been up a while. I debate just closing my eyes for a few more minutes, but mother nature is calling.

After going to the bathroom, I find Zac's discarded shirt from yesterday on the floor. I put it on and roll the sleeves up a little. I decide that it covers enough of me. I mean, the shirt stops mid-thigh; it could almost be a dress. I walk out in search of Zac.

I find everyone in the living room, everyone being: Zac, Bray, Dean, Reilly, Sarah, Holly and Ella. All eyes swing my way when they hear me walking in.

Bray wolf whistles, smirking at me. "Damn, Lyssa, are you sure you picked the right brother?"

Zac slaps him across the head as he stalks towards me. He says nothing, just turns me around and leads me back to the bedroom.

"*Umm,* Zac, as much as I'd love to play around again. I think you need to give my vagina some recovery time," I say.

"Sunshine, there are two hot-blooded males out in our living room. You need to put clothes on before you walk out." I watch as he walks into his wardrobe and comes out with a pair of my yoga pants I've left here, a sports bra and a shirt. He lays the clothes on the bed.

Roaming his eyes up and down my body, he says, "Maybe I should just kick them all out and leave you in that shirt all day. You look fucking good in that shirt, Alyssa."

Laughing, I grab the yoga pants and pull them on. "Zac, you're not kicking them out. You know Bray only says those things to get a rise out of you, right? I'm pretty sure he is hung up on Reilly."

Groaning, he says, "I know he does, and it works every damn time."

Zac watches intently as I strip his shirt off and put on the bra he pulled out for me. "It's such a shame to cover those breasts up. It's like covering up the Mona Lisa or the David. They are a bloody work of art."

I have no response to that. I just laugh and pull on the shirt—another one of his shirts—which falls down to my thighs. I tie the shirt up so it sits just above my waist line.

Zac groans. Running his hands through his hair, he says, "Really, sunshine, is there anything you don't look like every man's wet dream in?"

Looking down at myself then back up at him, I respond, "I'm literally in yoga pants and a shirt, Zac. Hardly the stuff dreams are made of."

Wrapping me up in his arms, he whispers in my ear, "You are more than what I ever could have dreamed up. You don't even know the effect you have on men."

I step back and towards the door, because, coffee, I need coffee. I look back over my shoulder to see Zac now staring at my ass.

Winking at him, I say, "It's a good thing the only person I care to affect is you then, *huh*?"

Walking into the living room, I notice Dean scrambling to pick up papers from the coffee table; everyone stops talking at once.

I smile sweetly at Dean and, with the sternest voice I can muster right now, I say, "I'm going to go make a coffee, then I'm coming back in here and you will tell me everything that you found out about this psychopath."

Dean's face falls; his mouth opens and closes. He looks behind me to Zac, as if searching for what he should do. I don't give either of them the chance to come up with anything to prevent me from finding out what they are all hiding. Turning around, I grab Zac's hand and start pulling him into the kitchen.

"Babe, can you help me figure out how to use that fancy coffee machine of yours?"

The minute we step into the kitchen, Zac picks me up, sitting me on the countertop before walking over to the coffee machine. He presses a few buttons and returns to me with a steaming cup of vanilla latte. Could this man get any dreamier?

He steps between my legs, rubbing his hands up and down my thighs, as I sip at the deliciousness that is my vanilla latte. Closing my eyes, I let out a little moan as I savour the flavours in my mouth.

"Sunshine, if you keep that up, I will not be held responsible when I fuck you right here."

He pulls me flush against him so I can feel how aroused he is when my core meets the hard length of his cock.

"As fun as that sounds, you have a house full of people just in the other room. And I have a conversation to be had with Dean."

As I try to push him back, so I can jump down off the bench, he grabs my waist and says, "We."

Confused, I scrunch my face and look up at him. "*Huh*?"

"*We* have a houseful of people," he explains.

I just roll my eyes and walk back into the living room, where once again, everyone stops talking at once.

"Okay, out with it. Someone had better tell me what is so bad that you all stop talking the minute I step into the room."

I look from person to person, all of whom are looking behind me to Zac, who in turn is glaring at each and every one of them.

"Seriously, somebody better start talking!"

It's Sarah that breaks. I knew she wouldn't be able to keep anything from me. "*Ah,* Lyssa," she says and then looks at Zac. "Either you tell her, or I will. You aren't scaring me with the scowl that's pretty much permanently planted on your face."

Zac pulls me over to the couch, pulling me down onto his lap as he sits down. Sarah's wrong about the scowl; it's never on his face when he looks at me. All I ever see written on his face are love, adoration and lust—okay, lots of lust.

"Sunshine, you know I'm not going to let anything happen to you, right?"

I nod my head but don't say anything.

"Okay, well, Dean went and helped himself into Caitlyn's apartment last night. He took some photos of something she had attached to one of the walls in her living room."

He watches my face. I'm not sure if he's waiting for me to break, or if he just wants to buy time before actually getting to the point.

"Okay, so show me the pictures. What was on the wall?"

Zac shakes his head no. "You don't need to see the pictures, babe. They were disturbing as shit for me to see."

Pretending to think this over and agree with him, I nod my head before I stand up to place my empty cup on the coffee table. That's when I move fast, picking up the big yellow envelope I saw Dean

shoving papers into. Tipping the envelope upside

down, I empty the contents onto the coffee table before anyone can stop me. I stare down at the images. Lots of images of Zac. Some of Zac and me together. In all of those, a big red cross is drawn across my face.

"Fuck," Zac grunts and curses as he turns me around. "Sunshine, I really didn't want you to have to see that."

I don't move or say anything for a while; a lone tear drops down my cheek. Zac is quick to wipe it away. I don't want to think about this anymore. I want to bury my head in the sand and pretend like everything is perfect. Then I remember the plans the girls and I made with Ella last night to go shopping together today.

"I'm going shopping with Ella and the girls today," I say to Zac, who has shock written all over his face.

Turning, I say to the girls, "Give me ten minutes to get changed and I'll be ready."

Then a fun idea comes to me. Turning back to Zac, I give him my biggest smile. "Can I borrow your car today, babe?"

If I thought Zac's face showed shock before, it has nothing on the look he has now. I hear Bray coughing and spluttering in the background.

Zac stands there, stumbling over his words. "*Uhh,* babe… *umm…* well… you know…"

He's looking for a way to say no. I'm not going to help him. I just stand there and smile sweetly.

Ella is laughing so hard she's rolled over, holding her stomach. "What's the matter, Zac, cat got your tongue?" she teases.

Dean laughs a little before adding, "Stay strong, bro. Don't do it."

Zac seems to recover from his shock. I watch as his face morphs into that cocky smirk that would drop any girl's panties. "Sunshine, I can drive you to the mall, and then come back and get you when you're done." He smiles like he just solved all of his problems.

Leaning up, I kiss him on his cheek, letting my lips just brush the corner of his mouth while pressing my breasts a little harder than necessary into his chest.

"That's sweet, babe. But really, I want to drive. Besides, it will be good for Ella and me to have some girl bonding time, don't you think?"

He groans, running his hands through his hair. I've learnt he does this when frustrated. "Sunshine, it's just that… well, I don't…" He doesn't finish his sentence.

Bray calls out, "Way to tell her no, bro."

Zac flips him off, then smiles at me, a light in his eyes. "How about we go shopping and I buy you your own car?"

Okay, well, now *I* drop my mouth open in shock. Reilly spits out the mouthful of water she was drinking.

Bray continues mocking Zac, "Damn, the boy is whipped!"

Zac ignores them all, smirking at my silenced face. Shaking off the shock, I say, "*Umm*, no, you are not buying me a bloody car, Zac. If you don't want me to drive your car, all you have to do is say so. I'll try not to be too offended, you know, considering you let Reilly drive it that one time. But it's okay. If you don't trust me enough to drive it, I'll survive."

Patting him on the chest, I'm about to turn and walk into the bedroom when Zac grabs onto my wrist, stopping me.

"Baby, I trust you completely. If you really want to drive, then you can take the car." He leans in, bringing his lips to meet mine.

Ella walks past and says, "Damn, that was quick."

I smile up at Zac. I can't help but laugh a little. "Thanks, babe, but actually, could you drive us? There's a new wine bar that I want to show Ella." I feel a little bad for putting him through that stress. I have to confess, "I never wanted to drive the Batmobile, you know, just curious if you'd let me."

"Damn, babe, that's harsh," Bray laughs.

Zac turns his attention to his brother, glaring him down. "Her name's Alyssa. She's not *babe* to you, asshole."

Then turning back to me, he very sincerely states, "You know, I'd give you anything you want, right? And I think the whole car shopping idea has merit. While you girls are shopping for whatever girly shit you shop for, Dean and I are going to buy you a car.

You should probably go get ready, babe." He accentuates the *babe* at the end.

Walking down the hallway, back to the bedroom, I call out, "You're not buying me a damn car, Zac."

I hear him laughing just before I shut the door. *He is joking, right?* There's no way he is actually going to go shopping for a car. That's crazy... of course he's joking. Clearing my head, I get changed into a pair of cut-off denim shorts and a tank top. I'm sitting on the edge of the bed, lacing up my Chucks, as Zac walks in.

His eyes travel up and down my bare legs. "*Uhh*, sunshine, I think you're missing some material on those shorts of yours."

Standing, I walk over to him, ignoring his remark about my shorts. It's December in Sydney—it's bloody hot out.

"Thank you for driving us. I really appreciate everything you do for me. You know that, right?"

He tilts his head. "Yeah, babe, it's my pleasure to do things for you. Are you okay?"

"Well, I feel a little bad about making you think I wanted to drive your car. You looked really stressed out there."

He wraps his arms around my waist. "Sunshine, I love you, so damn much. I wasn't stressed about you driving the car, and I know this will sound irrational, but I was worried about you being out without me. Especially right now, when we have no idea what Caitlyn is capable of."

I get he would be worried about my safety, but that stress was definitely more about his car. I raise an eyebrow at him silently. After a minute, he relents.

"Okay, maybe I was a little worried about my car too. But there is not a shadow of a doubt that I love you way more than I love that car, Alyssa."

Laughing, I reach up and kiss him. "I believe you. Now, let's get going. There's only two weeks until Christmas and I haven't bought a single present yet. Also, you know you *can* say no to me. I'm not a princess, Zac. I'm not going to have a tantrum if something doesn't go my way."

Zac walks over to his dresser and, as he pulls something out, he says, "I know, but I have the means to give you whatever you want, and the desire to see you happy. Here, I had this ordered for you."

He walks out the door, leaving me standing in his room holding a black credit card with my name on it.

I follow him out of the room while waving the card around like a looney and screeching at him, "*Umm*, Zac, this is a credit card. Why would you give me a credit card?"

He laughs. "I know what it is, sunshine. It's linked to my personal account—there is no limit." He looks at me like I'm the crazy one here, like he just hands out credit cards to everyone he meets. What is he, Oprah?

Bray swipes the card out of my hand. "Damn, you gave her the black card? Bro, you wouldn't even give *me* a black card." Bray whistles then looks at me.

"If you don't want this thing, Lyssa, I'll be more than happy to take care of it for you."

Zac snatches the card out of Bray's grasp. "Shut up, idiot."

He places the card back in my hand. "Sunshine, it's for you. Use it... don't use it. But I want you to have it, please."

"Okay, I'll hold on to this, but I'm not using it, Zac. I don't need your fancy money. I work too, you know. I have my own money. Well, maybe not like your money kind of money, but I have money." I'm rambling because the fact that he just gave me an unlimited credit card makes me nervous.

Does he think I'm with him for his money? That I need him to buy me pretty, shiny things to be happy? Oh god, is he going to expect me to become a kept woman? To stop working, stay home and go to brunch with the ladies? I look around at everyone, and they're all staring at me. Oh god, I'm hyperventilating. I don't think I can live up to those kinds of expectations. I went my whole life having to work and fight for everything I needed to survive.

"Sunshine, breathe in... out. It's okay. I've got you." I feel Zac's arms brace me.

"Zac, I don't think I'm the kind of girl you want. I will never be okay with being a kept woman. I can't become fully dependent on someone."

He rubs his hands up and down my back, then brings them up to my face.

Holding my face still so I'm looking into his eyes,

he responds quietly, "Alyssa, you are the only girl I want, however you come. I don't need you to be anything but who you are, okay?"

I nod, not able to form words right now. Zac leans down, kissing me until my body feels like it's melting into him.

He pulls back and questions, "You good?"

"I'm good. Sorry, I kind of had a tiny freak-out moment."

"I don't mind—just gives me an excuse to hold you longer before you disappear on your shopping trip." He smirks.

"*Uh-huh*, let's go." I turn around to see the living room empty. "Wait, where did everyone go?" I ask, looking around the now empty room.

"I told them we would meet them in the garage." Zac picks his keys up off the hall table and throws them at me. "Come on, sunshine, you're driving."

Ah, wait, what? Running out the door, I catch up with him at the lift.

"Zac, I can't drive that thing. No way. I can't. I mean, what if I scratch it? Or crash, or worse?"

Zac scrunches his eyebrows at me. "Babe, what could be worse than crashing it?" Laughing, he pulls me into the lift.

"I don't know, Zac. Stop laughing at me." I try to give my best glare, but he shrugs it off.

"Let's get you to the mall. I'm looking forward to seeing the look on Bray's face when I tell him he's going with you girls shopping."

"Why are you making Bray go on our girls' shopping trip, Zac? We will be at the mall. It's a really public place. Nothing will happen." I try to reason with his overprotective nature.

"You won't even know he's there, babe."

I look at him like he has lost his mind, because if he thinks Bray could be anywhere and not be noticed, then he for sure has lost the plot.

"Doubtful," I say as we exit the lift into the parking garage.

WE'VE BEEN in the mall for two hours and I still have absolutely no idea what I can get Zac for Christmas. I mean, what do you get the guy who has everything?

"What about socks?" Sarah asks, unable to keep a straight face.

"Socks? You want me to get the hottest man on earth socks for Christmas?"

"I object to that statement. He may be in line for

number two, but I definitely have the number one spot, sweetheart." Bray smugly smiles while draping an arm over my shoulder.

I look at the arm he has on me then raise an eyebrow at him. "You know your brother will probably lose his mind when he smells your scent all over me."

Bray immediately drops the arm. "Harsh, Lyssa, harsh."

"What about Victoria's Secret? I mean, the thing Zac seems to want most in the world at the moment is you, so why not get something a little sexy that he can unwrap off you?" Reilly suggests.

"You know, I'd be all for unwrapping you on Christmas morning, princess." Bray waggles his brows at Reilly, who is too busy examining her nails to acknowledge him.

"Hey, maybe I could do that for my boyfriend this year, since you think it's such a great idea and all, Bray," Ella so sweetly drops while winking at me.

Bray stops walking, turning around to Ella and pointing. "No, Ella, just no. Wait, you don't have a boyfriend, right? No, you're not allowed to have boyfriends yet, and you sure as shit are not allowed to wear anything from Victoria's Secret *ever*. Fuck."

"Okay, Bray." Ella shrugs her shoulders as she walks around him.

Ignoring Bray's little meltdown, Reilly links her arm with mine. "What do you think, Lyssa?"

"I think it's a great idea actually. Sarah, do you

think you could get your photographer friend to meet us at our place tonight?"

"Yeah, I'll text him now. Wait, are you doing what I think you're doing?" she asks.

Nodding my head, I respond, "Yep, I'm going to do a boudoir photoshoot. It's a good thing my best friend is a makeup artist. Think you can fit me in today?"

"It'll be tough, but I think I can manage." She smiles as we walk into Victoria's Secret.

Okay, I'll need wine, lots of wine, to have the courage to go through with this. I can't believe this is what I came up with. I mean, get me alone in a bedroom with Zac and I can be brazen. Posing in lingerie in front of a photographer, I'm not so sure. But I want to do this. I want to give him something that will blow his mind.

My phone blares "Stuck Like Glue" from my pocket. I still haven't gotten around to changing it yet. I quickly turn my phone to silent. Pulling it out, I see a text message from Zac and a smile automatically grazes my lips.

My own GQ: Sunshine, hope you're having fun. Quick question, if you had a choice between white or red, which colour would you go for?

Laughing, because I was literally just thinking the same thing standing in front of the red lingerie. I take a selfie in front of the rack and send it to him.

Me: Funny, I was just thinking the same

thing. I'm leaning towards the red. What do you think?

Immediately, the little dots on the screen start bubbling, showing that he is replying.

My own GQ: I think you just gave me a damn hard-on. RED!!!

My own GQ: Please tell me you are not in a lingerie shop with my brother right now. Dammit, I knew I should have come with you.

I knew that wouldn't pass his attention. I take a snap of Bray and Ella arguing with each other at the front of the store and send it to him.

Me: Don't worry, Bray is too busy arguing with Ella. Apparently, she is not allowed to wear Victoria's Secret. His words, not mine. Ella says she's been wearing Victoria's Secret since she was fifteen, and that she's had one of your fancy little black cards for a while and you're not very good at checking the receipts.

My own GQ: Please tell me you are joking!

Lyssa: Nope, sorry.

My own GQ: You have just ruined Victoria's Secret for me, thank you!!

Lyssa: So, you don't want me to buy anything?

My own GQ: Babe, you don't need fancy lingerie. You know I'm just going to rip it off anyway. But yes, buy red, lots and lots of red! Please.

Me: Mmm, since you asked nicely and all, I'll see what I can manage. Got to go, I'm heading into the changeroom now.

My own GQ: Cruel, you are being cruel!!! FaceTime???

Me: Not a chance. Have fun doing whatever it is you're doing... love you.

My own GQ: Right now, I'm trying not to let it be obvious that I have a fucking hard-on in the middle of Mercedes, because apparently all I have to do is think about my gorgeous girlfriend in lingerie for him to be at attention. Love you too, babe.

Putting my phone away, I pick up random pieces of red lingerie.

"*Ah*, Lyssa, not to burst your bubble or anything, but do you really think Zac is going to let some guy take photos of you in lingerie?" Bray grumbles behind us.

"Well, he won't know about it if you don't tell him, right, Brayden?" I glare at him.

"Sweetheart, if you think he won't find out, you're out of your damn mind." Ignoring him, I head for the changing room.

I've just sent Sarah out to get a size larger for the last lacy red teddy I want to try on. I hear footsteps outside of the dressing room and someone comes to a stop in front of the door. Thinking it's Sarah back with the teddy for me to try on, I'm about to open the door when I look down and see the shoes under the bottom of the door and freeze.

Whoever is standing on the other side of the door is not Sarah. I can hear heavy breathing of someone who sounds as though they have been running. I watch as the combat boots shuffle against the floor. I'm reaching for my phone, about to call Bray, when a piece of paper floats under the door, landing at my feet. I watch the boots disappear as fast as they appeared.

I'm frozen in place, standing in a Victoria's Secret dressing room in my bra and panties. I don't know whether to bend down and pick up the paper, or ignore it and leave it there. Curiosity gets the better of me. Picking up the sheet of paper, I turn it over, a blood-curdling scream escaping my throat.

I'm huddled in the corner of the dressing room on the floor. I can hear Sarah and Reilly banging on the door, attempting to open it while simultaneously attempting to coax me into opening the door for them. But I'm frozen. I can't seem to move. I stare at the photograph in my hands, a photo of my mother's headstone, only next to her headstone in the photo stands another headstone, a new one. One with my name and birthdate on it. Underneath the birthday, the tombstone reads:

Died too young, because she touched what didn't belong to her.

WHY, why is she doing this to me, to us? What have I done in my life to warrant this kind of treatment? How does one person attract two psychopathic stalkers in one lifetime? Not even a lifetime, in the span of just three years? Is the relationship I have with Zac worth putting up with this kind of torment? Am I prepared to face the devil with the possibility she may just be crazy enough to find a way to end my life?

I mean, she got past all of my friends and Bray without being noticed. Bray… With my breathing coming back under control, I can hear him arguing with Sarah and Reilly on the other side of the door.

He knocks lightly and coaxes, "Sweetheart, I need you to open the door for me, okay? Can you do that, Lyssa? Please open the door for me. I can call Zac for you; he will be here before you know it. But I need you to open the door."

It's at his mention of Zac that I'm able to answer my own questions. *Yes*. Yes, I am prepared to endure whatever kind of torment this bitch throws my way, because he is mine. And in this life, you fight for what's yours; you don't cower on the floor of a dressing room. With that resolve, I stand up and unlock the door. Bray takes one look at me before barging into the small dressing room, shutting the door behind him.

Sarah and Reilly are both on the other side of the door, arguing with him to let them in. He ignores them as he picks up my tank top from the bench, silently putting it over my head and threading my arms through. He then bends and pulls my shorts up my legs. There is nothing but genuine care in his eyes.

Once I'm clothed again, Bray pulls me into his arms. "What happened?" he asks.

Still unable to find words, I show him the piece of paper. "Fuck." He scrunches the paper in his hands, "I'm going to fucking kill her, I swear. Shit, I have to call Zac." Just as Bray is pulling his phone out of his pocket, I stop him.

"Bray, wait, don't call him yet. I'll call him and have him meet us at the wine bar." Taking in a shaky breath, I can do this.

Bray shakes his head no at me. "Lyssa, we have to tell him; he will want to know. Fuck, it's possible he will kill me if I don't tell him."

"I'm going to call him. I don't want him to worry or rush back to get here. I'm not letting this bitch ruin our day again, Bray." Then I smirk at him, needing to lighten the mood. "If you think he'll kill you for not calling him, what do ya think he'll do when he finds out you were in a dressing room with me while I was in a state of undress?"

The look on his face is hysterical—he looks tortured. I can't help but laugh out loud at his torture. "Don't worry, Bray, I'll make sure he doesn't kill you."

He shakes his head. "And how exactly do you plan to do that?"

Smiling, I say, "Simple, I'll just ask him really nicely to spare you."

Bray opens the door to all the girls on the other side. "How the fuck did I get lumped with you all. This is bullshit. Hurry up and check out, Lyssa. We need to get out of here."He storms off to the front of the store.

Eighteen

ZAC

*A*FTER DROPPING Alyssa and Ella at the mall to meet up with the other girls and Bray, I made my way to the Mercedes-Benz dealership. I smile as I remember the look of horror he had on his face when I told him he would be joining in on the girls' shopping. The horror faded quickly, turning into more of a scowl when he looked Reilly's way.

I'm sure I'm likely to get pushback from Alyssa about this purchase, but I don't care how much of a fight she puts up. She needs a car and I have the means to get her one. It's a no-brainer, really. We've been here for around two hours, and I've finally decided on the car. I'm waiting for the paperwork to be finalised.

Dean stopped asking if I was sure I knew what I was doing purchasing this car, and if maybe I should look at something smaller—a little coupe like I just got Ella for her eighteenth. I had to tell him to shut up and get onboard. He hasn't questioned me since, although I don't miss the inquisitive looks he sends my way. I've been ignoring them mostly, occasionally answering them with raised eyebrows, daring him to say whatever the fuck he's thinking.

We're sitting in an office, waiting on the salesman to come back in with the final paperwork. I'm working on getting my hard-on to go down after texting with Alyssa. Why the hell couldn't I be in the Victoria's Secret with her right now? I know she's in the dressing room trying on lingerie, and I can't stop picturing her creamy skin in red lace. Groaning, I shake the thoughts from my head.

Dean looks over at me. "What's up with you?"

"Alyssa is at Victoria's Secret, trying on lingerie right now," I say, needing no more explanation.

Dean laughs. "Man, you have it so bad. You know, I think she's good for you, keeps you on your toes."

Yes, she does.

"I know it's quick, but I'm one hundred percent certain that she's the one."

Dean processes this—that's what he does, always quietly processing and analysing everything.

"Then why the fuck are we shopping for a car and not a ring? Because you really should lock that shit down before she wakes up and realises what she's been lumped with."

Looking over at him, I think about it. "Do you think she'd accept a ring yet? We could go hit up

Tiffany and Co. next," I ask in all seriousness. Dean laughs as the salesman enters the office.

"All right, Mr. Williams, it's all ready. One red Mercedes-Benz G-Class G63 AMG, in the name of Alyssa Summers. The car will be ready for delivery on the twenty-second of the month."

At first, I was told I'd have to wait until February for the car—it's the middle of December now. When I not so kindly informed them that I'd be paying cash and I expected to have a car delivered prior to Christmas day, the salesman almost shit himself. He came through though. They always do when they realise you have money. I figured I'd put a big-ass bow on it and call it a Christmas present. She can't reject a Christmas gift, can she?

"I just need you to sign here, and here," the salesman says, pointing out where I need to sign. "You'll need to leave a twenty percent deposit today and the rest will be due two days prior to delivery." Pulling out my wallet, I hand over the black card and say, "Put it on this."

He takes the card, and standing, he goes out to the front, returning a moment later before handing over the card and paperwork.

I hand the paperwork over to Dean. "Hold on to this for me, will you?"

He looks at me confused. "*Ah*, why?" he asks. "Because I don't want there to be any chance that Alyssa finds out about this purchase before Christmas Day," I reply as though that should explain it.

Thanking the salesman, we make our way back out of the building. I'm about to get in the car when my phone plays "My Girl." I smile, knowing immediately that Alyssa is calling, with the hope she changed her mind on the FaceTime request while in the Victoria's Secret dressing room.

I throw the keys to Dean. "You drive," I say as I answer the call and walk around to the passenger side. "Sunshine, change your mind about a dressing room FaceTime call?" I ask, hopeful.

"Zac, hi. *Umm,* no… no FaceTime call, sorry." There's a slight hitch in her voice.

"What's wrong?" I ask, knowing something's made her upset.

"*Ah*, nothing's wrong. I'm fine… just, *umm…* wondering if you can meet us at the wine bar. We're heading there now. But if you're busy, that's okay. I'll just… just see you later."

Shit, she's rambling. There is definitely something wrong. "I'm never too busy for you, babe. We'll be there in about fifteen minutes, okay?"

I know she's not okay, but I also know she's not about to tell me that right now.

"Sure, I'll see you soon." Shit, she sounds fucking sad but before I can add anything, she quietly says, "I love you, Zac."

"Love you too, sunshine. I'll be there before you know it."

I'm trying to stay calm, to not let on that I know she's not okay. I don't want her to be any more upset than she already is. I can tell how much she is trying to keep it together.

"Okay," she says before hanging up.

"Fuck, get to the mall as quickly as you can, Dean."

In my head, I'm running through all the possibilities of what could have happened at the damn mall to make her so upset.

"What's wrong?" Dean asks.

"I don't know, man. I could just tell something was off. She wouldn't say, but I just know. Fuck. I should have gone with her. I should have had Bray go pick out the car."

Before I know what I'm doing, I'm dialling Bray's number. He's been with her… Why the fuck didn't he call me himself if something happened?

"Hey, bro, what's up?" he answers the phone in a way too cheery voice—that's his giveaway that something happened.

"What the fuck happened to Alyssa, Bray? And don't lie to me right now. I know something happened."

I hear the intake of breath, and the tell of a hand covering the phone, before he not so quietly says, "You didn't tell him? Damn, Lyssa," in the background.

"Bro, she's fine, okay? Not a hair out of place." Great, now he's trying to placate me. The longer they are not telling me, the more pissed off I'm getting.

"Bray, tell me *what-the-fuck-happened*," I demand. I

know I'm yelling, and if Alyssa is anywhere near Bray, she will be able to hear me. Taking a calming breath, I try again, voice quieter, "Please, Bray, I need to know."

"Okay, while she was in the dressing room at Victoria's Secret, someone slipped a piece of paper under the door. None of us saw anything. We were all in the store and we didn't see the person."

Closing my eyes, I'm doing everything I can to not yell right now. "What was on the paper?" I ask in a much calmer voice than what I am feeling.

"*Ah*, it was a photo of a tombstone," he says hesitantly.

A tombstone, someone slid a picture of a fucking tombstone under the door. What the fuck.

"Whose tombstone was in the picture, Bray?" I ask, needing more information.

"Look, she's okay, Zac. I've got her right next to me. Actually, she's so close to me it would probably give you a coronary if you saw."

He's probably right, but I also know he's trying to distract me.

"Bray, do me a favour and send me through a picture of the piece of paper. Keep her fucking close. I swear… if anything happens to her…" I let my sentence drown off, because the thought of anything happening to her is inconceivable.

"Okay, I'll send a picture. See you when you get here, bro." He hangs up before I can reply.

Bray sends the picture through straight away. The

KYLIE KENT

moment I've zoomed in on the image, my blood goes cold. There are two tombstones, one older looking one. I can barely make out the name on it to be Sophia Summers. The other tombstone, a newer looking tombstone, has Alyssa's name on it. Her name and date of birth.

"Zac, we're here, man." Dean shakes me out of my frozen state.

Looking around, I see that we're in the mall's carpark. I don't recall any of the drive here. How long have I been staring at this image? I'm going to fucking kill her. I've never killed a woman before, never even thought I'd have it in me to do it. But the woman who is threatening Alyssa's life? I would enjoy watching the life fade out of her as I cut off her air supply.

"Zac, snap the fuck out of it. You can't go in there like this. You'll scare your girl more than she already is."

Dean's right. I know he's right, but he hasn't seen the picture. He doesn't know the inferno that was just set inside me. I will burn down this whole damn town until I find the bitch.

"Dean, I need you to get copies of all the cameras inside the Victoria's Secret store here. Find out what cemetery Alyssa's birth mother is buried in and send someone out there. I want to know if this picture has just been cleverly edited, or if that psychopath put a tombstone there."

Dean scrunches his eyebrows. "Tombstone? What tombstone?"

"Someone slid a piece of paper under the dressing room door while Alyssa was changing. It was a picture of a tombstone. A tombstone with Alyssa's fucking name on it." I hold up my phone to show him the picture.

Dean nods his head. "Send me a copy of that. I'll get on it."

"Thanks, man. Take the car. We'll get a ride back with Bray. Meet me at mine in a few hours?" I ask.

"Yeah, sure. Do you want to look at hiring personal security for Alyssa? It might be a good idea; we don't know how far Caitlyn's prepared to go."

I'm not sure how Alyssa will take having bodyguards.

"I'll think about it. I don't plan to let her out of my sight again in a hurry anyway."

WALKING INTO THE BARREL, the new wine bar that Alyssa wanted to take Ella and the girls to, I notice her table straight away. I hear her laugh; it registers deep within my soul. I stand there for a while, taking in the room. It's rustic, old wine barrels randomly placed around the middle of the room stand as bar tables. The edges of the room are sectioned off with brown Chesterfield lounges and wingback chairs.

Alyssa is sitting in a lounge next to Bray—the fucker is way too close to my girl. I continue to watch her for a moment. As much as I want to run up to her and wrap her in my arms, I enjoy watching her in moments like these. She's unguarded, a flush stains her cheeks. She's laughing at something Reilly says at the same time Bray is scowling towards the fiery redhead. I watch as she brings a wine glass to her lips and sips, running her tongue along her bottom lip when she pulls the cup away. Fuck, now is not the time for a hard-on. Just as she's about to raise the glass to her mouth again, she looks directly at me. It's almost like she can sense when I'm in the same room as her. I can never stay hidden for long.

A huge smile grazes her face; her eyes light up. Nudging my head, I indicate for her to come to me. I need a moment alone with her, away from the prying ears of our family and friends.

Putting her glass on the low centre table, she says something to Bray before standing. He looks over, nodding his head in acknowledgement. I glare back at him, because frankly, he looked way too comfortable that close to my girl. Bray smirks back at me. *Fucker.*

I watch as Alyssa saunters towards me in those little fucking shorts, her long legs on full display for everybody to get a look at—which, right now, I can clock at least five men who let their gazes linger a little too long on her. I give them all a glare, at which point they advert their gazes.

As soon as she's in arm's reach, I pull her into me, slamming my lips against hers. She instantly melts into me. The taste of sweet white wine lingers on her tongue, as she meets me stroke for stroke. I get so lost in the moment that I forget where we are. I forget about the picture that had my blood run cold. I forget it all as I try to communicate with her just how much I fucking love her with this kiss.

Pulling back, she smiles up at me. "*Mmm*, hi."

"Hi, sunshine. How are you feeling?" I ask, not wanting to ruin this moment but also needing to know if she really is okay. I pin her with my eyes as I wait for her answer.

"I'm better, now that you're here," she responds, batting her eyelashes at me. I laugh and damn, it feels good to laugh.

"How are you really feeling? I saw the picture. Alyssa. You don't need to pretend, or to hide your feelings from me. You know that, right?"

I feel like I need to reassure her that, no matter what, I'm not going anywhere. I know she hasn't had that much in her life, always moving from one foster home to the next and constantly being let down by the people who were meant to care for her.

"I had a little freak-out when I saw it. But I made a decision not to let this crazy psychopath ruin my day, or your day. And I'm not about to let anybody scare me away from you, Zac. You are mine, not hers. I don't care what anyone says—you are mine." She stops to take a breath.

"I like being yours, sunshine. And we will not let anyone ruin what we have. This…" I say, pointing between the two of us. "This is a once in a lifetime kind of love. I'm not about to let that go." She blinks up at me a few times then smirks.

"You know? I get it," she says.

"You get what?" I hope that she gets just how much she means to me.

"How someone can become so crazily obsessed with you. I mean, you're kind of a catch, the complete package. I'm surprised there's only one crazy ex on the loose."

She thinks I'm the complete package. Maybe I should book in that trip to Tiffany and Co. for a diamond after all. I smile with this thought, then the rest of her speech registers. Crazy ex on the loose? Wait, does she think I had some kind of relationship with Caitlyn? Just the thought of that makes me shiver in disgust.

"Sunshine, we will come back to the part where you think I'm the complete package at a later date. But let me be very clear, so there is no misunderstanding. I did not, at any point in time, have any kind of relationship with this woman other than a professional one. She was my employee—that's it. Did I constantly turn down her advances and flirtation? Yes. Was there ever a time where I thought I'd want to fuck her? Absolutely not, not ever."

The only thing I want to do with Caitlyn is strangle the goddamn life out of her for threatening Alyssa.

"Okay, I believe you, Zac. Now let's enjoy our afternoon with your family and my crazy-ass friends," she says, pulling on my arm.

I stop her, pulling her back into me. "Our," I say, correcting her mistake.

"Our what?" she questions.

Smiling, I tell her, "*Our* family and *our* friends. There's no *mine* or *yours* anymore, sunshine. There is only *ours*."

Leaning up, she kisses my lips before ever so quietly saying, "There'll always be a tomorrow together for us." She says it so reverently and quietly, it's almost like a prayer falling from her lips. I don't even think she meant for me to hear it, but I did.

Leaning down into her ear, I tell her the same promise we tell each other every night before we go to sleep, "There will always be a tomorrow together for us, sunshine. I promise."

WE'VE BEEN SITTING HERE in this wine bar for an hour and a half. I can't say I've ever been to a wine bar before, but I'm enjoying myself. I'm enjoying seeing Alyssa relax and have fun. Everyone has gotten louder with each empty bottle of wine that's been left on the table. I have learnt that Alyssa loves any kind of sweet white wine, and I make a mental note to get a supply sent to my office and the penthouse.

"Oh, Lyssa! We need to go. We have to get home!" Sarah exclaims.

My body tenses. Like fuck is she taking Alyssa home. I look to Alyssa, to her mischievous smile as she gazes up at me.

"Oh, babe, I have to do something at my town-house. I forgot until just now," she says like that's all the explanation I need.

"What is it you have to do?" I ask. I know she's very tipsy, and if she thinks I'm letting her go anywhere without me, she's bloody nuts.

"*Umm…* I, *umm…* I have to… you know…" She's looking to all the girls to help her. Help her what?

What could she possibly have to do that she can't tell me?

"Told you he'd find out. You're a fucking hopeless liar, Lyssa." Bray laughs at her.

"Find out what?" I ask very pointedly to Alyssa, who is squirming in her seat.

"*Argh*, it's a surprise and I'm not telling you because it's a surprise for you. But you can't see it because it's a Christmas sort of surprise." She whacks Bray in the arm, then immediately shakes her hand out. "Man, do you have bricks lining your shirt? Damn you, Bray. I told you not to tell."

Bringing her fingers up to my mouth, I kiss each one better. "I didn't tell him, Lyssa. I just knew that he would find out, and I can't wait to see his face when he does." Bray smirks at her.

Now, I'm really intrigued as to what the surprise is, but I'm not going to ruin any surprise she wants to give me. I decide to let it drop. I'll drive her to her house, and even if I have to sit in the car the whole time, I will be there... just enough to not ruin the surprise for her.

Alyssa turns to Bray, a triumphant smile on her face. "Yeah, well, I can't wait to see the look on his face when he finds out you were in the dressing room with me when I was only wearing my bra and panties —" Her mouth stops, and it registers with her what she just said. Everyone at the table goes quiet and watches me.

My body has gone stiff, shoulders tense. *I can't kill*

my brother. I can't kill my brother. I keep replaying the mantra in my head as I breathe in and out. Alyssa looks back and forward between Bray and me before trying to fix what she just said.

"*Ah*, babe, it's not how that sounded!"

"Are you sure, sunshine? Because I just heard you say that my brother was in a dressing room with you while you were naked?" I ask her, my voice strained.

"Oh, for fuck's sake. She had just screamed the whole damn store down with a blood-curdling scream. Of course, I would barge in to see what the hell was wrong. And for your information…" Bray points to me. "I dressed her before anyone else saw her." He nods his head like: *That's that… I should be thankful that he was the only one who saw my girlfriend naked.*

"Plus, I wasn't naked. I had underwear on," Alyssa adds.

So not helping like she thinks she is. I don't know what to think, other than my brother saw my girl naked. I'm so fucking mad at myself for not being there. For not being the one who was there to help her when she needed help.

Blood-curdling scream? Bray said she let out a blood-curdling scream. That's a little more than a *tiny freak-out,* as Alyssa had told me she experienced when she picked up that picture. Fuck, I'm grateful for the foresight to send Bray along with the girls today. I'm grateful that he was there to help her, and I know, without a doubt, he would have been nothing but respectful towards Alyssa. I know my brother, and as much as he clowns around, deep down, he is a fucking decent guy—one of the best I know.

"I think you broke him," Reilly says, a slight concern to her voice.

Before I can respond, Alyssa slams her lips down on mine, swiping her tongue along my lips until I open for her, granting her the access she is seeking. *As if I'd ever deny her.* I can feel the tension leave my body with each stroke of her tongue against mine. I've never loved kissing anyone as much as I love kissing her. I think I could sit here and kiss her all day and not get bored.

Pulling back from the kiss, she looks at me. "I'm sorry, really sorry. Please don't hate me," she pleads.

Hate her? What the fuck? As if I could fucking hate her...

"Sunshine, I could never hate you. I slightly hate my brother right now, but I'll survive. I'll get over it... maybe."

Leaning into me, she whispers in my ear, "He was a true gentleman; he put my shirt on and shorts on without even saying a word. He didn't touch me at all, I promise. But if you tell him I said he's a gentleman, I'll deny it."

I laugh at that. He would hate being referred to as a *gentleman*.

Leaning in, I whisper in her ear, "Babe, I know he would be respectful. I know my brother. I never doubted his intentions. It's just a little fun to watch him squirm for a bit. But I'm glad he was there to help you.

I just wish that it was me. I should have been there."

"You can't be with me all the time, Zac. It's not how life works. Now, I need you to drive Sarah and me to our townhouse, because I have someone meeting me there."

Who does she have meeting her at her place? I want to question it, but when I remember how happy she was when she talked about how she has a surprise for me, I can't bring myself to question her. Like I just told her, I trust her completely.

Nineteen

ALYSSA

*Z*AC PULLS UP to the front of my townhouse. The drive here has given me time to sober up, which has returned the nervousness of what I'm about to do. *Think of Zac. Think of Zac.* Repeating that over and over in my head, I can see him on Christmas Day, opening a photo book filled with pictures of me in a range of red lingerie.

I've never felt more desired than when I'm with Zac. He has unintentionally given me a self-confidence boost I didn't know I needed. It's not like I hated my body image before he came along. I knew I was attractive enough, more like a girl next door kind of attractive. But Zac, he makes me feel like I'm more than that. He has no shame in letting anyone and everyone know how much he wants me all the time.

I can see the outline of a growing erection in his pants. The way he moves and tries to not so subtly rearrange his crown jewels also gives away that he's a little turned on right now. I'm actually not sure that he has an off switch. It seems like he's in a constant state of arousal. I didn't know it was possible for a guy to be so ready all the time.

Shit, these thoughts are just getting me all hot and bothered now. I look over to Zac, and he gives me that trademark smirk. His emerald eyes darken as he rakes his eyes up and down me, lingering on my heaving chest—which I'm sure anyone who cares to look can see the outline of my hardened nipples through the thin material of my tank top. Dammit, get it together, Lyssa. You've got a job to do. You can *do* Zac later tonight, many times over, no doubt.

"Okay, thanks for the lift, babe." Leaning over, I quickly peck his cheek. My attempts at a quick escape are halted as he grabs my wrist, stopping my hasty exit from the car.

"Sunshine, if you think for one minute, I'm just leaving you here, then you've lost your goddamn mind!" he exclaims.

Turning the car off, he opens his door and as I'm conjuring up ways to get him to leave, he makes his way over to my side of the car, holding his hand out to help me out. *Ever the gentleman.* I sigh, accepting his hand as I jump down from the car. Bray has a big SUV Mercedes-Benz. I like it a lot; the seats are air-conditioned. I mean, I didn't even know you could get air-conditioned seats, but apparently, they exist.

"I think I'm in love with your car, Bray," I say, turning to see Sarah, Ella and Bray all just staring at me, all three of them making the motions of eating popcorn, invisible popcorn. Rolling my eyes at them, I turn back to Zac. He has a weird, satisfied grin plastered on his face—I have no idea what that's about. But I know I need to get him out of here.

"Babe, you know I would usually invite you in and all, but you can't stay. I just need two hours, tops."

I turn to Sarah to see if my time estimate is right. She gives me a silent nod and a thumbs up, before returning to her imaginary popcorn. Dammit, okay, I'm gonna need to pull out the big guns to win this battle.

Facing Zac, I tilt my head up to look at him. Blinking my eyes, I stick out my bottom lip and ever so quietly plead with the most sugary-sweet voice I can muster, "Please, Zac, don't ruin your surprise. I really want to be able to give this to you. I promise I'm not leaving. I'll wait for you to come back and take me home to your place. And then I'm all yours for the rest of the night, to do with as you please." My voice morphs from sweet to sultry by the end of my plea.

"Fuck. Dammit, sunshine. You know it's bloody impossible to say no to you, right?" He pulls at the ends of his hair. I know he's torn between giving me what I want, and the need to protect me. Finally, he relents. "Okay, I won't come in. But Bray's staying with you."

Just as I'm about to open my mouth to argue that Bray is not staying, he says, "Not negotiable, babe. If I'm not able to be with you, then Bray will be."

I look over my shoulder to Bray for help, but the bastard just grins. Zac tilts my head up towards his. "Sunshine, please don't ask me to leave you unprotected. I can't do it."

Great, it seems I'm not the only one who has mastered the puppy-dog pout.

"Okay, thanks, babe. Love you. See you soon." "Ella, sweetheart, do you want to stay here or come back with me?" Zac asks.

It amazes me how this man, who I know can be ruthless as all hell, is such a big softy with his little sister. I envy how strong the relationships are with these three siblings. I wish I had that.

As a child, I spent many nights lying awake, dreaming of how different my life would have been if my mum didn't die. If I had siblings I could count on to be there in hard times... When I have kids, I definitely want at least three, so they all have each other to lean on.

Hold the front door. Where the hell did that thought just come from? *When* I have children?

What the hell happened to the girl who would literally have a panic attack at the thought of having kids? Zac happened—that's what happened.

I can see how much of a great dad he will be. He stepped up and took over raising a thirteen-year-old girl and a seventeen-year-old teenage boy. That could not have been easy by any standard. But he has never made it out to seem like a chore; he's never complained about having to grow up before his time. He loves his siblings, unconditionally. I know, without a shadow of a doubt, he will love our kids the same.

I'm brought out of my thoughts as I zone in to Bray and Zac arguing. "Zac, take her home. She does not need this level of influence—trust me on this," Bray is saying. Oh crap, he will let the cat out of the bag if he doesn't shut up.

Looking over to Ella, I plead silently with her. She gets it immediately.

"Don't worry, Bray. I'm going with Zac. I'd be bored out of my mind waiting around here anyway. It's not like I haven't seen or done these things with my friends before."

I can tell she is just trying to rile her brother up. There is no way sweet, innocent, little Ella has done this, *right?*

"Take that back, Ella. You can't say shit like that to me. Don't think I won't lock you up in that tower you live in and take away your keys." Bray is fuming. I'm sure a whole lot of unhelpful thoughts of his little sister are going through his mind right now.

"Okay, I'm out. Got things to do. Leave your sister alone, Brayden. Let's go."

I know I'm a little demanding, but I need to get out of this situation before Zac questions what it is I'm really doing here. Walking towards my front door, I don't look back. I'm doing this. I'm really, really doing this.

Okay, I can totally do this.

SITTING IN SARAH'S ROOM, I'm staring at my reflection in the mirror. She has transformed me from your average, sandy blonde girl next door to a 1950's pin-up model. My hair is made up of big barrel curls, pinned back with diamante hair pins. How she gives my hair this kind of shine, I will never understand. No matter how many times I watch her and attempt to retrace the steps on my own, I just can't seem to figure it out.

My eyes are smoky. She put on glue-on eyelashes, so my lashes are long, thick and dark—with dark eyeliner running along the bottom of my eyes before turning up into a wing on the tops of my eyelids. She has contoured my face, giving me much more defined features than I would normally have. My cheeks have a shiny, golden hue to them and my lips are painted in a bright red, wet-look lipstick.

"Wow." Turning to Sarah, I say, "I think you have really outdone yourself this time."

"Please, it's easy when what you're starting with is already a masterpiece," she says.

I hug her tight. "I know I haven't seen you as much these last few weeks, but I love you. You know that, right?"

"I love you too, and don't beat yourself up. I have been plenty busy myself over the last few weeks." A dreamy look briefly crosses her face before she continues. "I'm so happy that you are finally getting your happily ever after, Lyssa. If anyone deserves it, it's you. That it just so happens to come wrapped in that fine piece of ass is a total bonus," she says with a wink.

I laugh. "It really is one fine ass. I bet I could bounce a coin off it." I make a mental note to enquire about what or who her *busy* is later. "Okay, I can do this. We're doing the pictures in here, right?" I ask Sarah's very gay photographer friend Tom. I smile as I recall Bray's internal struggle with letting the photographer in the room with me.

"Yes, hon. Ready when you are, beautiful," Tom says.

I turn my face back to Sarah, partly so he doesn't see the blush working its way up my neck and face, while also trying to steal some of my friend's courage from her. Sarah would do this without even batting an eye. Me? I have to give myself internal pep talks and think about Zac, think about what his reaction will be.

Picking up the Victoria's Secret bag, I head for the bedroom door. "Okay, I'm going to change in my room. I'll be back in a sec."

"I'll help and also make sure you don't chicken out and make a break for it." Sarah's laugh follows me down the hall.

Our rooms are separated by a shared bathroom. Opening my bedroom door, my steps halt, Sarah running into the back of me.

"What the…" She doesn't finish the sentence. Or, at least, I don't hear her finish the sentence as I take in the scene in front of me.

No, no, no, no. This is not happening. Closing my eyes and reopening them, I attempt to change what they see. It doesn't work. This cannot be real; I must be dreaming. I'm frozen as I observe what used to be a somewhat orderly bedroom.

Everything has been thrown around, drawers opened… My clothes are shredded everywhere. I mean, literally, they are in shreds like someone has taken a pair of scissors and just hacked right through them. There is paint everywhere, red paint splashed all over the room, on the floor, on the walls—it's even on the ceiling.

The message that's written above what used to be my bedhead is what breaks my frozen stance and has me screaming at the top of my lungs. The message painted in what I'm hoping is red paint says:

I'm coming for you.
We will meet soon. xxx

OH MY GOD, all of my things, everything I have worked so hard to get, has been destroyed. Running to my wardrobe, I'm scrambling to the mess. No, she cannot have ruined it. I'm crying, rummaging, trying to find it. I can't find it. Why can't I find it?

Strong arms wrap around me and pull me back, stopping me from looking.

"No, I have to find it. It has to be here," I say as I fight my way out of his hold.

"*Shh*, sunshine, I've got you. I've got you. It's going to be okay."

It's not going to be okay; it's never going to be okay. Why doesn't he know? This is what my life is, one fucked-up situation after another. He would have been better off never having met me. But I can't think about that right now. I need to find that picture.

"I need to find it. It's here, somewhere. Please, just help me find it," I'm begging for anyone to help me.

Sarah gets down on her hands and knees and starts digging through the mess. She doesn't need to ask what she's looking for; she already knows.

Zac is still trying to hold me still. "Alyssa, I'll buy you another one. It's okay. Please stop." I hear his voice crack.

I turn to look at him, tears running down my face. "It's the only picture of my mother I have, Zac! You can't buy me another one!"

I feel defeated. Slumping to the ground, I curl into myself and let myself break.

Sarah wraps herself around me, whispering in my ear, "Lyssa, honey, you need to let Zac take you home. I'll stay here. I'll keep looking. I will find the picture for you and bring it to you. Please, just let Zac take you home, Lyssa."

I can't tell if it's Sarah's cries I hear, or my own. I'm only vaguely aware as I'm lifted into Zac's arms, and he carries me out of the house.

Twenty

ZAC

I'VE BEEN STANDING out front of Alyssa's townhouse for an hour. I was never planning to leave her here. Ella made sure I knew how much she did not like the fact I had called Dean to take her home.

Pulling my phone out, I give him a call to make sure Ella didn't put him through too much hell on the drive home. The phone only rings twice before he answers.

"Yeah?"

"I'm judging by the fact that you answered, you're still alive and my sister didn't manage to find a way to kill you yet?" I laugh.

I don't know what's going on with those two; Dean and Ella used to be really close. Lately, it's like they can't stand being in the same room together.

"I wouldn't put it past her to be plotting my

demise as we speak. She is your sister, after all," he says.

"Don't I know it."

I'm about to ask him what's up with the two of them when I hear someone scream. No, not someone, Alyssa. I hear Alyssa scream.

"Fuck!"

I'm holding the phone in my hand as I run towards Alyssa's front door, my heart pounding as I take the stairs two at a time. Barging my way past Bray and some other fucker in the doorway of Alyssa's bedroom, my heart feels like it's just been ripped out of my chest.

The room is a fucking mess. Where is she? Turning around, I spot her on the floor at her wardrobe, rummaging through shit while mumbling about needing to find something. *Fuck.* Grabbing her, I pull her back into my arms. She fights herself out of my hold, begging me to help her find whatever it is she's looking for.

Trying to reassure her that I can replace anything she needs, I freeze as her next words to me just break my fucking heart.

"It's the only picture of my mother I have, Zac! You can't buy me another one!"

That's not something I can replace. I watch as her body crumbles to the floor; she bends over herself and cries. I can feel the tears running down my own face. I haven't cried since my parents' funeral five years ago.

But the sight of Alyssa on the floor, looking so fucking broken, I can't take it.

I'm about to pull myself together, scoop her up, and put her back together. I can fix this. I have to fix this. Sarah leans over her, whispering in her ear. She's also fucking crying. She looks up at me.

"You need to take her home, Zac. Get her out of here. Please," she pleads with me.

I can see that she's looking to me to put her best friend back together right now. I'm not sure how I will do it, but I make a promise to anyone who will listen that I will do just that. I will do anything to take away Alyssa's pain.

I pick her up and walk down the stairs with her in my arms. Bray follows me down.

"I'll drive," he says just as Dean comes running through the door.

He takes one look at us and asks, "What happened?" looking at Alyssa's limp form in my arms.

It's just registering with me that she's not clinging to me like she usually would when experiencing a panic attack. This is different. I don't like how limp and unresponsive she's being. I know she's conscious to some extent; she's still crying and mumbling about finding that damn picture.

"Can you stay and help Sarah upstairs? Don't leave her alone. Bring her to the penthouse when she's finished here."

I can't even tell him what happened. I can't bring

myself to find the words, confirming that Caitlyn has finally managed to break down Alyssa.

Getting her home, I take her straight into the shower. She's stopped crying; she's just silently staring into space. She won't answer anything I ask her other than nodding or shaking her head. I honestly don't know how to help her. Should I call a doctor in? A trauma specialist, maybe? Fuck, I just need to figure out how to help her.

"Baby, please tell me how I can help you? What can I do?"

I keep my voice quiet, calm, or at least, I try to. But I'm breaking on the inside too. I'm breaking from seeing her like this. This is not Alyssa, not my sunshine, so full of life and promise. The girl standing in front of me, with her once beautiful blue eyes that are now dull, seems to look through me.

She doesn't answer me, so I continue to remove her clothes so I can get her in the shower. Just as I've pulled her tank top over her head, she says, "You can't help me, Zac. No one can."

Like fuck, I can't help her. I know that right now, she believes that, but she will see. We will get through this.

After washing her hair for her, I dry her and bundle her up in one of my shirts. I watch as she brings the material up to her face and inhales. That one little gesture shows me she is still my Alyssa. Mine, and fuck anyone who thinks they can take her from me. I lie down in bed with her and hold her.

Whispering to her, I promise to fix this. I promise her that, no matter what, our tomorrows will always be together.

IT'S BEEN two weeks since I carried Alyssa out of her bedroom in her townhouse and brought her back here. Two weeks and I still have no fucking clue where the fuck Caitlyn is holed up. I've had teams of private investigators looking for the bitch. I can't find a single fucking trace, and it's doing my head in.

It's been two weeks since Alyssa has left the penthouse. She puts on a brave front to everyone. She didn't fight me when I told her she should put in for a couple of weeks leave at work, which tells me she's not as good as she keeps insisting she is.

She can pretend to be fine, but it's the way she jumps at loud sounds, the way her hands shake a little, the way she clings to me when she becomes over-whelmed... All these little things tell me she is not okay at all. She is spooked, she's angry, and she's anxious about what's next.

Alyssa didn't get out of bed for two days. She barely ate. She spoke only in answer to a direct question and, even then, would only give two-word answers. On the third day after I brought her home, Sarah turned up, having found the photograph of Alyssa's mother. Fortunately, the picture was not damaged, and now lives locked inside the safe in my home office. After she received the picture back, Alyssa's spirits lifted again, and slowly, I saw my sunshine coming back to life.

Still, her laugh is not as full as it was, her smile not as bright. I didn't know my heart could hurt so fucking much, but the last two weeks, watching Alyssa struggle and fight with her fear, has fucking wrecked me. I feel useless right now. The only time she seems at total peace and relaxed are the times when it's just her and me in the bedroom. Every night, we have been up for hours, me wringing orgasm after orgasm out of her until I wear her out enough that I know she will get some sleep.

You won't hear me complaining about that task though. I will happily give my girl whatever release she needs, anywhere, anytime.

One thing I know for sure is that she is it. She is the girl I see my future with, the one I want to wake up next to every morning. And I will take her any way I can have her. If that means I spend the rest of my life fighting to bring life back, to restore the sunshine and happiness to her eyes, I will. If I have to spend every day proving to her that she is safe with me, that I'm not about to let any motherfucker get their hands on her, then that's what I'm going to do.

I'm lying in bed with Alyssa in my arms and I couldn't think of waking up any other way. It's Christmas Eve. I have her car in the garage with a huge fucking bow on it. I just have to figure out a way to get her to accept it. I've been lying awake for hours, conjuring up ways to get her to accept the car and accept the question I'm planning to ask her tomorrow morning. But first, today, the car.

Alyssa stirs, slowly opening her eyes. She is the definition of *not a morning person*. Grumbling, she smiles up at me.

"Morning, babe." She leans in and kisses me gently before settling her head on my chest.

"Morning, sunshine. Sleep well?" I ask, kissing the top of her head.

"*Mmhmm*, I always sleep well next to you," she mumbles back.

Huh, she's in a great mood today. Rolling her over to her back, I pin her down and kiss her. She responds immediately, opening for me. I pull away before I take things any further. A look of disappointment crosses her face as I get up.

Chuckling, I say, "Stay here. I'm going to get your coffee. I'll be back."

Not waiting for her to reply, I make my way out to the kitchen and set up the machine to make her coffee. As I'm walking out of the kitchen, Bray walks through the living room.

"Morning, how is she?" He asks the same thing every morning. He's been sleeping here for the last two weeks, around to help with whatever I needed, without question.

"She's good," I tell him and can't help the smile that appears on my face. Because for the first time in two weeks, I actually feel like it's the truth.

"That's good, bro. I'm taking Ella last-minute shopping today. Apparently, there is more shit she needs to get. Call if you need anything," he says as he walks into the kitchen.

"Thanks, man," I call after him.

Walking back into the bedroom, I'm greeted with the sight of Alyssa sitting up in my bed, smiling at me. Maybe it's the coffee she's smiling at, but I'll take it.

Holding her hands out, she says, "Give me, give me, give me."

Laughing, I hand over her vanilla latte. I watch as she takes a sip and her face morphs into an expression of pure bliss as a moan escapes her. Dammit, I want to be the reason for those moans. I want to hear her screaming out my name in ecstasy. Reaching down and readjusting myself not so subtly, I see her smirk over at my discomfort.

Tilting her head, she says, "So that does still work, I take it?" pointing at my crotch region.

Oh, she did not just say that. Hell no. Does she think it wasn't working?

"Sunshine, my cock has never not worked. Why the fuck would you think it was broken?" I ask her, mortified that she's questioning my manhood.

"For the last fourteen days, I've woken up to that being buried deep inside me. I thought maybe you had a little problem or something this morning?" She shrugs.

Is she fucking kidding me right now? I look around the room in search of the hidden cameras, not seeing any.

"Babe, I tore myself away from you this morning because I didn't want to get caught up in bed all day. It's Christmas Eve and we have shit to do today. It has absolutely nothing to do with my manhood not working."

"Oh, okay," she says like that's the end of this conversation.

Ah, hell no. Crawling up the bed, I straddle her legs.

"I'm more than happy to show you just how not broken he is. Name the place and time and I'm there," I tell her, leaving the ball in her court.

She looks from me to her cup of coffee, back and forth, like she's trying to decide. Please god, do not let me lose out to a fucking cup of coffee right now. Finally, she sets the cup down on the table, reaches up and pulls my face down to hers, slamming our lips together.

Home. That's what this kiss feels like; it feels like returning home after a long absence.

"How about right now?" she asks, raising her eyebrow. Well, she doesn't have to ask me twice. I do, however, look carefully at her face, reading her expression.

"Are you sure?" I ask.

"I've never been more sure of anything in my life," she says.

I make quick work of removing her shirt—well, my shirt that she's been sleeping in. Cupping her breast in my hands, I lean down. Taking a nipple in my mouth, I audibly groan.

"*Mmm*, I missed these beauties," I say as I show the other breast just how much I missed it by sucking, nibbling and biting at it.

Alyssa laughs. "It's only been four hours since you last saw them."

Looking up at her, I respond, "Babe, ten minutes without seeing these beauties is ten minutes too fucking long."

Tilting my head back down, I get back to work, worshiping the fuck out of her breasts.

Alyssa is making the most beautiful sounds, moaning, shivering and squirming beneath me.

"I'd love to take this slow, babe, but I can't hold out. I need to be inside you now—it will be rough and quick. But I swear I'll make it up to you later."

Holding the sides of her lace panties between my hands, I rip, tearing them from her body. She gasps and arches her body while I trail my finger between the lips of her pussy, making sure she is ready for me.

I'm pleased as fuck to find her pussy wet and weeping for me.

"Look how wet you are, sunshine. Is this pussy starving for my cock? Has she missed him?"

I feel a gush of wetness escape her as she takes in my dirty words. I settle between her legs, lining my cock up to her entrance.

"Ready?" I ask her.

"Oh god, Zac. Hurry up already and put that in me!" she exclaims.

Slamming into her, I still. Fuck. I'm really not going to last long. This feels too fucking good. I move slowly, thrusting in and out in careful, precise, slow motions. It's not helping. I can feel my orgasm building. Reaching between our bodies, I rub my finger in circles around her clit

"I need you to come for me, sunshine. Come now!" I demand.

She doesn't disappoint. She comes hard, screaming out my name. Her pussy clamps down around my cock, milking me for all that I have to give. Falling onto the bed next to her, I pull her into my arms. We're both a sweaty mess, both breathing heavily, sucking in air, attempting to catch our breaths.

Alyssa's breathing slows, her body relaxing into mine. "You okay?" I ask her.

"*Mhmm*, never been better. God, I love when we do that."

"Yep, you and me both, babe, but what I love

most is this, just lying here, holding onto my girl with a feeling of bliss."

"Zac." Alyssa's voice is quiet. She tilts her head up so she looks at me.

"Yeah, babe?"

She's pensive for a while before speaking again. "I know I haven't been the easiest person to live with these past few weeks. But I want you to know that I'm really trying."

Her voice breaks a little. I'm about to say something when she continues, "I am trying. But the images, they keep playing in my mind. I'm not scared of her, you know, Caitlyn. I'm scared that she will succeed. That you are going to finally have had enough and leave me. I don't know if I can survive that kind of loss, you know?"

"Sunshine, there is nothing anybody, and I mean fucking anybody, can do to make me leave you. I will stay in this apartment for as long as you need me to be with you. Until you're ready to go back out to the world. Until then, I'm happy staying here with you." Kissing the top of her head, I continue, "Always have tomorrow together, right?"

I don't know how else to reassure her I'm not going anywhere. Hopefully, tomorrow she will get the picture that I'm in this forever.

"Always," she whispers. "It's not just the Caitlyn stuff. It's the holidays."

"What about the holidays?" I ask her.

"Well, I've never really had a good relationship

with Christmas before. I've never had a family to celebrate with, to exchange gifts with. I mean, ever since I
met Sarah in college, she has taken me home to her
family every Christmas. But it's not the same. I've
always just felt like an outsider."

Shit, why did I not think of this before? Of course
she hasn't had a real fucking Christmas. "Well, you
have a family now. And you just might question the
sanity of the family you've joined when tomorrow
morning you're woken to the screams of Bray
carrying on like a child. Because I can promise you
that is exactly what's going to happen."

She lets a small giggle escape. Good, if Bray being
his usual idiot self will get a laugh out of her, then I'll
make sure he amps it up more than usual tomorrow.

"Thank you. For everything, for being you. For
not leaving me alone the last few weeks." She leans up
and kisses me. I need to get her back to a better
mood, back to happier thoughts.

"So, it's Christmas Eve, babe. I've got an early
Christmas present for you."

She sits up, eyes wide, and then they turn watery.

Shit, I fucked up. What the fuck did I say?
"What's wrong?" I ask as I rub her arms.

"Your present, I didn't get to make your present
the way I wanted to. I mean, I got part of it done that
day you went into the club and Sarah and her friend
came over. But it's not very good, and it's not what I
wanted to give you," she says with tears running down
her face. "I… I don't have anything else to give you."

That's what she's upset about? *Jesus.*

"Babe, the only thing I need from you is *you.* If you want to gift me something, I have an idea of what you can give me." An idea starts to build in my head.

"What is it? Anything, I will do my best to get it today," she says eagerly.

I laugh and get up before she can reach out and slap me. "Your gift to me will be your acceptance of any and all gifts I give you over the next two days, without argument." I raise my eyebrows at her, waiting for her to respond.

She stands up, completely naked, as she saunters over to me. Leaning up, she kisses me on the lips. "Okay, but—"

Before she can add a *but*, I place a finger over her lips, stopping her sentence. "No *buts.* All I want to hear is: *thanks Zac, or yes.* Now get dressed. I need to take you downstairs to give you your first gift."

I head into the walk-in wardrobe, of which I have now designated half the space for Alyssa's things. Not that she has a whole lot yet, but that's about to change tomorrow when she wakes up to see it full.

I had Reilly sworn to secrecy and handed over my credit card to her to replace all of Alyssa's clothing, shoes, and bags that were destroyed. Not that Reilly complained one bit about doing that shopping. I've seen the bank statements from her shopping trips. I know she hasn't skimped out. She's going to be in here tonight to set it all up with Holly and Sarah. I just have to keep Alyssa occupied in the home gym.

Alyssa comes out of the bathroom, and I swear every time I see her, she takes my breath away. Even now, she's wearing yoga pants and one of my shirts, but she still steals my breath with how beautiful she is.

Smiling, I hold out my hand. "Ready?"

Taking my hand, she smiles, a little sceptical at what I'm about to give her. "As I'll ever be," she says, following me out to the elevator.

Twenty-one

ALYSSA

I'M STARING at a huge, freaking shiny red car with a huge, shiny white bow on it. *Merry Christmas, Sunshine* is written across the windscreen. What the actual fudge?

"*Ah*, Zac, that's a car!"

Turning to face him, I can see an enormous smile on his face. I'm taken aback. I haven't seen him this happy for a while. I know he's been hovering over me and trying to make sure I'm okay. It has taken a toll on him.

"Well, it has four wheels and what looks like a steering wheel inside it. So, yeah, it possibly is a car." He laughs.

I'm stunned, not sure what to do or say. No one has ever given me a gift like a car before. I mean, what do you say to a gift like this? *Oh, thanks, I love it!* just doesn't seem enough.

I've been standing in the same spot, just staring at

this huge, bright red car for too long. I can feel Zac's gaze burning into me. Finally, he takes my hand, leading me to the driver's side door. Opening it, he picks me up and places me on the seat before walking around and climbing into the passenger seat.

"I don't even know what to say," I tell him, shaking my head as I look around the car.

"I believe the words we agreed on were: *thanks, Zac.*" He laughs.

Looking around, it dawns on me that this car is exactly the same as another car I've been in recently.

"Wait, is this the same car as Bray's?" I ask.

Smiling, he says, "You said you loved Bray's car, so I figured you could only love the model higher up from his even more."

Not sure what to say to that, I lean over to him and kiss him, hoping that this kiss shows my appreciation of him, of his thoughtfulness, of the care and devotion he constantly provides me.

Pulling apart, I look him in the eye. "Zac, I freaking love this car," I shriek, "but you really do not need to be buying me these kinds of gifts. It's really too much."

He stops me, placing a finger to my lips before I can tell him he should take it back.

"Sunshine, the car is yours. It's in your name. You can do whatever you want with it, but I am not, under any circumstances, returning the damn car. So, before you even think about it, it would mean the absolute world to me if you accept this gift—not to mention the peace of mind it will give me, knowing you can drive yourself around in a safe car for those rare occasions I can't drive you myself."

"Okay." Kissing him lightly on his lips, I whisper, "Thank you, Zac. I freaking love it."

He laughs before grabbing my face in his hands, tilting my head and deepening the kiss. Climbing over the centre console, I settle on top of Zac's lap, grinding against him as he continues to assault my mouth with his tongue.

Groaning, he finally slows down his kiss before pulling back. "As much as I would love to christen this car, I don't think a garage where our neighbours can walk by is the place to do it."

Looking back over my shoulder, I peer through the windscreen to see an older couple waiting at the lift.

"You know when you kiss me like that, I lose all common sense. I wouldn't notice who was watching."

Zac grabs my ass in both hands. Squeezing, he says, "I don't share, sunshine, and that includes letting any other fuckers see this ass that belongs to me."

I grind my centre along the hardness of his cock. Holding my hips still, he says, "Do you want me to show you all the features of the car, or should we move on to your next gift already?"

"If the next gift is your cock in my pussy, then yes, let's move on already!" I exclaim.

Opening the door, he pulls me out of the car with him before placing me on my feet.

"That's not your next gift, but you never know it could be something even better."

Shaking my head, I follow him back to the lift—not that I have any choice, considering my hand is tightly clasped in his. His grip is so firm, it's almost like he thinks I'm going to run.

"Not sure anything could be better than that," I mumble behind him. By the little chuckle that escapes his lips, I know he heard.

I'M SITTING cross-legged on the floor in the gym, in a pair of running shorts and a sports bra, waiting for Zac. He told me to meet him in the gym, to be ready to work out with him. Secretly, I'm hoping that the workout he has in mind involves the clothes I'm wearing being removed. All day, he has been surprising me with little gifts, randomly coming up with a box or gift bag in his hands when I'm least expecting it. No one has ever wanted to give me gifts like this before, not to mention the freaking car, which I still can't believe.

Everything from a beautiful silk scarf to a pair of diamond studs, which I can tell are real and probably of some carat I didn't even know existed. The smile on Zac's face when I open each gift is what has kept me accepting them all day with something like a *thanks, Zac, I love it!* response. He seems genuinely excited to see me open gifts. I haven't been able to wipe the smile off my face all day.

Hearing the click of the door opening, I look up, only for my smile to falter when I see Bray sauntering in and not Zac.

Making a dramatic scene of sniffing under his armpits, he says, "Nope, I don't smell. I don't know why you're looking so disappointed to see me walk through the door, Lyssa. Do you realise how many ladies would swap places with you just to sit and watch me get all hot and sweaty?" He waggles his eyebrows up and down at me.

I can't help but laugh a little. "I was waiting for Zac. Have you seen him?"

Bray heads over to the weight bench, pulling his shirt over his head before lying down on it.

"Who?" he asks as he lifts the weight bar over his head.

How he is lifting that thing is beyond me. The weights on it look like they weigh a ton.

"Funny," I say, getting up from my spot, walking over to him and glaring down at him.

"Where's your brother, Bray? He told me to meet him in here. I've been waiting for fifteen minutes already."

Bray continues to lift the weights up and down from his chest. "I saw him just a minute ago with Ella. She needed his help to wrap some shit. I'm sure he won't be long. But feel free to stand there and enjoy your view for as long as you want," he finishes with a wink.

"Oh, okay, I'll just wait then. And *eww*, not even if you were the last man on earth, Braydon." With that, I turn and head back to sit on the floor.

"You hurt my feelings, Lyssa. You know I have fragile self-esteem issues, and you go and say mean things like that to me. I thought we were friends." Bray puts the bar back in its holder before sitting up and pouting at me.

"Oh my god, self-esteem issues? Yeah right. If your ego was any bigger, your head wouldn't fit out the door. And stop pouting. It's not a good look on you," I say with a little giggle.

Just then, an idea comes to me, something I have been thinking about for a while now.

"Bray, since we are both in here and it seems I have some time to kill, how about you make yourself useful to me and teach me a few fighting moves?"

Putting on my brightest smile and fluttering my eyelashes does nothing to wipe the look of shock and despair crossing over Bray's face.

"Do you really hate me that much?" he asks in all seriousness.

Confused, my eyebrows pull together. "What? Why would you think I hate you? Of course I don't hate you."

Bray just stands there, glaring at me. "You're trying to get me killed, aren't you?" he asks.

I shake my head no. I have no idea what his problem is.

"You're asking me," he says, pointing to his own chest, "to teach you," he emphasises as he points to me, "to fight?"

"Well, yeah. Last I knew, you were a professional fighter. So, I figured, who else's better to teach me to knock someone on their ass than you?" I shrug, really not understanding what the big deal is.

"Lyssa, sweetheart. If I taught you to fight, it would be the last thing I ever did," he declares.

I think he actually believes that. However, I still don't understand why he has such a problem with it.

"Why on earth would it be the last thing you did? Do you have some kind of medical issue I don't know about? Like if I accidently punch you in the head, are you going to have an aneurysm or something?" I ask.

"Or something," Bray says. "If I teach you to fight, you're likely to get hurt in the process, not bad but probably a bruise here or there. If you get hurt because of me, I'm a dead man, because that crazy as fuck boyfriend of yours will kill me."

At this, I laugh. I laugh so long and so hard at him I have to wipe tears from my eyes.

Noticing the tears, he adds, "Well shit, now I've made you cry, so I might as well go and dig my own grave."

Shaking my head, I pull myself together. "Bray, Zac won't kill you for teaching me how to protect myself. And if he wants to kill you for it, well, I'll just tell him not to."

Standing up, feeling energised suddenly, I bounce on the spot.

"Okay, so what's the first thing I need to know?" I ask as I punch him in the arm then shake my hand out because, damn, hitting his arm was like hitting a brick wall.

"If I get killed, I'm coming back to haunt your ass until you're in hell with me."

He walks over to a shelf and retrieves a pair of gloves. After securing my fists into pink and purple gloves that look like they must belong to Ella, I bounce around, feeling the excitement building.

"First, you need to stop jumping around like a damn lunatic on speed. Hold your fist up like this." He models holding his fist in the air in front of his face. "Hold your left arm up, protect your face, and jab with your right, like this." He jabs out stopping just before he makes contact with my face. His hand comes at me so fast I don't even notice it until it's stopped just an inch away from my face. "You would have just been knocked out cold. You didn't even try to block."

"That's because I didn't even see it coming, jerk."

Bray bounces around me in a circle, throwing out pretend jabs my way, each time calling out, "KO!"

It's starting to annoy me. I can feel myself getting worked up. He notices the change in my mood.

Stopping in front of me suddenly, he says, "Good. Now that you really want to hit me, give me all you got."

That's what I do. I punch, or at least I try to land punch after punch to his face, his torso. Each and every time, he blocks with what seems like little effort. It's pissing me off more that I can't actually land a punch on him.

I don't give up though. I keep trying to punch him for what seems like hours, my arms burning. I can feel the sweat rolling down my back. But as I continue punching, I feel like a weight is being lifted off me. Who would have thought this would be so cathartic?

I don't notice as the door opens, and I don't stop trying to land a punch as Zac's voice booms across the room.

"What the fuck do you think you're doing?"

Bray stops blocking and slightly turns towards Zac. That's when I see my opportunity and I swing my right arm out, landing a punch on his face. Where? I could not tell you, but I definitely felt the contact.

You can't miss the dramatic yell from Bray, "*Ah,*

goddammit, Lyssa! You fucking punched me!" He holds his hand up to his face, covering his left eye.

Oh god, I stop in place. The high feeling of making contact and landing a punch turns into a feeling of dread. I think I hurt him. I can't believe I actually punched him. Sure, I really wanted to land a hit on him, but I didn't want to hurt him.

"I'm so sorry, Bray. I… I didn't mean to. I just got carried away." I try to explain myself. At the same time, I try to not let the tears fall that are threatening to come loose.

Zac wraps me in his arms. "Sunshine, he's fine. He's being dramatic. Don't worry about him."

Wiggling out of his arms, I don't miss Zac's scowl as I reach up and pull Bray's hand away from his face, a gasp leaving my mouth. Holy shit, the skin around his left eye is red. Zac stands behind me, wrapping an arm around my waist before he starts laughing.

"It's not funny, Zac. I hurt him. I hit your brother. Oh god, I'm so, so sorry, Bray. Let me get you some ice."

Zac tightens his grip around me as I try to move away.

"Babe, he's fine. You probably bruised his ego more than anything else."

Bray tilts his head, examining Zac. "You know, there was a time you would have stuck up for me if I got sucker-punched," he says, pointing at him.

Meanwhile, Zac continues to laugh as he pulls me out of the room, calling out, "Be thankful it was her that landed that punch, because if she didn't, I was already planning to. Don't teach my girl how to fight, dammit. What the hell were you thinking? She could have gotten hurt." I can feel Zac getting worked up as he stops and turns back to Bray.

"She asked me to. What was I meant to do?" "Say no," Zac says.

"Yeah, how's that work out for you? Saying no to her?" Bray asks and then adds, "When you figure out how to do that, let me in on the fucking secret. It might just save my life one of these days."

I pull on Zac's hand, tugging him towards the door. "Come on, I need a shower. And he needs to ice his face."

I'M SLOWLY PULLED from my sleep and my hot AF dream I was having about a sex god, a sex god who is currently peppering my neck with kisses.

"*Mmm.*" Rolling over, I face him and open my

eyes. "I was having the best dream," I tell him. "I was naked, you were naked, and it was good."

I can feel his body shake as he laughs. "How about I make that dream a reality?" he asks as his hand slowly makes its way up my shirt to cup my right breast.

Lifting my hand up, I cup his face. "I'm all for…" My words die off as something shiny reflects off my left hand. Something freaking big and shiny! Sitting up suddenly, I look around the room frantically, realising I am, in fact, in Zac's bed in his penthouse and not in a hotel in Vegas somewhere. I hold up my left hand. Yep, it's still there. Sitting on my ring finger is probably the biggest princess-cut diamond I've ever freaking seen. I'm speechless. I don't know how this got here.

Oh my god, did Zac propose and I've forgotten the whole thing? How could that even happen? I remember going to bed last night. I remember having a shower with Zac, a very long and rewarding shower. What I don't remember is getting a ring put on my finger.

"Babe, you okay?" Zac asks, sitting up next to me.

Am I okay? Is he freaking serious right now? Does he not see this rock sitting on my finger? Oh shit, maybe I'm hallucinating. I must be. I've finally lost the plot.

"*Umm,* Zac, honey, do you see anything on my hand? Anything at all?" I ask, my voice a little quiet and unsure.

Zac grabs my hand and pulls it close to his face, turning my hand from front to back and inspecting it.

"Well, I can see you've still got five fingers, clear skin, no signs of a rash." Turning my hand back over so the diamond is facing him, he adds, "Other than that three-carat diamond on your finger, I don't see anything else. What am I supposed to be looking for?" Still holding my hand, he looks up at my face.

"*Umm,* Zac, how exactly did that diamond come to be on my finger?" I ask, still staring at the huge rock.

"I put it there of course," he replies. That's it, no other explanation.

"Okay, but I think you forgot the part where you ask me a very big question before you put a rock on my finger?"

Zac raises my hand and kisses just under where the rock sits. "I didn't forget. I was waiting for you to wake up. I thought I'd get a better answer when you're conscious and all."

"*Mmhmm.*" I continue to stare at the ring. Zac grabs my face, tilting my chin up so I'm looking at him.

"Sunshine. Alyssa. I was going to do this differently, more romantically, but I couldn't wait. I love that the first thing I see in the morning when I wake up is your beautiful face. I love that that's also the last thing I see before I close my eyes at night. I love how you have brought so much light and joy into my otherwise dark and dim world.

"The word love doesn't even begin to describe what I feel for you. I don't think there is a word to describe it. It's like you are a part of me. When I'm not with you, it's like I'm short of oxygen. I would love nothing more than to wake up with you in my arms every morning for the rest of my life, to spend the rest of my life loving you the way you deserve to be loved. Alyssa Summers, will you marry me?"

The tears are running down my face uncontrollably. No one has ever loved me like Zac loves me. As I'm processing everything he just said to me, I can hear Ella and Bray squealing down the hall.

"Babe, I don't want to rush you to answer or anything. You can take all the time you need to think about it. But we have about two minutes before that door is busted open."

Laughing, I lean in to kiss him. "I don't need any time, Zac, yes. Yes. Yes. Of course I will marry you!"

I barely get the words out as Zac pins me down to the bed and rolls on top of me, kissing the ever-loving hell out of me.

Our moment is broken when Bray barges through the room and jumps on the bed. Jumping up and down, he screams, "Mum, dad, it's Christmas. Get up, get up, get up!" I don't know how the bed is not giving out with how much he is jumping around.

"*Argh*, make him stop, Zac, please," Ella grumbles from the end of the bed.

Zac rolls off me, pulling me up while kicking at

Bray's legs. Bray stops jumping. Landing on the end of the bed, he sits down.

"Come on. Why aren't you up already? It's Christmas!" he yells.

It's then that I really look at him and see the shiner on his face. He has a black eye. I gave him a black eye. *Shit.* Sitting up, I move across the bed and reach my hand up to touch his face.

"Oh my gosh, Bray, I can't believe I gave you a black eye."

Before my hand reaches his face, he snags my wrist, holding my hand still.

"What the fuck? Lyssa, do you know there is a rock on your finger?" he asks.

This makes Ella look up and squeal, "*Ah*, yes, yes! I'm finally getting a sister!" She is jumping around and then suddenly stops. "Wait, you said yes, right?"

Bray and Ella both look at me expectantly.

"Of course she said yes," Zac answers for me before continuing, "Now let go of her fucking hand, Braydon." Zac pulls me back as Bray drops my hand.

"I can't believe you said yes to that, Lyssa!" he says before laughing. "I am thrilled to be able to call you my sister though. Lord knows I needed an upgrade on the one they gave me first. *Ow!*" He rubs his arm where Ella just punched him.

"Thank you, both of you. It means a lot you're okay with this. I know it's quick, but, well, I don't really have an answer for that."

Zac kisses the side of my head. "Babe, this would

be happening whether they liked it or not. It's just easier on them that they like it."

Looking over to Bray and Ella, I see them nodding their heads.

Bray stands up off the bed and pulls the blankets off with him. "Now get up. I've got presents to open."

He walks over to the door and bends down to pick up something off the floor, before he walks back, holding out my saving grace, a coffee cup filled with coffee.

"I think I love you right now, Bray. Thank you," I say as I take the cup and sip at the deliciousness, ignoring Zac's grunts behind me.

"Get out. We'll get dressed and meet you out there. Don't start without me," he warns Bray.

Standing up, I head into the walk-in wardrobe, only to stop at the entrance, Zac right behind me.

"Oh, my god, Zac. What? When? How?" I shake my head. I am staring at what Zac calls my side of the huge walk-in, which is now filled to the brim with clothes, everything from dresses, shirts, skirts, pants... There is even a whole section of shoes. A dozen bags are placed in neatly arranged rows on the top shelf.

"I had a little help, sunshine. But I believe the words you're looking for are: *thank you, Zac.*" Kissing my forehead, he says, "Merry Christmas, my beautiful fiancée."

I melt at hearing him call me his fiancée. I mean, who the hell wouldn't? "Thank you, Zac, you really didn't need to do this," I say as I turn and wrap my hands around his neck.

"You're welcome, and I know I didn't need to… I *wanted* to. I want to give you the world, Alyssa, but I'll start with a closet."

What am I meant to say to that? Pulling away from him, I rush to the drawer where I was hiding his present, thanking the stars it's still there. Whoever put all these clothes in here had the good grace to leave it. Picking it up, I'm nervous now. My gift pales in comparison to everything he's done for me.

"Okay, so, this isn't much, and it's not how I wanted it to look, but Merry Christmas." I hand over the gift box.

"You are a gift—the fact that you said yes is the best thing you could have ever given me, sunshine. I don't need anything else from you, just *you*."

Nodding my head, I motion for him to move on with it and open the box. The moment he lifts the lid, I know what he sees. Me, in lingerie, all variations of red lingerie. I'm nervous as he lifts the first picture and sees that there is another underneath it. Suddenly, he sits on the floor, cross-legged with the box in front of him, lifting picture after picture out.

He still hasn't said anything and it's driving me crazy. Does he hate them that much? "I know they aren't that good, and I was planning on the pictures being printed into a book, but I ran out of time and had to settle."

He looks up at me with an undecipherable look in

his eyes. "Sunshine, these look fucking amazing. I'm torn right now between how much I love these pictures and the knowledge that someone had to take them, which means someone was looking at you in this lingerie. But don't for a second doubt how goddamn sexy you are."

He goes back to the box and continues to pull out the pictures in silence. Sitting in front of him, I wait for him to say something. As he gets to the last picture, he looks up at me.

"Do you have all of this lingerie still?" he questions.

"*Umm*, yeah. I took these pictures just last week. Of course I have it all."

He nods his head. "Good, because I counted twenty pictures. That means, for the next twenty nights, I get to have you in each piece of lingerie. In fact, I think we should cancel Christmas and start right now."

Laughing, I say, "We're not cancelling Christmas, but I will wear each and every piece one day at a time."

"Thank you, sunshine. No one has ever given me a gift like this. It's hands down the best gift I've ever received, apart from you."

Yeah right, like he hasn't been given better gifts. "*Uh-huh*. Hopefully, over the course of our lives, I can figure out this gift-giving thing and get as good at it as you are. There's always tomorrow, right?"

"There will always be a tomorrow for us together,

sunshine," he declares, just like he does every night before we go to sleep.

"Promise?" I ask.

"I promise. There is nothing in this world that could tear me away from you."

Even as he makes this promise, I have a lingering feeling that some things are out of even his control.

Twenty-two

ZAC

*S*PRAWLED across the couch, watching some 90s Christmas movie with Alyssa in my arms, I could not be any more content. We've spent the day exchanging gifts and indulging in a gourmet Christmas banquet fit for a king and queen.

I've always attempted to give Bray and Ella a family Christmas and follow on with the traditions that mum and dad had started. Christmas has never felt as complete as it did today though; Alyssa joining our little family has made today more than I could have ever wished for.

I haven't been able to wipe the smile from my face all day, seeing Alyssa enjoy herself so much, knowing that she said yes, without a doubt, to being mine forever. It makes me fucking happy. I can't remember a time I've been happier than I am right now in this moment.

Alyssa yawns as she snuggles into my chest. "Tired, baby?"

Burrowing in deeper to my chest, she says, "*Mmm*, who would have thought Christmas could be so tiring."

Standing, I lift her into my arms. "Come on, let's get you to bed."

"I can walk, you know. You don't need to put your back out carrying me. Put me down."

Laughing, I hold her tighter. "Never, I will never let you go, and please, I could lift ten of you and still not put my damn back out." She gives up her protest and relaxes into me.

Laying her on the bed, I undress her so she can sleep more comfortably, leaving her in just her panties. I make quick work as I undress and climb in behind her, holding her in my arms.

"Sweet dreams, baby. We'll have tomorrow together," I tell her. She's already out of it as she murmurs something in response.

THE LAST FEW days have been bliss. I've spent almost every waking hour with Alyssa, wanting to get in as much time before we both go back to work today. I tried, very unsuccessfully, to get her to quit and come work at the club with me. If it wasn't New Year's Eve, I think I would camp out at the hospital throughout her entire shift, just waiting for her.

As much as I want to do just that, I can't. New Year's is a big night for the club, and I can't continue to palm my responsibilities off to Bray and Dean. We're also holding the first fight since the holiday break. Bray's been training like crazy the past few days, *shredding the holiday weight* he put on—his words not mine.

I'm also keen to get back to work and expand on the hunt for fucking Caitlyn. It's been nearly three weeks since she trashed Alyssa's room at her townhouse and there hasn't been a sighting of her. No more threats have been delivered either. But I know something is coming. I can feel it in my gut. The sooner we catch the crazy bitch, the sooner I can relax and know my girl is safe.

Alyssa's alarm starts blaring on the bedside table. She reaches out, blindly swatting at her phone. Laughing, I roll over top of her and turn the alarm off.

"Morning, sunshine." I kiss the top of her head. "Don't move. I'll get your coffee."

I hear her mumble something incoherent as I walk out of the bedroom.

Returning with her coffee, it does not surprise me to find her sound asleep again. I take a sip of the sweet crap she calls coffee and then put the cup down. Leaning down, I gently roll my lips over the top of hers, urging her mouth open with my tongue. She doesn't disappoint. Opening for me, she meets my tongue with strokes of her own.

"*Mmm*, you taste divine," she says as she slowly comes to. Laughing, I pull back, pulling her up into a sitting position.

Handing her the coffee cup, I suggest, "Drink up, sunshine. Just think, if you quit your job and come work at our club, you won't ever have to wake up at these ungodly hours again."

"I'll be fine once the caffeine hits my system." She continues drinking, purposefully ignoring my suggestion. I'm not giving up though. I know I'll wear her down, eventually. From what I've seen and heard from her friends, she doesn't even like her job.

"I'm gonna hit the gym for a bit. Do you need anything before I go work out?"

"I'm good. I'm just going to finish this coffee and have a shower."

I kiss her once more. "Okay, but I'm just down the hall if you decide you need me to wash your back, or your front, or your hair."

Laughing, she says, "I think I'll manage, but good to know you'll wash all those hard-to-reach places."

Leaning in, I kiss her again. I don't think I'm ever

going to get enough of her kisses. It's like a drug and I'm addicted.

"Anytime, anyplace, babe," I say with a wink and leave her to get ready.

I'm not surprised to find Bray already in the gym as I enter. Jumping on the treadmill, I start my warm-up. Bray eyes me suspiciously.

"What happened? Did Lyssa kick you out already? If so, I want her to get custody of me in the divorce."

"Fuck off. There won't ever be a fucking divorce, idiot."

"Then why the hell are you up at this hour? I haven't seen the likes of you this early for well over a month."

"Alyssa's going back to work at the hospital today."

I shrug, like it doesn't bother me at all that she's going to work and I won't be able to be with her all day.

"Shit, man, is that safe? I mean, we still don't know where the fuck Caitlyn is hiding out," Bray questions.

Like I haven't fucking thought of that already. "I tried to talk her into quitting and coming to work at the club, but she won't have a bar of it."

"Well, at least now I know why you're in such a cheery mood." Bray smirks.

"She also wants to drive herself to work in her car," I grunt as I speed up the treadmill to a slow jog.

"What time is she planning on leaving?" he asks.

"In about an hour, around six. She's doing a twelve-hour shift and is meeting me at the club when she finishes. Why?"

Shrugging, he grabs a towel and wipes his face. "I need to visit a mate at the hospital. She can give me a lift."

I nod, knowing full well he's full of shit. He doesn't have any mates in the hospital, but I'm grateful for the lie if it means she won't be driving by herself.

"Thanks, man," I say as he makes his way out of the room.

AFTER PUNISHING myself for forty-five minutes in the gym, I wander back into the bedroom in search of Alyssa. She should be just about ready to leave. I find her sitting on the edge of the bed, bending over, tying the laces on her joggers. For a moment, I just stand in the doorway, enjoying the view. I forgot how damn good she looks in those scrubs. Then again, Alyssa would be hot as fuck in a burlap sack.

Groaning, I adjust the growing erection forming in my shorts. Alyssa finally looks up, pausing momentarily where my hand is adjusting my cock.

Smirking as her eyes meet mine, she asks, "Good workout?"

Shrugging my shoulders, I make my way to her. Kneeling on the floor in front of her, I trail my hands up her legs from her ankles up to her inner thighs.

"There are much better ways I prefer to get my cardio in these days."

Alyssa laughs while attempting to push me away. As her hands meet my chest, I think my heart literally stops for a minute. There is something huge missing from her left hand. My eyes should be met with a fucking diamond on that hand, a huge fucking diamond that I put there just a week ago. Grabbing her hand, I rub her ring finger, her bare fucking ring finger.

I take a deep breath before gritting out, "Where the fuck is your ring, Alyssa?"

As much as I try to get my voice to remain calm, I don't succeed. I know my words come out harsh.

She looks down at her hand, then back at me before answering, "Zac, I can't wear that ring to work."

I hear her words, but they make absolutely no sense. "Why the fuck not?"

Staring at her hand, I'm racking my brain for

reasons she would not want to wear my ring out in public. Has she changed her mind already? I don't think I'd survive if she says she doesn't want me anymore.

Alyssa reaches up, touching my face, and pulls my eyes up to meet hers. "Zac, honey, I'm still marrying you. There is nothing in this world that could stop me from wanting to marry you. I can't wear my ring because it's just too big—it's not practical. I have to put gloves on and off all day. I won't be able to do that with the ring on."

Although I feel like a weight has been lifted, knowing she's not leaving, I still don't like the thought of her walking around without the fucking ring on her finger. I want the world to know she's taken and taken by me. There's also the fact that that particular ring has a GPS tracker in it. I know, not my finest moment putting a tracker on my fiancée, but given the circumstances, I think if I ever had to actually use it, I won't regret putting it there. She of course does not know that her ring has this extra feature. There is no way I'm letting her walk out of this apartment without that ring on her.

Standing up, I ask her, "Where is it?" as I look around the room.

Alyssa walks into the walk-in wardrobe and retrieves the ring from the island bench. I don't tell her that she just left a four-hundred-thousand-dollar ring sitting around like a piece of costume jewellery. I'd never get her to wear it if she knew that stone's value. Instead, I open a drawer and pull out one of my gold chains. It's thin enough and long enough that she can wear it under her shirt.

Threading the ring through the chain, I then place the chain around her neck. Alyssa doesn't move; she doesn't question my actions. Once the chain's clasp is secure, I tuck the ring into the inside of her shirt, letting the stone rest between her breasts.

Damn, for a moment, I'm lost while staring down into her cleavage; that is, until Alyssa clears her throat.

"Thank you. I didn't even think to put it on a chain."

Wrapping her arms around my waist, she buries her head into my chest. I hear her inhale and I smile. I love that she always inhales my scent like it's her favourite scent in the world, even though I'm pretty sure I come second to the scent of coffee.

"It's not too late to change your mind, you know," I whisper my last-ditch attempt at getting her to stay with me rather than go to work.

"As much as I'd love to stay in our little bubble and be with you all day, we need to get back to reality, and reality is *I have a job*. A job that I'm going to be late for if I don't leave now."

"It was worth a try, and you know you don't actually have to work, right? I have enough money that neither of us would have to actually work another day in our lives. We could just move to a deserted island and continue to exist in our little bubble, just the two of us." As the idea runs through my head, I'm liking it more and more.

"Zac, do not buy a bloody island retreat anywhere. We are not leaving our family. Now walk me to the door and kiss me goodbye."

With that, she turns and walks out of the room. I'm left there smiling like a fool. She said *our family*. It's the first time she's referred to my family as her own, as *ours* and not just mine.

"Zac, I'm leaving," I hear Alyssa call from down the hall. I meet her in the living room just as Bray comes running down the hall at the same time.

"Lyssa, sis, thank god you haven't left yet. I need you to give me a ride." His words rush out like he's in a hurry to get somewhere. I work hard to hide the smirk that's trying to form on my lips. He really does go all-in when he's on a roll.

"What's wrong?" Alyssa questions as she pats Bray down with her hands, inspecting for an injury of some sort.

Pulling her back into my chest, I stop her inspection of my brother's body.

"He's not hurt, Alyssa. He's just a fucking idiot," I inform her while sending Bray a death glare.

"Your concern for my wellbeing means everything to me, brother. I'm fine. I just need to visit someone who's laid up in the very same hospital you're driving to. So, can you give me a lift?" Bray asks.

Alyssa looks sceptical, glancing back and forward

between Bray and myself. Shit, she is too damn smart for us. She already knows he's full of shit.

"Bray, visiting hours don't start until eight. It's only six now. What are you planning on doing, sitting around the door for two hours to visit a friend?"

I look at Bray pleadingly. I know he'll come up with something; he's always been able to talk his way out of anything.

"Okay, well, I didn't want to tell you this because, well, just because… But you see, there's this nurse I just met, and she wants me to meet her before her shift at the hospital. A before work hook-up, some might call it. It's the next Tinder."

Alyssa shakes her head and screws her face up. "First, gross. Second, I think you're full of shit. You've been moping around for the last four weeks, trying to get Reilly to pay you some attention and now, all of a sudden, you've moved on to someone else? Really, Bray?" she questions him.

Bray looks almost pained when he says, "Reilly won't give me the time of day, so yes, I'm moving on. Let's go. I can't keep a lady waiting—it's not polite." We both watch Bray as he presses the button, opening the doors on the lift.

Alyssa turns to me and whispers, "I can't wait to see what excuse he comes up with tomorrow when he needs a lift to the hospital." Reaching up and laying a quick kiss on my lips, she says into my mouth, "I love you so damn much. I'll see you tonight."

Holding her tighter, I tell her, "I love you more

than I thought it was possible to love someone. Text me when you get there. Also, I'll meet you on your lunch break."

Biting onto her bottom lip, she looks at me like she's unsure of what she's about to say. "*Umm*, well… lunch… I kind of already told Sarah I'd meet her in the hospital café. It's just that I haven't seen her since before she went to her parents for Christmas and, well, I've been a shitty friend lately and haven't really spent any time with my friends. The only one I see is Reilly, and that's only because she works for you and is always dropping stuff off here."

I lean down and kiss her. She's rambling; she does that when she's nervous.

"Sunshine, you can see your friends whenever you want, you know that, right? I'm not going to ever stop you from meeting up with your friends. Have fun with Sarah and I'll see you at the club tonight. Also, you are not a shitty friend. Anyone who can call you their friend should thank their lucky stars."

She nods at me. "Thank you. I don't know how I got so lucky to have you."

"Come on, lovebirds, I have somewhere I need to be. I can't hold this button forever, you know," Bray calls out from inside the lift.

Laughing at him, Alyssa pulls away and walks into the lift. As the doors close, an unsettling feeling returns to my gut. I try to shake it off as separation anxiety. That's all it is… I haven't been separated from her for over three weeks now. She's safe at the hospital; there is security everywhere to protect the staff and patients.

LOOKING AT THE CLOCK AGAIN, I note it's just nearing one o'clock. I've been at the club for the last three hours, going over everything we have on Caitlyn. There's nothing giving any possible whereabouts, or indicating where she could be now, and it's pissing me the fuck off. The foreboding feeling I have in the pit of my stomach hasn't left me all day. Something isn't right; we're missing something. I just don't know what. I've been texting Alyssa all morning, and now and then, she will send a brief response. I have had no response since 11:20 a.m. though. I'm telling myself it's because she's busy, or at lunch with Sarah, and just hasn't checked her phone.

"We will find her, Zac," Dean says from where he sits on the sofa in my office.

"We have to. She had a fucking headstone made up, man. A headstone with Alyssa's fucking name on it."

I know he already knows this. It was him and Bray

who smashed that headstone to pieces when they located it at the small cemetery three hours away in the little rural town. Right next to her mother's fucking grave. I haven't told Alyssa that it was actually there, that the photo she received in that dressing room was, in fact, an actual photo and not something edited just to scare her.

"How the fuck have we not found her yet?" I ask.

Dean may be my best friend, but he is also the head of my security, and I want him to do the job I fucking pay him to do and find this bitch.

"I've been working day and night on this, not to mention still ensuring everything in this club gets handled in your absence. I know you're stressed and worried, but Caitlyn is a ghost right now. There's been no activity on any of her bank accounts. She has no traceable family. Nothing… It's like she's vanished off the face of the earth."

"I know, man, sorry. I know the last three weeks haven't been easy around here. But fuck…"

I'm pulling at my hair in frustration when my phone blares from my pocket. It's not the ringtone I want to hear right now though; it's not my sunshine calling. When I look at the screen and read who the caller is, my blood turns to ice, knowing immediately something isn't right.

"What's wrong?" I ask Sarah as I answer the call.

She should be at lunch with Alyssa right now. The only reason she'd be calling me is if something were wrong.

"Where are you hiding her, Zac? You have to learn to share, you know. She was mine first. I've been waiting in this damn café for an hour."

"Fuck!" I yell out, tempted to throw the phone. Sarah's tentative voice comes through the speaker.

"Zac, she's not with you, is she?"

"No, she's not fucking with me. She was meant to be with you right now. Have you tried to call her? Text her?" I ask.

Maybe she's running late, got stuck in the ER. As I think this, I know that's not the reason she didn't show up for lunch.

"I'm heading to the ER now; I'll ask the nurses' station to find her," Sarah says in a huff. "I'm sure she just got held up."

"Don't bother. I'm locating her now."

I place the call on speaker as I open the tracking app on my laptop. It takes only moments before the app loads her exact location on a map, the red dot showing her location is moving.

"What do you mean you're locating her? How the fuck are you locating her, Zac?"

Ignoring Sarah's questions, I stand, grabbing my keys. Dean is already holding the door open. "Sarah, I'm going to get her. I gotta go."

As I hang up, I hear Sarah screaming at me, "Don't you dare hang—"

Putting my phone in my pocket, I tell Dean as I make my way down the hallway, "She's got her; she fucking has my sunshine. Get a team to follow us. We need to go."

"Where? Where did she ping?" he asks while he loads the tracking app on his phone.

As his app loads, he curses, knowing where she's heading.

"She's already got two hours ahead of us." Stating the fucking obvious, Dean follows me into the carpark behind the club. "I'll drive. You keep tracking," Dean says as he climbs into the driver's side.

I don't argue, knowing I'll probably kill us both in the state I'm in if I get behind the wheel.

As we peel away from the club, I pray to a god I don't even believe in that she's still alive. That I can get to her in time. Looking in the side mirror, I see not only Dean's team following behind but also Bray's SUV behind them. I will get there... I will get her back... There is no other alternative.

A half hour passes and the red dot on the tracker has stopped. She's at the cemetery, the one where that fucking psycho had a headstone made. I know she's planning on burying her next to her mother.

"She's stopped at the cemetery," I grit out to Bray as he speeds down the highway.

"Fuck, we're still at least an hour and a half out. Put a call through to the men in Glenvale and get them to the cemetery now. She's there now." Dean speaks into the headset he has on.

"You have guys already in Glenvale?" I ask him.

How did I not know this already?

"I've had two guys there on standby ever since we found the headstone. They're only five minutes away from the cemetery."

"Thank fuck. I want her alive. Caitlyn, I want to be the one to fucking end her," I tell him.

"I know." Dean smirks my way.

Twenty-three

ALYSSA

*M*Y HEAD IS POUNDING, I reach up to touch my forehead and find my movements restricted. My hands are tied with rope. *What the hell?* I try to look around, but it's dark. I'm in a small, cramped space. I'm in a goddamn car boot. Closing my eyes, I try to keep my breathing even and recall how I got here.

I remember being at work. I was doing obs on an elderly patient. I remember an orderly entering the room and that's it. I can't remember anything else. I just need to breathe, to stay calm. As much as I want to scream out, I know I need to stay calm. The longer whoever put me here thinks I'm still out of it, the longer Zac has to realise I'm missing and start searching. Oh god, the thought of Zac brings tears to my eyes.

This is meant to be the start of our forever. What if we don't get a forever? What if this morning was the last time I would get to kiss him? Hug him? I should have listened to him. I should have quit my job and just taken any random job he would give me at the club. At least then, I wouldn't be in this predicament now.

Has he realised I'm missing yet? He will be out of his mind once he notices that I'm missing. I don't know how much time has passed, how long I've been passed out in this car boot. I can hear movement outside and the boot opens, letting in the sunlight. Squinting my eyes, I try to focus on whoever the person is that opened the boot. But I know who this psycho is without even looking. I know it's Caitlyn. I know she wants to follow through with her threats to get rid of me so that she can have Zac to herself.

"Oh good, you're awake. I was hoping you'd be conscious when I make you take your last breath. It would be such a shame to not see the look in your eyes when you realise that I won." She laughs while pulling on the rope that binds my hands. "Get out, bitch. It's time to end this."

I'm roughly yanked from the car, my legs giving out beneath me as I fall to the ground. Whatever drugs she injected into me haven't worn off yet. As I'm trying to find the strength to stand, something hits my head, making me fall onto my back, my vision going blurry. Not something, a foot. She just fucking kicked me in the head. Grunting, I hold in my cries of pain.I will not give her the satisfaction of hearing my anguish.

"Why are you doing this?"

"Why?" she screams into my face, grabbing me by the hair and pulling my face closer to hers. "I gave you the chance to leave him alone. He's mine!"

She lets my hair go, pushing my head back down to the ground.

Pointing to herself, she says, "Mine, I know he loves me. He doesn't love you. He doesn't want you. And once he knows the lengths I'm prepared to go for him, he will know I'm the one he should be with."

As she's pacing up and down in front of me, I look around, trying to identify where I am. When I look to my left, I know exactly where she's brought me. I've only been here once, when I turned eighteen. I found out where my mother was buried and came here. I haven't been able to bring myself to come back. Dread settles in deep within me. I'm three hours away from the city. There is no way Zac will know to look for me here. This really is it.

I wanted to have it all. I wanted what Zac promised, to always have a tomorrow together. I wanted us to be a family, an actual family. I wanted to have kids with Zac. I haven't admitted that to anyone, too scared of what that means. I've always thought I could never have kids myself because they would grow up on their own, without a mother, just like I did. But I know that Zac and his family, our family, would never let our kids grow up alone, even if I ended up with the same cancer that killed my mother.

I wish I had told him I wanted his babies. I wish I

had the chance to tell him how much happiness and love he has brought into my life in the short time I've had him. I've never felt love like the love that Zac so easily and freely offers me. I'm thankful that I got to experience that kind of love. I just wish I could thank Zac for giving it to me. I wish he could know just how much I love him.

Finding the energy, I sit up and push myself over to lean against my mother's headstone. I tell her, "He will never love you." I know I shouldn't taunt her, but she's going to kill me anyway.

Caitlyn pulls a gun out from behind her back, pointing it at my head while screaming at me, "Shut up, shut up, shut up!"

Then I hear the gunshot… I feel a burning, searing pain in my arm. I can't help but yell out in agony. She shot me. Looking down, I see that my arm is now covered with blood, so much blood. My head is dizzy. I can't even cover the wound; my hands are still tied together with rope.

I'm trying to figure out a way to get myself out of this situation, trying to free my hands of the rope that binds them together. My arm is burning, tears run freely down my face, and my wrists are red, raw from the rope burn as I twist and turn them in attempts to free my arm.

Then I hear it, another gunshot. I hold my breath, and close my eyes, waiting to feel the pain of being shot again. Waiting to identify where she has shot me this time. The pain doesn't come. Opening my eyes, I see Caitlyn just before she falls to the ground.

Wait, did she shoot herself? No, she wouldn't have. My head is spinning. I know I need to stay awake. I can't give in to the darkness that calls me to close my eyes right now. A man dressed in black stops and squats down in front of me.

"Alyssa, it's okay. There's an ambulance on the way. Just hold on, okay?" he says as he cuts my wrists free from the rope. I don't know who this man is. I don't know how he knows my name, but right now, I don't care.

"Zac, I… I… I need Zac," I plead with whoever this stranger is.

"He's going to meet you at the hospital. It's okay. You're safe now."

I hear the sirens getting closer and I let go. Closing my eyes, I give in to the darkness and let it take over me.

BEEP, *Beep, Beep.* Oh god, someone shut off the damn alarm. The noise continues, my eyes flutter open slowly, and I take in my surroundings. The smell of antiseptic, the beeps of machines, the chill in the air... I know I'm in the hospital. Confusion wraps around my brain. Am I at work? Why is my head pounding? I attempt to lift my arm but a burning pain pauses my movement.

"*Argh,*" I groan out loud.

"Sunshine, baby, don't move. Let me call for the doctors."

Zac... Zac's here. He's squeezing my hand like he's afraid I'm going to run off somewhere. He reaches above my head, pressing a button.

"Wh... what happened?" I ask him as I look around the hospital room.

"Alyssa, I am so fucking sorry. This should never have happened to you. I should never have let this happen to you."

Zac bends his head down, leaning his forehead on the hand he has in a death grip. I wriggle my fingers to get him to loosen his grip, which he does, slightly.

"Zac, what happened? Why am I in the hospital?" I ask again.

"You don't remember?" he asks, looking up, concern creeping across his face.

I shake my head no, wincing as pain slices through my head.

"Where the fuck is the doctor?" Zac questions,

looking towards the door. "Sunshine, I didn't do my job. I didn't protect you properly."

I have no idea what he's talking about. I close my eyes briefly—the light is really too bright.

"Shit, sunshine. Please open your eyes. Don't go back to sleep yet, please," Zac pleads.

My eyes pop open immediately. "Zac, I'm right here. I'm not going anywhere."

"I was so fucking scared I was going to lose you. When we discovered Caitlyn had taken you, it felt like my world dropped out from under me."

I tighten my grip on his hand in an attempt to reassure him that I'm not about to disappear.

"She took you to the cemetery, the one where your mother is. Three fucking hours away. By the time we realised she had you, she was two hours in front of us."

"How did you find me?" I ask.

Zac shakes his head. He looks a little nervous. "I *uhh*… well, I…"

I wait for him to decide on what he's about to tell me. His hesitancy is making me nervous.

"Okay, I had a GPS tracker put into your engagement ring. I'm not sorry either. I know it's probably all kinds of wrong, but it's also the only reason you're still alive right now. The only way we knew where you were."

I look down at my left hand, where my engagement ring currently sits. I remember it was around my neck while I was at work, so I'm not sure how it landed back on my finger, but I think I could probably guess. I look back at Zac.

"Okay, let's keep it there," I tell him, honestly not bothered at all that he can track my location through the ring.

Zac sighs like a weight has been lifted. "Yeah? You're not mad? Sarah said you'd be pissed when you woke up and found out I had a tracker on you. You can be pissed at me, sunshine. I can handle it."

"I'm not mad; it's a little disturbing that you did it without telling me. But I'm glad you could locate me easily. I'm glad you got to me before she finished what she started." As I go to move my arm, the pain shoots down again. "What happened to my arm?"

"Caitlyn shot you in the arm," Zac grunts out, "and I didn't get to you in time. Dean had two guys near the cemetery for the last few weeks. They got to you, not me."

I rub my fingers over his hand. "It's because of you that those men were there."

The door to the room opens and a doctor and nurse walk in.

"It's about fucking time," Zac bites out.

"Miss Summers, I'm Dr. Ryan. How are you feeling?" the doctor asks, while holding a light pen to my eyes.

"My head hurts, my arm feels like it's on fire but other than that, I'm okay," I tell him honestly.

The doctor nods. "That's understandable. You had a nasty hit to the head; you had ten stitches placed on your hairline." The doctor picks up my chart, noting something on it before adding, "The bullet grazed your arm, and you lost a fair bit of blood, so you will probably feel weak for a few days."

I take in everything he says. The bullet only grazed my arm. That's good—still hurts like hell.

"What about some pain relief. What are you giving her? She's in pain." Zac's question comes out harsh.

"It's okay," I tell him, trying to keep him calm.

"No, it's not, sunshine. You're hurting. It's not fucking okay."

The doctor looks down at the chart in his hands. "She's on the best pain relief we can safely give her," he says to Zac. Looking down at me, he adds, "You're doing great. We're going to keep you in overnight for observation, but you should be able to go home tomorrow. I've ordered an ultrasound tech to come and check on the foetus, just to be cautious. All your bloods came back good."

I noticed Zac stiffen during the doctor's spiel. He is looking down at me as he watches my face. I run back through what the doctor said; it takes a minute but then it clicks.

"Wait, what?" I question the doctor.

"All your bloods came back good." He places the chart back over the foot of the bed.

"No, go back a bit. Foetus? What foetus?" I ask him.

"You didn't know you were pregnant?" the doctor asks.

I shake my head, unable to speak, and look over at Zac, who has not said a word. He is still looking down at me, watching for my reaction. It's almost like he's holding his breath, too afraid to move.

The doctor continues, "My guess is it's early; the scan will tell us more."

Pregnant. *Pregnant. I'm pregnant.* How did this happen? Of course I know *how* this happened. I smile at that thought. Then something lingers in the back of my mind.

"Why don't I remember what happened?" I ask the doctor.

"You were injected with propofol. You were asleep for most of your ordeal, I believe."

I nod my head. Well, that explains why I can't remember anything.

"Will that hurt the baby?" I ask the doctor. As I do, Zac looks up to the doctor while squeezing my hand.

The doctor shakes his head. "No, the baby should be fine. Let's get the scan done and find out how far along you are," he says with a reassuring smile.

I'm about to thank him, but before I can, Zac breaks his silence. "*Should be?* Should be fine is not good enough."

He pulls his phone out of his pocket, dialling someone and looking back down at me briefly, before the call connects.

"Dean, find the best OBGYN in Sydney. Get Alyssa an appointment with them tomorrow." He listens for a bit. I can't hear what Dean says but Zac answers, "Yes, I don't care how much," before hanging up the phone.

The doctor looks down at me and smiles. "I'll find out where the ultrasound tech is."

I nod and thank him, unsure what to say right now. With that, he walks out the door. When the door closes, I look back to Zac, who is again staring down at me, like he's waiting for something.

"I'm sorry," I tell him. What if he thinks I got pregnant on purpose? That I'm trying to trap him or something?

"You have nothing to be sorry for, sunshine," he says while absently placing his hand over my abdomen. I don't even think he's consciously doing it.

"I don't know how I got pregnant," I say, to which Zac arches his eyebrow at me. "Well, obviously I know that part, but I didn't once miss a pill, I swear. I didn't lie to you. But I will understand if you don't want this. I can do it. It's okay—"

Zac leans down and kisses me, kisses the hell out of me, cutting off my rambling thoughts. When he leans back, he smiles so wide. "Sunshine, you are crazy if you think I would ever let you do this by yourself. Or that I wouldn't want a child who is made up of us, of our love." Tilting his head, he looks at me, waiting.

"What are you looking for?" I ask him after a few

moments.

"I'm wondering where the panic attack has gone. You once had a panic attack on me at the thought of having a child, but you seem so calm right now. It's a little off-putting."

That's why he went stiff and quiet when the doctor mentioned a foetus. He was worried about my reaction.

I smile at him. "I realised that it doesn't matter what happens to me. If I end up having a shorter life like my mother, this baby will still be loved, will still have a family. I won't be leaving this baby alone in a world that can be so cruel."

"I'm not going to let anything happen to you, sunshine. You're never leaving my side again."

He looks serious, like his word is law and nothing will ever happen to me. I'm not as convinced it's that easy.

"I want this life you've given me, Zac. I want a family with you. I want to have this baby." My eyes tear up at the thought of everything I ever wanted coming true. "I want to always have a tomorrow with you," I tell him.

"Sunshine, I want nothing more than to raise a family with you. For all of my tomorrows to be with you. I love you," he says while wiping the tears from my eyes.

The door opens and the ultrasound tech rolls in with a trolley machine. The girl introduces herself before blushing profusely, a reaction that often comes when Zac introduces himself to any woman. Rolling my eyes, I look over at the screen as she places the wand on my abdomen.

This is surreal. I can't believe this is happening right now. After a few swipes of the wand over my stomach, the unmistakable sound of a heartbeat rings out through the room.

"What's that?" Zac asks, like he's ready to go into battle, making the woman jump.

"Relax, you're going to give her a damn heart attack. That sound is the baby's heartbeat. Our baby's heartbeat." I have tears running down my face again.

Zac reaches up, wiping the tears. "What's wrong?" His voice is soft, concerned.

"Nothing, I'm just really thrilled right now."

I stare at the screen, where there is a still picture of my womb. You can't see anything other than a blip on the screen. The ultrasound tech finishes with her measurements, and wiping the gel off of my stomach, she says, "You're about five to six weeks pregnant. Everything looks good. The heartbeat's good, strong. Congratulations."

"Thank you," we both reply as she unplugs her machine and leaves the room.

I look at Zac. "I can't believe this is real; we're having a baby."

"We are, and you should probably get some rest while you can. I've told everyone they can visit you tomorrow, so expect to be inundated with visitors you can't get rid of when you wake up."

I smile, thinking of how hard he must have worked to get my friends to wait until tomorrow to come barging in here. "I don't know how you got the girls to agree to wait until tomorrow."

"I didn't. They're camped outside in the waiting room now, refusing to bloody leave," he grunts.

That sounds more like my friends. "You should probably let them in for a bit. They won't leave otherwise."

"I'm selfish, I know, but I want you to myself. I don't want to share you and this baby with anyone yet." Zac shrugs.

I nod, slightly agreeing that I don't want to share either. "I know, but we always have tomorrow together, right?" I ask him.

"Always," he says.

"Promise?"

"Promise. We will always have a tomorrow together, sunshine."

Want more?
Get the bonus Zac & Alyssa wedding scene
here: Zac & Alyssa - The Wedding

Continue reading for a sneak peak at the next instalment in this series Fused With Him, featuring Bray & Reilly

Acknowledgments

I am thankful first to you, the reader, the one for whom this story was written. And I hope that you enjoyed the characters and the world of Alyssa and Zac as much as I enjoyed writing them.

For months, Alyssa and Zac lived within me, urging me to get their story told. Being able to translate my random thoughts and daydreams into a real-life written story is a dream come true to me. Having people read and enjoy my story is icing on the cake, so thank you, readers!!!

I am thankful to my wonderful husband, whose support and endless encouragement never fails. Nate, I could not have accomplished this without you.

Thank you, Reilly, the very real feisty red-head I like to call my best friend. Your eagerness to live in the world of Alyssa and Zac alongside me was endearing. Thank you for the constant nagging for the 'next chapter' instalment as you read through chapter by

chapter as they were written. Thank you for being my sounding board, and for never tiring of me talking and rambling on about Alyssa and Zac. Thank you for falling in love and claiming Bray as your very first book boyfriend!

Thank you, thank you, thank you to Shannan, my very wonderful and patient editor. Thank you for helping me along the journey of publishing my very first book baby. Thank you for your endless positive reinforcements and encouragements along the way. I could not have gotten to this point without you.

Last but not least, thank you to all of the awesome and inspiring authors and readers I have met through social media over the course of this process. Thank you for welcoming a newbie like me into your author communities and taking the time to answer questions and encourage me along my journey

About the Author

Kylie made the leap from kindergarten teacher to romance author, living out her dream to deliver sexy, always and forever romances. She loves a happily ever after story with tons of built-in steam.

She currently resides in Sydney, Australia and when she is not dreaming up the latest romance, she can be found spending time with her three children and her husband of twenty years, her very own real life instant-love.

Kylie loves to hear from her readers; you can reach her at: author.kylie.kent@gmail.com

Let's stay in touch, come and hang out in my readers group on Facebook, and follow me on instagram.

Made in the USA
Monee, IL
07 February 2023